Murder Lies Waiting

By Alanna Knight

a&b

Murder Lies Waiting

A Rose McQuinn Mystery

ALANNA KNIGHT

Allison & Busby Limited
12 Fitzroy Mews
London W1T 6DW
allisonandbusby.com

First published in Great Britain by Allison & Busby in 2018.
This paperback edition published by Allison & Busby in 2018.

A CIP catalogue record for this book is available from
the British Library.

10 9 8 7 6 5 4 3 2 1

ISBN 978-0-7490-2219-8

Typeset in 10.5/15.5 pt Sabon by
Allison & Busby Ltd

The paper used for this Allison & Busby publication
has been produced from trees that have been legally sourced
from well-managed and credibly certified forests.

Printed and bound by
CPI Group (UK) Ltd, Croydon, CR0 4YY

To George and June McKenzie,
with love

CHAPTER ONE

'You'll be safe enough there,' said husband Jack about my intended visit to Bute. He called it a neat, tidy island. Nothing exciting ever happens, the only murder – and that not-proven – was twenty years ago. You'll be safe enough there. His final words, somewhat cynically expressed, related to the fact that wherever I went, murder always seemed to be waiting for me.

Safe enough. Those words were to haunt me.

But to go back to the beginning. A clash, between my essential appearance as a lady investigator on a client's behalf in the court at Glasgow – details of which have no place in this narrative, including the possibility that matters might not be concluded in one day – and Chief Inspector Jack Macmerry's long-planned annual family holiday: dates non-negotiable and set in stone by the Edinburgh City Police, daughter Meg's half-term school holiday and, most important of all, his parents' golden wedding day at Eildon, a farm in the wild Border country near Peebles.

Sadie Brook, our housekeeper at Solomon's Tower, had been given a week's holiday. 'Seemed grateful and delighted, probably had plans of her own. And if you don't go with us, Rose, then she will feel obliged to cancel them. And who is to look after you?' Jack added anxiously.

'No need for that, I am used to being here on my own. A few days will hardly be a hardship.' In a curious way, I hated to admit that I was rather looking forward to having the Tower on my own when I returned from Glasgow, no immediate investigations and time to attend to much neglected domestic matters, discarding items from Jack's much loved but extremely shabby wardrobe, Meg's outgrown clothes and toys, as well as the contents of forgotten cupboard shelves.

'Are you sure? You're still not yourself again,' Jack said.

I found his concern touching. I was hardly at death's door, merely recovering from what seemed a lingering head cold and cough. Listening to that cough disturbing his night's sleep, Jack said desperately: 'You're not well, Rose, you're needing this holiday. A change of air and some of Ma's cooking will work wonders. Make a new woman of you.'

'Do you really want a new woman of me?'

He grinned: 'You know the woman I want.' His accompanying look said it all and proved that even after ten years it could still bring a blush to my face.

He went on to enthuse about the golden wedding long regarded as an exciting local event, a rare gathering of the clans, not to be missed. The Macmerrys were a popular couple and families from miles around would converge on the farm, none too young or too old to be excluded, as long as they had breath in their bodies and were capable of eating and drinking, particularly the latter, and with the inevitable ceilidh, for those not rendered completely legless.

The prospect of a whole week of social invitations to more remote farms and cross-country bone-shaking journeys, more food, drink and hangovers, very bad fiddle playing and ear-splitting shrieks from would-be dancers, did not, if I am honest, seem that enticing.

But as all the arrangements had been carefully planned by his mother Jess, Jack was furious with the clash of dates. She would be so disappointed. Although as a high-ranking officer in the Edinburgh Police he was liable to cancel more personal engagements than he had hot dinners, and frequently both, as I knew to my cost through the years, it was a totally different matter for his wife. I tried to muster interest in his suggestion that I might come for part of the week as the Glasgow meeting might involve two days' travelling with little in the way of transport – unless he collected me from Edinburgh on my return. I knew from the slight frown and immediate change of subject that this idea did not appeal to him.

'They'll be getting enough of me. I'll be here when they come back with you next week.'

Andrew Macmerry's birthday also marked his retirement, the farm handed on to his nephew having long ago been declined by Jack, who decided to be a policeman, much to his parents' disappointment.

Jess Macmerry wistfully fancied a few days in Edinburgh, with memories of her one and only visit on their honeymoon fifty years ago. She had never been to Solomon's Tower and there were hints that a large amount of luggage might also be transported separately – Jess would be indulging in an orgy of baking and food preparation and since Jack's motor car could barely squeeze in Meg and I, plus Thane, there would be little room for another passenger. And there was no question that Thane would be travelling too. He went everywhere with us and was a popular favourite with Jack's father, who declared Thane the most extraordinary dog he had ever set eyes on, something most folk would agree with.

I sighed. Although they both boasted to being fit as fiddles, as Pa Macmerry was fond of stating, Jack decided that an aged couple used to living in a low-lying, one-level farmhouse should not have to cope with an ill-lit perilous and ancient spiral staircase, the only access to the Tower's upper floor.

We often slept in Jack's study in winter, cosy and close to the warm kitchen when the rest of the Tower was impossible to heat, and Sadie was set to work immediately transforming the Guard's Room into a pleasant bedroom.

We had no idea where the name for the study originated, but I suspected from similar rooms on the upper floors that the Tower had once served as a soldiers' barracks. Solomon's Tower, resting on the now peaceful slopes of the extinct volcano that was Arthur's Seat, had Edinburgh's grim history confirmed by relics of battle – rusted swords, helmets and even the occasional skull – unearthed from time to time through the passing centuries.

My change of plan being discussed, I looked around the supper table. Angry, tight lips from a now grumpy Jack. Meg seemed slightly sad and was making all the right noises – but those grandparents in Eildon, who could resist them? She loved the farm and the animals, to say nothing of the overindulgence.

Like all young creatures she didn't seem to feel any discomfort from cold draughts, doors left wide open and faulty chimneys belching forth smoking fires. Certainly not with so many good things to eat, all proudly home-baked and with a loving grandma who also applauded her desire to help in the kitchen and learn how to cook, seeing in Meg the potential for what she called growing up to be 'a real woman', unlike her daughter-in-law, Jack's wife, seriously neglecting family duties by doing an unwomanly and potentially dangerous job involving nasty people and occasional dead bodies, activities best left to the police.

Jack had another cup of tea and was considering a final plea. He had also observed that there wasn't much work for the 'lady investigator, discretion guaranteed' coming my way in Edinburgh at the moment. It wasn't as if I was turning prospective clients away from the door, he said.

That was true, I had to agree. A temporary hiccup or perhaps Edinburgh society was also becoming more modern, in keeping with King Bertie and that loosening of the shackles of tight morals, a code put down, sternly fixed and adhered to in his mother's long reign.

Her son, perhaps because of that stern upbringing, showed more understanding of the frailties of human nature. And that, most folk agreed, was a good thing. 1906 was the twentieth century after all, and ready for a lady investigator.

CHAPTER TWO

The following morning Jack left for work and after waving goodbye to Meg as she hurried down the road to the Pleasance and the convent school run by the Little Sisters of the Poor, I sat in the big kitchen enclosed by the grim and ancient walls, and the lost history of Solomon's Tower.

Life was becoming a little dull. Sadie was washing the breakfast dishes. She looked across at me, heard me sigh and smiled. 'Is it as bad as all that? Anything I can help with? Here, have another cup of tea, still warm in the pot,' she added, her favourite antidote to all ills.

Sadie had been invaluable during the past two years,

showing remarkable abilities as a nurse as well as running our lives with her customary efficiency, duties awakening memories of childhood afflictions and the devotion of her aunt Brook to whom Chief Inspector Faro frequently abandoned his two daughters, Emily and me, during our stay in Sheridan Place from Orkney on our annual school holiday.

Grandma Faro had taken us to live with her in Kirkwall after our dear mother died when I was eight, giving birth to a stillborn baby, the son she and Pa had longed for.

Sadie took a seat opposite, and the next moment, I was drinking more tea and pouring out my tale of woe, glad to have someone whose sympathetic ear I could bend for a change. We had become close in recent times – Sadie Brook the housekeeper had suddenly become Sadie the companion and secretary. I needed help and she was so good, not only keeping the house but also keeping my study in order. While I was laid low recently, she had taken the opportunity to update my filing system, which would make life much easier in future, that is if Jack's dismal prophecy of my lack of clients was not fulfilled.

She had said apologetically: 'I hoped that you would be pleased. That it would help. You are always so busy taking care of Mr Jack.' I had on request dropped the respectful title of Mrs Rose and guessed that she understood from observing, without my putting it into words, that sometimes I had problems with Jack. We were happy together and had much to be thankful for, in harmony most of the time, but like all married couples there were brief moments when we stared angrily at one another across that kitchen table and harsh words were not always bitten back.

I sighed. 'Forgive me. I am at this moment in danger of being sorry for myself.'

'And you have every right to be,' she said firmly. 'You're not your usual self at all. You've been very poorly with that wretched cold and that takes its toll—'

I shook my head. 'This golden wedding and my absence has brought it all to a head. I should be ashamed to admit any of this to anyone. I have absolutely no reason for moans.' Feeling defensive and that an excuse was needed, I added: 'Jack is a great husband and we have had ten years of a good marriage.'

She sighed. 'Aren't you lucky! Sounds wonderful to me.'

Such statements like 'good marriage' always suggest perfect happiness to the unmarried and I said: 'I might as well tell you I have another reason for not being tempted by a whole week at the farm. A brief visit is quite enough. Jack's parents are somewhat stoical – I'm not implying mean . . . just careful – about heating cold rooms and keeping doors shut against draughts.' That I always felt cold was a matter of amusement, and dare I add, even contempt to my mother-in-law, who saw it as a slackening of the moral fibres to admit to such weakness.

Sadie's eyebrows rose. 'Considering this house is not the warmest, perhaps they just think that you are used to the cold.'

I looked around me and smiled. 'I never get used to

15

it, but I love living here so much.' And looking out of the window at the vast height of Arthur's Seat, I added: 'Living here in an ancient tower that looks as if it was built from the very boulders and stones that flew down millions of years ago at its last eruption as a volcano, is a rare and exciting kind of home. I feel privileged. I would never want any other place.'

She followed my gaze, a grey dull day outside, and she seemed surprised. 'Not even one of those grand houses in the New Town,' she said wistfully, 'if Mr Jack had that kind of money?'

I laughed. 'Not even then. Besides, as you know well, we live mostly in this kitchen.'

She smiled. 'I hope it's always warm enough . . .'

'It is indeed. And you make sure that our bedrooms are too.'

She stood up and put the kettle on to boil. 'You know, it is quite natural for Mr Jack's parents to be disappointed. They are devoted to him and Meg, and so proud of you and all your achievements.'

'Are they? I wonder. I'm not at all sure about that. Perhaps I have never been quite forgiven for not presenting their only son with an heir for the farm.'

'But they have wee Meg and they adore her.'

That was true and I made no comment, but it had long been obvious that I was not the light of my in-laws' lives. That position was unassailably and rightly held by Jack, always had been, and in more recent years by his daughter, ever since Meg came into the Macmerry family six years ago. A newcomer, a ready-made granddaughter, she was their flesh and blood, after all, and blood was for them far, far thicker than water.

I didn't say any of this to Sadie because she just believed that Meg was my daughter and I was happy to let her go on thinking so. She had made another pot of tea and as she handed me a cup I thanked her and said: 'I'm afraid Mrs Macmerry never quite approved of a daughter-in-law tainted by a life investigating crime. She's very proud of her chief inspector son but crime and other such sordid things – that is a man-only business, very brave and commendable, but definitely not for women!'

I paused, wondering how best to rephrase Meg's arrival. 'As soon as we had Meg, she firmly decided that I should have immediately cast aside my career and devoted every moment to my new role—' I stopped just in time. I almost said 'as stepmother'. Although to give Meg her due, she regarded me as her mother, the only one she had ever known.

'Mrs Macmerry is like most women, you can't blame her for that.' And giving me one of her intense looks, Sadie went on: 'You are quite different, a new species, a career woman, it's not her fault if she doesn't quite understand that. She's puzzled by you, I expect.'

I smiled wryly. 'I know. I see it in her eyes each time we meet. She looks at Meg and then at me and I feel that I am falling short by not fulfilling what she regards as a woman's only role in life. That is, spending all my waking hours cooking, sewing and making clothes, darning socks and being quite content to wait on my two, hand and foot.'

I stopped, suddenly embarrassed as I realised this described Sadie's role as a housekeeper exactly. With sudden compassion, I wondered how she felt about it and whether she had secret ambitions stretching way beyond biding her time in Solomon's Tower.

Sadie seemed unaware of my discomfort. 'But you are much more than a career woman. I noticed from various things in your study that you are also fighting for votes for women. And I approve of that.'

'You do? Well, I am glad to hear it.' For another convert in the making, I added enthusiastically: 'You must come to our next meeting.'

'I'll be delighted. I should like to join your movement, take an active part, become a suffragette.'

My eyes widened at that. The word 'suffragette' made Jess Macmerry blanch and I tried my best to keep that other piece of grey evidence against me well under wraps, with visions of a mother-in-law's agonies concerning this weird woman her son had brought into a respectable God-fearing family. Grievances suppressed under a polite and smiling surface but doubtless unearthed as the door closed on our visits and poured into Andrew Macmerry's long-suffering ears, used as they were to considering only the vicissitudes of poor harvests and sheep-farming matters.

Sadie was clearing the table, opening cupboards to make a list of what we needed for a meal that evening. Leaving such matters to her, I was only to be consulted on special occasions like birthdays and entertaining visitors.

'Such a pity you have to go to Glasgow midweek,' she said, 'if it had been Monday or a Friday you might have been able to go with them.'

'Jack knows there is no way I could be in both places on this important day. We've discussed it plenty, as you well know.'

She had been present, trying to look invisible through sharp discussions, seeing Jack looking angry and resentful, and me making matters worse with reminders about how often being a policeman's wife, not to mention a policeman's daughter, arrangements had been changed in the past.

I said: 'My sister Emily and I had our childhood blighted by hardly ever seeing our father, without a mother; we grew up in many ways closer to your aunt Brook when we visited Edinburgh.'

She smiled. 'Aunt Brook was wonderful. She brought me up after I lost my parents.'

I remembered that in Orkney this summer for Emily's husband's funeral, Pa and I had thrown a safe bridge to travel over this sad omission of parental care. We loved each other, and having much in common he was well pleased and proud of his daughter's role as a lady investigator.

Sadie was about to take my bicycle down the Pleasance and then into Princes Street. 'I have parcels to collect from Jenners for Mr Jack,' she said.

That would be the wedding anniversary present for his parents and from the children's department something special for Meg to wear, chosen by Jack on their visit to the shops while I was ill.

Sadie left and I went into my study. I had nothing to do and the Tower now so still and empty, I felt very alone. Being sick had drained me of energy and enthusiasm. Sorting idly through papers on my desk, my mind backtracked to my soul-bearing with Sadie. I thought of her collecting the parcel for Meg and that I should have been the one to decide what she would wear. It was no comfort to know, as I had always known from the moment she came into our lives, that given a straight choice, however much Jack had once loved me, now he would always choose Meg.

She was his child, she was his image and these days I noticed an increasing movement of our world around 'Meg thinks . . . Meg says . . . Meg wants . . .'

Not for a moment must this imply that I was resentful, the wicked stepmother. I loved Meg with all my being. She was the child I had never borne, the replacement for that beloved infant son with my first husband Danny McQuinn. The baby who still lived in my heart, whose frail ghost still rose from the unmarked grave in the Arizona desert that I had dug with my own hands and laid him to rest.

After several miscarriages I knew I was unlikely to bear Jack a child. The St Ringan's curse my sister Emily and I called it, by which all Faro women could bear only one live child. If Jess Macmerry never forgave me for Jack's baby I had lost in those early months and was at that particular time my only reason for getting married at all, I had sought and found a granddaughter for them, reunited with her father but with no past memories. She loved both of us, her mother and father. But Jack was first – and the thought came unbidden and sometimes too often that now in my early forties, I was almost there, stepping over the threshold into middle age. With a loving husband and step-daughter, I had nothing to complain about, but it didn't help to know that somehow I had failed as a wife.

I was not – or ever likely to be – the first person to live and die for anyone's love; for blood, as previously mentioned, is thicker than water and that no amount of devotion can equal. Once I had prided myself, preened secretly, that I was first with Pa – now he had Imogen, happy together and settled in Dublin. Now there was no one wanted me above all others, and that included Thane, rushing to Meg's side, tail wagging in delight, as soon as the door opened or he heard her footsteps on the stair.

I made a resolve that morning. Unburdening myself to Sadie had been a catharsis, a confessional Meg would have said, like the Catholic pupils at the convent. Yet Sadie had seemed impressed, even envious.

I stood up, cleared away the papers from my desk and made careful notes of what was required for the Glasgow court, telling myself to get a grip, stop feeling that life was slipping away. Be grateful, and be like Meg, say thank you, God, for every day. And go now, feed Thane.

Yes, there was Thane, my beloved deerhound. What about Thane? Thane had always been Meg's from the first day they met, his allegiance was to her. He would go with them to the farm, sure of a warm welcome, indulged by Andrew Macmerry. And give Thane his due, he knew when he was on to a good thing.

Sadie had returned and smiled as she unpacked the groceries. 'You're looking better, Rose. A bit more cheerful than when I left.'

'I've been gathering the threads, busy with things, that's always good for the spirit.'

'I was going to ask you something,' Sadie hesitated, frowned. 'I've been thinking just now. If you had been going with them, I would be off on a week's holiday. Now that you are staying—'

'No! You must still have that holiday. I insist. You deserve it, you work so hard for us all the time. And I can look after myself for a few days.'

'Are you sure?' She looked at me doubtfully.

'Of course I'm sure. Have you somewhere to go?'

'Yes. I was planning to go to Bute, catch up on old relations,' she added.

'Is that where your family came from?'

'My parents, yes.'

I laughed. 'I had no idea. I thought Mrs Brook being your aunt, Edinburgh born and bred . . .'

She nodded vaguely and I realised that was a foolish presumption as she said: 'I was born near Rothesay.'

She said no more, retreating up the spiral stair to tidy Meg's bedroom and put out her change of clothes when she returned from school. Scrambling about with Thane outside on the hill in her uniform was strictly forbidden after one or two disasters.

Suddenly I was aware of how little I knew about Sadie

or of what had been the pattern of her life before coming to Solomon's Tower.

She came downstairs, looked at me and said: 'I've just had a great idea.' Pausing, she smiled eagerly. 'Why don't you come with me, Rose? To Bute.'

CHAPTER THREE

Sadie's suggestion took me by surprise. The idea of going on holiday with her had never entered my mind. I had never been to Bute, although Pa had long ago and he once compared it to Orkney. He liked it, reminding him that he was also an islander, an Orcadian born and bred, he said proudly.

Sadie was saying: 'Look, I have to go through Glasgow, change trains there for Wemyss Bay, go across on the ferry.' She laughed excitedly. 'Why don't we go together? I'll do some shopping while you're at your court case, then you come to Rothesay with me. You like islands, don't you – brought up on Orkney with your grandmother? You'll love it,' she ended enthusiastically.

I think we both realised that a change of scene was called for and I suspected that apart from my slow recovery from what had seemed a particularly bad cold, another reason for my discontent might well be that I was perhaps now entering what the ladies of my acquaintance delicately whispered as 'the change', something all women dreaded, heralding the approach of middle age. The idea hadn't occurred to me so far to be scared, but maybe the symptoms were imminent and at that moment Sadie's suggestion seemed like a small miracle. The perfect answer, and I was certain that Jack would be happy about it too, with his insistence that I needed a holiday.

I considered Sadie as a possible holiday companion. Thirty-six, unmarried, she had no objections to being what they called a spinster or 'being on the shelf', as she laughingly described herself. I discovered that she had made a lot of man friends through the years and she always seemed to have some chap on the go. And that worried Jack more than it did me, especially when we met her in Princes Street, walking in Holyrood Park or Salisbury Crags' Radical Road nearby. And always on the arm of yet another man.

'Never the same one twice,' and Jack would frown. Once pressing on, with polite bows exchanged, but no introductions, he whispered: 'I was wondering, do you think we're paying her enough?'

'What do you mean?'

'Come on, Rose, surely the same thought must have occurred to you – that she's maybe making a bit of extra cash on the side.'

'Jack! That's awful. What a dreadful thing to say.'

But now that he had mentioned it, I gave Sadie's behaviour a certain amount of thought. Certainly there was nothing in her appearance to arouse such suspicions. She didn't behave flirtatiously towards Jack, she didn't dress flashily nor was she a beauty, a stunner as men called them, although she had pretty chestnut hair and elegant hands – what Grandma Faro called a lady's hands. She used to say they were a real giveaway of age too. Something you can't disguise, she insisted, and made me very self-conscious in childhood about my short fingers and toes, haunted by the fear that they might be webbed, like those of my selkie Orcadian great-grandmother.

Certainly with Sadie, it was more than pretty hair and elegant hands that gave her that mysterious sex appeal, an irresistible chemistry that had men flocking to her side. If I had ever attempted to discuss such matters with Gran, she would have been quite shocked that I could let such notions ever pollute my innocent young mind. She would have said firmly she knew about such disgusting things and that particular appeal I was referring to, in her opinion, had more to do with the farmyard than the farmhouse. They belonged in the same category as rude or naughty words that, when uttered, I had to go and wash out my mouth, but alas there was no means by which I could wash out my childish mind of certain sordid and unexplained images.

Discussing this with Jack, I told him how at school long ago I had encountered any number of Gran's wicked women. We laughed and concluded that in another age

Sadie might have had the right qualities for a courtesan, a breed where beauty was not quite enough.

Once, I decided while we were sewing together to cautiously ask why, since she was so domesticated, she had escaped the matrimonial net. She shrugged and said she knew men and she liked them, they liked her too but marriage – she held up the sock she was darning – no, that was out of the question. I nodded sympathetically; she was one of this new age of emancipated women, like many of my suffragette colleagues, who refused to abandon their freedom and become men's slaves.

The subject closed, I decided wryly that perhaps she saw too much of what it might become, aware of those threadlike cracks in my marriage. Jack was a good husband and a fine policeman, but he was also a very ambitious man and had no scruples or hesitation in putting every hour of his career ahead of his domestic life.

Later I was to be told that when she was orphaned in Bute in her early years, she had been fostered by a couple who seemed right enough, but behind closed doors there was a horror story. Strangely enough, although the man abused her, it obviously hadn't put her off men altogether.

My thoughtful look at the suggestion of a holiday in Bute hadn't gone past her. 'Oh, do come, Rose, you'll love it,' she repeated.

'Where will we stay?'

'My family connections are near Rothesay, an ancient castle, and if any of them are still alive – it's twenty years since I left – I thought I might look them up.' She shrugged. 'Remote cousins.'

The mention of an ancient castle was enough to make me shudder and have second thoughts. Although Solomon's Tower was what it said, an ancient pele tower built some centuries ago, I never wanted to live anywhere else. But while it was dear to my heart, I wanted a change from stone walls that seeped in draughts, cold, vaulted ceilinged rooms with only the kitchen warm enough to survive the winters. The thought of a voluntarily chosen holiday in another ancient ruin sounded like utmost folly.

Sadie observed my doubtful expression, and smiled. 'I know what you're thinking, but what I have in mind is this chap I met in Duddingston – his uncle has a first-class hotel. It has all modern luxuries, as well as lifts, a bathroom for each floor, bedrooms overlooking the bay. All the rich folk from Glasgow go there, so it really is something. And we can stay there. Plenty of room out of the main tourist season.'

'How much will it cost – sounds very expensive?'

She shrugged. 'If you can pay your way, Rose, don't worry about me.' A small hesitation. 'I have savings put by – you and Mr Jack are very generous with my weekly wages.' And as my thoughts drifted inevitably to Jack's outrageously wicked suggestion about her extra cash, she added: 'I have a small legacy, from another aunt, put by. So I can afford it.'

And that finally made up my mind, I decided that I owed it to myself, and at this moment what I needed most was a warm, luxurious hotel for a few days, and Sadie's description had definite appeal.

It remained to persuade Jack. Sadie was with me when

he came in from work, as if for moral support. I need not have worried. He thanked her and, I fancied, with a sigh of relief, making me wonder if perhaps he knew more about those threadlike cracks than I thought and that, after ten years of marriage, the petals in that bed of roses were beginning to wilt a bit. But as Sadie went out, with a delighted smile, Jack gave me one of his big hugs and kisses, making me feel guilty of such disloyal thoughts.

'If you can't come to the farm then this seems the perfect answer,' he said reassuringly. 'A great opportunity going with Sadie, a nice woman I can trust to take care of you.' I had no chance to register a protest about needing care as he continued: 'A great place Rothesay, very popular, especially for ordinary Glasgow folk with big families in the old queen's reign. They called it going "doon the watter".'

Warming to the subject, he nodded eagerly. 'I've been there a couple of times and one of our lads from there was never tired of singing its praises. So go for it!' A wide grin spread as he grasped my hand across the table. 'The change of scene will do you a world of good. I know that hotel too, but it's very expensive, top-class.' He frowned. 'We can manage, but what about Sadie?'

'No. It was her idea. The uncle of a man she knows owns it and she assured me that she can afford it.'

Jack's eyebrows rose at that. 'Can she indeed? Hardly from what we pay her.'

'She has savings, apparently, a legacy she inherited from an aunt. Not our Mrs Brook.'

Jack gave me one of his wry looks and shook his head. I

could read his thoughts, which took me back to our earlier conversation about her making a little extra on the side.

'I don't doubt her, Jack,' I said sharply. 'Perhaps this fellow from the hotel is getting her a discount. Especially as she is from Bute,' I added indignantly.

'She never told us that,' Jack said. 'We thought she was from here, being Mrs Brook's niece.'

Meg who had been listening silently to our conversation came over, took my hands and wailed: 'I'll miss you, Mam. It won't be the same without you. And Thane will miss you as well, won't you?' she added, giving him a pat.

At which Thane looked wise as always, not having anything dog-like to add in the way of words.

I didn't say a word to Meg but Thane was one of my chief worries these days. How old was he? I had no means of knowing his age when we first met on Arthur's Seat, where he seemed to be living wild when I returned to Edinburgh from the wilds of Arizona, after the disappearance and presumed loss of my first husband, Danny McQuinn. The huge deerhound, who appeared in my life and saved me from rape by drunken tinkers, looked fully grown and I would have said in the prime of dog life.

That was in '95, and although eleven years had fled, Thane didn't look a day older. He hadn't aged like the rest of us and yet I knew, having made careful enquiries, that hounds as large as Thane don't live as long as the smaller breeds. I often sighed, aware that the inevitable must happen, preparing myself mentally for when, sooner now than later, he must leave us. A day as inevitable as life itself but we couldn't bear to think about it.

Jack and I were well aware that Meg would be inconsolable. He was so much part of the furniture of our lives, of Solomon's Tower and Arthur's Seat. Jack tried to be very philosophical about it all, insisting that Thane was 'just a dog, after all', despite the many instances I had recorded through our years together that he was more than just a dog. He had remarkable qualities, a kind of telepathy that existed between him and Meg – and me. He knew when we were in danger, knew when we needed him. Difficult to explain to anyone, but we were very conscious of it.

At this moment Jack and I shared a rare moment of telepathy. He squeezed my hand gently and said: 'Go and enjoy yourself and stop worrying about Thane, he'll be waiting for you when you get home again.'

And so the plan to visit Bute went ahead, Sadie saying she would let the hotel know, as with our heads together we went over timetables of trains and ferries. Each day it drew nearer, Rothesay with its luxury hotel, when my dreams of having a few days relaxing in warmth and comfort would soon become the reality of prepared meals and sitting by a window overlooking the sea. Sadie's ancient castle and her odd relatives I had mentally resolved to avoid at all costs.

When the day of departure arrived, Jack saw us off on the Glasgow train, surprised at our lack of luggage, just one large case each. He grinned. 'Is that all? I expected hatboxes and sundry small cases and valises,' to which I responded sharply:

'You know me better than that.'

I had a good training. The years of my life in the Wild

West with Danny had not included the acquisition of possessions beyond the minimum required for surviving attacks from hostile Indians and bandits.

Jack grinned. 'You're looking very smart, in your best city costume – for the Glasgow court, no doubt.' His eyes widened. 'And a hat too. That's a rarity.'

I never wear a hat if it can be avoided, at constant war with my unruly mass of yellow curls resistant to combs, brushes and the passing years. However, I have a code of dress for business assignments, which Jack doesn't often see.

He smiled at Sadie. 'You travel light, for a young woman. I wondered if the motor car would be large enough for all your luggage.'

She laughed. 'Spinster ladies have to adapt. We do not always have escorts and porters can be expensive.'

On the platform, I was saved a dreaded tearful farewell from Meg, who was not allowed by the nuns to miss school except *in extremis* – sickness or a death in the family – into which category seeing her mother off on a week's holiday could not be included.

The train slid towards us, and halted noisily, billowing steam. Jack saw us into our compartment; luggage stowed, he kissed me and shook hands with Sadie. The whistle blew, we were off, Jack left behind on the retreating platform, a diminishing smiling figure, hand raised.

As we sat back in our comfortable seats, Sadie sighed. 'We're on our way, Rose.' She clasped her hands. 'On holiday! Oh, isn't this just marvellous?'

I love trains. Even the shortest journey is exciting for

me, although shrouded by a landscape lost under heavy grey skies with the threat of imminent rain offered nothing worthy of note and had us both resorting to magazines from the newspaper stall.

And as Edinburgh retreated, folded back into the gloom, I found myself remembering last night as Jack and I prepared for bed. Maybe he was having second thoughts about me leaving when he said: 'Bute's a neat, tidy island. Nothing exciting ever happens; only one murder and that not-proven was twenty years ago. You'll be safe enough there,' he added with a somewhat cynical laugh.

'Safe enough . . .' The train's wheels whispered. Those words were to haunt me.

CHAPTER FOUR

At the end of an uneventful, dull journey for a train-lover who yearned for splendid landscapes, we arrived in Glasgow, left the station and walked across the square in the direction of the court. With no idea how long my presence would be required and the delay that might be involved to our onward journey, I had warned Sadie that I might have to meet her in Rothesay, but thankfully all went smoothly and with a modicum of preliminaries and a few statements to witness and sign, my part in the proceedings was ended in a couple of hours and I was free to leave.

Free. I caught up with Sadie as arranged in the nearby railway hotel and she grinned cheerfully. She had done some shopping for things that might be scarce in Bute. She added that you never knew with ferries: a spot of bad weather, wild seas and we could be stranded, our return journey delayed. I sincerely hoped not, with the vision of Jack's parents in Solomon's Tower and no Sadie – an imposing presence as our housekeeper – there to greet them.

With her usual efficiency she had been busy, consulting timetables and brochures. 'There's one in thirty minutes and we leave at the terminus, Wemyss Bay station, and catch the steamer across to Rothesay.' She seized my hand and laughed. And as everyone seemed anxious to assure me: 'You'll love it.'

We learnt that we were too late for the last train to Wemyss Bay that would connect with the ferry. 'Might as well take it, anyway. Better than spending the night here in Glasgow.' She looked around at the lounge and frowned. 'Staying here will be costly. Unless you know anywhere?'

I had to confess that I didn't know Glasgow well and the only hotel accommodation provided by the court for judges and visiting lawyers or witnesses was, I suspected, even costlier than this railway hotel.

My negative response didn't worry her and I learnt something else about Sadie. Her efficiency included being very knowledgeable about Wemyss Bay and where we could get cheap lodging for the night.

'Don't worry. Leave that to me. I know it well, had my first job there. When I was fourteen, some people I got to know in Rothesay had rich friends with a holiday home there. They got me a job as assistant lady's maid. Maid of all sorts would have been nearer the truth.' She added that she had seen little of her employers, and spent most of the time doing endless piles of washing and ironing and keeping a kind of peace between eight unruly children between the ages of two and fourteen.

I was increasingly thoughtful. Greater even than my excitement about trains was a growing apprehension regarding the ferry crossing tomorrow morning. The weather had not improved and as well as rain there was now a high wind. With my tendency to seasickness I prayed for a good day with a smooth sea, grateful that Sadie kept my full attention and fears at bay with her knowledgeable information as we waited on the platform and at last took our seats on the Wemyss Bay train.

The railway line had been opened some forty years ago in 1865, advertised as being superior to other local lines, such as Greenock. And Wemyss had one attractive difference to recommend. All the carriages contained proper seats. Before the advent of railways, steamboats had been the fastest means of transport, five hours from Largs to Glasgow at 7/6d cabin fare, single. Wemyss reduced the journey to an hour and a half and an all-in fare of 2/7d. An hour to Glasgow. I was aware that railway travel had revolutionised public transport, enabling people from all levels of society to travel about the country, but I must have looked surprised at Sadie having all these details at hand.

She smiled. 'Fares may have gone up but I remember it well. The family I worked for that summer went back and forth to Glasgow, the father to keep an eye on his business and the women to spend money on gadding about. They had inherited their fortune from forbears in the slave trade, although he pretended it was sugar.' She laughed. 'Sugar, for heaven's sake! Well, money was no object and he didn't mind spending it, taking the whole family, servants as well, practically everything but the kitchen stove went with them on holiday.'

The outskirts of Glasgow had given way to Paisley and rural areas around the Clyde – there was even a glimpse of a loch. A pretty journey for a hopefully sunny day tomorrow as at last we steamed into Wemyss Bay. Gathering our cases, we stepped off the train and Sadie said: 'Lovely, isn't it? Well, twenty years ago, there were two platforms and two steamer berths, and to complement the large private homes being built in the area around the station – what the newspapers called mini-Balmorals – it was vitally important that the station did not lower the tone.'

Outside the station, she pointed triumphantly across the road to the treelined hill. 'There it is, still there. That's the house.'

It was huge. I gasped. And she laughed. 'Yes, a big mansion, and this was just a second home. Oh yes, these holiday homes were for rich folk and industrialists from Glasgow and others who could afford to pack off their wives and hordes of bairns for the summer. Not too far away, near enough so the lord and master could travel back and forth with ease.' She grinned and shook her head. 'And I would be prepared to bet there were more than business deals in the offing, a chance to sow some more of those wild oats while the wife was safely offstage.'

She looked thoughtful for a moment, remembering. 'Things were different on Bute, though. Rothesay was for the poorer folks, crowds of a new breed of workers and their families escaping the grime and toil of industrial Glasgow to breathe some fresh sea air into their lungs for a change.'

We walked across the road on the lookout for a suitable place to spend the night. Sadie pointed. 'That one looks promising. They are advertising vacancies.' It didn't look prepossessing, but I was tired after the day's travelling.

'Let's try it.'

Our night's lodging was modestly priced and despite the somewhat shabby exterior, it proved to be welcoming and comfortable, the beds clean with fresh white linen, fleecy pillows, and towels provided. We were apparently the only guests that night and the proprietor, a plain, balding man of mid sixties, had a deferential manner immediately reminiscent of a retired butler who had seen better days with a wealthy employer. If we had stayed longer I was sure we would have found much about him that my powers of observation and deduction had failed to detect. Was he widowed or perhaps just lonely, I asked Sadie later when at last we made our escape after he had seized us as a unique opportunity to wax lyrical over Wemyss, and the station complex.

'You'd never credit it now, but the original station building and a much-improved pier were made from ground redeemed from the sea, with twice the platforms and steamer berths and without any interruptions to the passenger services,' he added proudly. 'Mind you, the better ferry service was greatly appreciated, a great relief to passengers trying to get from train to boat. Aye, that had led to frustration and angry words with families with bairns frequently losing connections and having to face all the physical discomforts of travelling, particularly in rainy weather.'

He paused to regard us solemnly. 'That was when my predecessor opened this guest house. He knew he was on to a good thing and it was greatly appreciated.'

Sadie was already halfway up the stairs as he bid us goodnight.

I slept well to awaken to a sunny morning. A hasty look out of the window: my prayers had been answered. The water across to Rothesay was smooth as silk. After a handsome breakfast served by our talkative proprietor, we settled the modest sum and he seemed reluctant to let us continue our journey, singing the praises of his lodging.

'Couldn't be better. You can watch the ferry standing at the window here, see it coming from Rothesay and take your time,' he added proudly. 'Just a few steps across the road to the station, ladies, knowing you'll have ample time for another cup of tea with still enough left to comfortably buy your tickets.'

We politely declined his offer and as he solemnly shook hands with us at the door he bowed and I had that butler image again as he said: 'It has been a pleasure having you to stay. Any time you are in the area, ladies.'

As he spoke and in all his conversation with us,

although his gaze politely included us both, it had lingered on Sadie and I wondered, perhaps wrongly, had she been the reason for our extra-friendly reception?

He was just an ordinary-looking elderly man, rather stout, and I looked again at Sadie. There was nothing exceptional about her appearance either, she had made no witty asides to his long, drawn-out commentary last night. But she had made an impression and as I turned at the gate he was watching her, his wave I was certain included a sigh, his expression sad to see her leave.

As we hurried across to the station again, Sadie said it had been redesigned and upgraded a few years ago. 'Another tribute to our new king, with all physical comfort in mind and of utmost significance,' she added as we walked swiftly down the short walk between platform and pier. Above our heads, the large circular, glass-fronted interior with its vast array of plants in hanging baskets also provided protection from bad weather.

Watching the ferry arrive and the passengers disembark, we boarded the slightly swaying though stationary vessel and I insisted that we took outside seats, which seemed to surprise Sadie, but was always advisable if one has a tendency to *mal de mer*. I soon discovered that my fears were groundless and I sat back, enjoying a cool breeze, blessed with a lovely day and the delight of a half-hour crossing on a smooth sea. Over our heads, the ferry was accompanied by an escort of seabirds – not the raucous greedy variety haunting the harbours in Leith and Granton, but with muted calls reminiscent of distant mocking laughter, as if they were happy creatures.

At last, as land grew closer, we were almost at our destination, too soon for me as I would have enjoyed remaining aboard and cruising endlessly around the island. The soothing motion of the ferry, its gentle engine sound had a soporific and pleasing effect, like drifting into sleep.

But here was Rothesay and its approach struck a bell and awoke the timeless feeling of yearning that belonged to and had always linked my life to Orkney. If I closed my eyes I would not have been surprised to find myself transported to Kirkwall or Stromness, the harbour and ferry landing and engine smells were the same and linked to an excited expectancy that welled back from childhood days, a feeling of homecoming that I recognised and understood.

It was as if those vast undulations and mounds, mere grassy, boulder-strewn lumps in the ground visible from the ferry, covered earlier pre-civilisations when a new evolution had taken place. Where creatures walking upright were just learning what was to be their lot surviving as humans, that race of almost-men who lived, built and died centuries before the Vikings sailed their dragon-headed ships across the seas. They had vanished into their burial chambers under the mounds of earth carrying their secrets, their dark rituals with them, gods worshipped and long lost, leaving behind no recorded history, only a few standing stones for future civilised men to interpret as they wished. And over the succeeding centuries, in the passage of time their interpretations led them to draw their own lofty and possibly inaccurate conclusions.

Sometimes I wondered if it was a natural part of my Orkney inheritance, this burning desire to solve puzzles that had turned me into a crime investigator and also formed a link and extended to unrecorded history. Each time I saw a chambered cairn or a standing stone or carved emblem of some mysterious past, I was intrigued and closing my eyes longed for an interpreter, someone from another time, with the magic to summon up dark and no doubt gory glimpses into that other lost world. Were these earliest of dwellers perhaps strange beings who had taken refuge on our planet when their own collapsed and died?

At my side, Sadie said: 'You're very thoughtful. Care to share it?'

'Just cairns and old tombs.' I tried in vain to find the right words to convey what all this meant to me.

Sadie merely laughed. 'Not for me. I like the present. And wait until you see the hotel – that will chase all your hobgoblins away.' With a sigh, she stretched her arms above her head. 'Oh, for a nice cup of tea, that's all we need.'

Leaving the ferry, she had remembered the shortcut as we headed towards The Heights, a tall, imposing hotel whose presence commanded a panoramic view of the surrounding area as well as across the bay.

Bute had few crimes according to Jack and Rothesay was a peaceful, uneventful holiday resort. A tragic family accident that had become notorious as murder two decades ago was still a talking point amongst the older members of the community and remained of considerable interest across the whole of Bute.

And hardly had we set foot ashore, walked across to the hotel and climbed the handsome staircase to our rooms with windows overlooking the bay, than I was to discover that instead of the promised week of happy relaxation away from the minor trials and tribulations of my Edinburgh life, I was to find myself on the receiving end of solving a twenty-year-old mystery.

Safe enough, Jack had called this holiday. But that was only the beginning, there was worse, much worse to come. And had I known a mere fragment of what lay in store that day, I would have been on the next ferry heading back home alone to my safe haven, at Solomon's Tower.

CHAPTER FIVE

At my side, Sadie looked up at the hotel's vast structure and giggled. 'Isn't it magnificent?' And another surprise. 'I was a servant here once. I heard from the fellow whose uncle owns it that the last owners had sold it at a great profit. Wait a moment.'

As we walked up the flight of steps, she paused and rummaged in her luggage to withdraw a somewhat shapeless navy-blue hat and settled it on her head without any apparent need of a mirror. In moments, with the matching tailored costume, she had become a uniformed and very correct lady's maid.

'Good, isn't it, ma'am?' She grinned, walking a few steps behind me.

I stared at her wide-eyed, astonished since I could not imagine any earthly reason for this sudden transformation. It certainly did her no favours, although I should have known but did not realise at that moment that just looking ordinary was the perfect disguise. I was to remember Pa and Jack saying they were the most difficult criminals to catch. The ones who had no outstanding features, the ones who wouldn't merit a second glance and would blend invisibly into a crowd.

Those are the ones we cannot watch, they said, the dangerous ones who if they were caught, their lack of any memorable appearance would render the word of any likely witness doubtful or be completely useless in an identity parade. Yes, such criminals would remember that just looking ordinary was a better disguise, a camouflage devised by nature and beyond the most accomplished actors.

As we reached the grand entrance she whispered, 'If I hadn't been with you' – she grinned, squeezed my arm and added mockingly – 'my lady, in the old days it would have been me for the servants' entrance.'

The door was opened by a splendidly uniformed footman. Frowning at our lack of impressive luggage or transport, which suggested that we were not wealthy customers, and although madam had her personal maid, he did not see the necessity of calling a porter. A discreet line had to be drawn somewhere.

He indicated the reception desk and a well-dressed, good-looking boy appeared out of a nearby door, bowed politely to me and recognising Sadie under the hat, rushed forward, and gave her a dazzling smile and a smacking kiss on both cheeks. Who was he? The schoolboy son of the owner with rather exaggerated manners for welcoming guests?

'Welcome, Sadie. So good to see you again. A good journey?' He looked as if he would like to keep holding her hand but was suddenly aware of me. 'Harry Godwin, Mrs Macmerry. Welcome to The Heights.' Another tender look at Sadie and a formal bow in my direction. 'If you will follow me. I can summon the lift' – he pointed – 'if madam would prefer.' I shook my head indignantly. Surely I didn't look that old and frail?

'Not at all,' I said shortly.

He bowed and nodding towards the staircase seized our two pieces of luggage. Following him, I wondered who on earth this sixteen-year-old could be. Getting in some holiday training and pocket money as a fledgling porter, perhaps?

He turned and smiled. 'You'll meet Gerald later.' He grinned. 'He keeps me in order.'

As he led the way, Sadie whispered: 'I thought I told you. Harry is the manager.'

That was a surprise. Who was this Gerald who kept him in order, then? Certainly, he looked far too young for the job of managing a great hotel. I am not very good at judging anyone's age, but I considered that a schoolboy would be a fairly accurate speculation. As he led the way up the richly carpeted steps of the handsome oak staircase, I decided this could not possibly be the same fellow, the acquaintance Sadie claimed she had met in Duddingston.

The staircase was lined with impressive portraits that I learnt later were of earlier owners, the empty spaces filled with a selection of seascapes. Pausing at the first-floor landing of a handsome twisting staircase with an oak banister overlooking the marble tiled ground floor far below and the reception entrance, I complimented him on the splendour around and he laughed proudly.

'Indeed. We even have electric light, which is more than the rest of the island can claim in their houses – and for that matter, it is well ahead of general domestic use across the length and breadth of the country. Homes everywhere are still feeling lucky in most rural areas to have gaslight instead of candles.'

That was still true of big cities, and living on the remote southside outskirts of Edinburgh, we were having a long, hard fight to be connected with the electric grid.

Harry smiled again at Sadie and turning to me, said: 'You ladies are very fortunate travelling today.' He shook his head. 'Things were very different twenty years ago.' As he spoke, a door alongside us opened and the bearded face of an old man peered out, frowning, obviously disturbed by Harry's voice.

'Are these our new guests you're showing round? Where's that fool Gerald gone now?' he demanded. 'That's his job.'

Presumably Gerald was the absent manager, I thought, as Harry frowned and the rest of the old man emerged, a bit the worse for wear, unshaven and exuding an unpleasantly strong odour of sweat and alcohol. But this was the voice of authority and I was conscious that Sadie had moved from my side into the shadows, that servant's hat pulled well down.

Harry was shuffling his feet, looking unhappy. He wasn't pleased at this sudden apparition.

'My Uncle Wilfred,' he murmured to us and to the old man, rather loudly, speaking the words clearly as if he was also deaf, 'Just showing our guests to their rooms.' His uncle did not move but remained staring at us, and Harry obviously feeling an introduction was necessary said loudly: 'This is Mrs Macmerry from Edinburgh and her maid.' I was conscious of Sadie melting closer into the shadows.

Uncle Godwin took both of us in in one long stare. He wasn't impressed and said to Harry, 'Tell our guests how lucky they are not to be working-class folk who made up the bulk of holidaymakers when I was young.'

Harry smiled uncomfortably and seemed about to say something when Uncle Godwin brushed him aside and stood in front of me, a captive audience. 'In my day, whole families crowded into single rooms in a tenement, often all that was on offer they were glad to take it. Landladies could pick and choose and they filled their houses to bursting point. During the Glasgow fair fortnight, it was not unknown for desperate families to arrive on the island and on finding no rooms left they would sleep outdoors in the Skeoch Woods. Not missing much, since some of the accommodation was just chalk marks on the floor showing the area they were to sleep in.'

He paused, grinning, and the whisky odour increased volubly. 'Aye, as more folk rolled in, the marks were rubbed out and packed closer together. The lucky ones who could afford to negotiate with private houses often included the owner giving attendance. The beginnings of the normal bed and breakfast ritual—'

It was quite an alcohol-induced speech as an introduction to the hotel.

As his uncle paused for breath, staggering somewhat, Harry seized the opportunity to escape and hustled us down the corridor murmuring, 'Sorry about that.' Deprived of his audience, Uncle Godwin's door banged shut behind us, and Harry's smile was one of relief.

'He doesn't appear in public much these days, getting rather frail, losing the place a bit, but he still likes to keep an eye on things so we let him pretend he is still in charge. That keeps him content.'

We had reached our rooms. He opened the door and ushered us inside, his hand on Sadie's arm. 'I hope you will be happy with your stay with us. You'll meet Gerald later.' And pointing to the bay window, 'Best view in town,' he added proudly.

Setting down our indifferent luggage he turned to me: 'Madam, Sadie's—I mean, your maid's room is through there.' A bow. 'I expect you are weary after the journey so I have arranged to have afternoon tea sent to you.'

As the door closed, Sadie took off the hat and flung it on a chair.

'Phew. That was close! When old Godwin looked out, I thought he recognised me again. I had to keep out of sight, but I think it was his drunken state I have to thank. That saved me.' She sighed and looked worried. 'This is going to be a problem.'

'After twenty years, surely not?'

She shrugged. 'I thought he would be dead by now.'

'Well, he is an old man, and probably his eyesight isn't all that good, either,' I said consolingly. 'And you were just a servant, after all, one maid among many,' I reminded her, 'so what are you worried about?'

'Nothing,' she frowned. 'Just thinking out loud.'

By the time we had unpacked and hung our clothes into the depths of adequate wardrobes, a tap on the door heralded the maid with afternoon tea, delicious scones and cakes. If that was an example of the standard of food we might expect, I prepared to relax and relish every moment of staying in such luxurious surroundings.

Sadie replaced her second cup of tea on the tray, pushed aside the tempting biscuits with a sigh and said:

'I have something to tell you, Rose. Something I think you should know.' She frowned. 'I hope you don't mind but I told Harry that you were a famous authoress writing a book about the island. If word gets around that you are a lady detective, and I am sure it might, then everyone will be dying to tell you about Rothesay's still most talked about crime. Although it's twenty years ago, old Godwin will certainly remember it.' She paused, sighed again. 'Harry would just be a youngster, he's quite a bit younger than me – I can't even remember him.'

I doubted if Harry would have been born then, but said: 'Don't worry, I am only concerned with domestic crimes in Edinburgh, and well used to dealing with these kinds of encounters.' However, I was rather worried about this false identity and being passed off as an authoress. That was an unknown territory, the additional famous category would be a considerable embarrassment, especially if asked about the books I had written.

Regarding my real profession, however, Sadie's concern was unnecessary. I reassured her that I frequently met such people in Edinburgh, the more genteel curious to know what had led me to choose such a strange and outlandish profession for a lady, and how I discovered clues that led to a criminal's apprehension, while the bolder were eager to know if I had solved any particularly gruesome murders and were eager for an eyewitness account I might have of hangings.

'I'm only concerned with the present,' I told her, 'but I'll be ready to listen politely to yesterday's crimes.'

Sadie frowned but she didn't look happy and after a moment's hesitation she shook her head and said: 'This case was twenty years ago.'

This must be the case that Jack had mentioned as she continued: 'It drew more than the usual rather morbid interest because the main suspect was a sixteen-year-old girl, Sarah, Lady Vantry's step-daughter, who it was alleged but never proved had pushed the only son and next laird down the stairs at Vantry – to his death.'

She paused and I nodded. 'Murder has to have a motive, Sadie, and rivalries between siblings are not all that rare. You just have to look at the history books. Kings and princes were at it all the time—'

She held up a hand. 'Do you know who it was, this Sarah Vantry?'

I shook my head. 'I never read anything about it.

Twenty years ago I was in America and we didn't have the luxury of newspapers where we lived in Arizona and they certainly wouldn't have reported a murder in Bute.' I smiled at her. 'Go ahead, I am quite intrigued.'

Sadie was staring at the window, biting her lip, hesitating as if searching for the right words and sighing, she drew a deep breath, turned and looked at me.

'That girl, Sarah Vantry. It was me.'

CHAPTER SIX

I stared at her in open-mouthed astonishment, unable to take in what I was hearing. Sadie Brook was telling me about a murder in which she had been personally involved, the accused was none other than herself, my companion and new friend who had suggested this holiday in Bute.

Sadie Brook, better known in Rothesay by her baptismal name Sarah Vantry.

She was shaking her head, trembling, her eyes tearful. 'I know it is awful for you, a bit of a shock.'

The revelation was more than a shock, it was horrifying. I could find no words.

I looked at her, wide-eyed, speechless, as she went on: 'I decided you had better be told right away. After all, there might be someone we meet in Rothesay who remembers me. I can tell you, I was really scared when the first person we met happened to be Harry's uncle. I'm sure he remembered me, that's why I tried to keep out of sight.'

I had been holding my hand to my mouth with shock. I tried to return to normality and looked at her intently and with a vestige of calm, trying to see this thirty-six-year-old woman as a sixteen-year-old girl and potential murderess.

Another shock wave, one for immediate consideration. I knew for a fact that where local murders are concerned, residents in small communities have particularly long memories, even though the facts become somewhat more lurid and subject to exaggeration over the years – what Jack calls subject to conversational embroidery.

I blinked rapidly, wondering if I would ever recover from the shock of this moment. The woman sitting beside me at the window was related to Mrs Brook, Pa's highly respectable housekeeper at Sheridan Place, a well-beloved substitute-mother for my sister Emily and me when he was called away on official duties during our Edinburgh holidays.

I was prepared to bet that Mrs Brook had never known or dwelt on the fact that she had a most remarkable niece. Sarah Vantry, a girl whose name in Bute was synonymous with murder. She had kept that secret very dark indeed. Small wonder that this niece Sadie was so competent and such an excellent housekeeper, having started off earning her livelihood as a servant at fourteen years old, and she probably owed her social accomplishments to the big house at Wemyss Bay and its wealthy, cultured inhabitants.

Fourteen? There were still two years to be accounted for in which she had returned to Rothesay, stopped being a servant and become a potential murderess. This would take some explaining and accepting when I got back home. I could hear myself telling Jack this extraordinary story. He would be astonished, that's for sure, and to put it mildly, shocked that a woman once tried for murder had been in charge of his precious little daughter, Meg.

Sadie was watching me, biting her lip, awaiting my reactions. She shrugged and having cast aside the navy-blue hat, her maid's disguise, she looked more like the Sadie Brook I knew. 'I had to tell you because . . . well, as I said, what if someone remembered me?'

I shook my head. 'That is most unlikely, you are worrying about that quite unnecessarily. A sixteen-year-old girl can change a lot in twenty years. That's a long time, Sadie,' I insisted.

She looked very doubtful and not at all consoled but I believed the possibility of recognition was remote indeed, that the physical appearance of even quite striking sixteen-year-old girls will be obliterated by the passage of time, forgotten and changed beyond recognition at thirty-six. Although I could not tactfully say so, she certainly did not fit into that category.

She was shaking her head, insisting: 'You never can tell. And when I saw old Godwin out there, I was sure he recognised me, despite the hat.' She gulped. 'You see, he was rather fond of me, wanted to make something of it and tried to seduce me, got me into a corner on more than one occasion. I had to fight him off – once when we were alone in the kitchen, I used the frying pan.' She smiled wryly. 'I wonder if he still has the scar?' A pause. 'Oh, Rose,' she said desperately, 'don't you see? I just had to tell you, it would be terrible if you had heard the story from someone else. What on earth would you have thought of me then?'

I shook my head, still trying to work out what I thought of her now, feeling that discovering this version of Sadie was going to be like peeling the layers off an onion.

'You had better tell me the whole story,' I said, trying to sound businesslike, for those were the words I used to calm prospective clients.

'All of it. Right from the beginning,' I added, pouring a cup of now lukewarm tea remaining in the pot, wishing for something more fortifying while trying to persuade my mind not to be distracted by longing for the peace, recently offered but now utterly shattered, of the magnificent view across the bay.

Right from the beginning, I thought, wondering how much of her glowing reference from Mrs Brook by which she had been introduced into Solomon's Tower as our housekeeper was true. Surely Mrs Brook must have known?

Sadie sighed. 'My father was a younger son of the Vantrys, not in line to inherit the title. The usual procedure. The heir, the first one out, gets that, the second goes into the army or navy, the third takes what is left over. In this case tragedy struck and the two elder sons died in childhood, one in a riding accident and the other of the sweating fever. So it was left to my father, who was a bit of a lad; he got married, not for love but one of those dynastic arrangements with property and dowries involved.'

She paused. 'Are you still with me? When he died, Lady Adeline didn't want to appear like the wicked stepmother, she didn't immediately send me off to an orphanage, that would have ruined her popularity in her role as lady of the manor. Even her husband's illegitimate small girl had her uses. Anyway, I had a fairly miserable time: I don't remember much about my childhood except – except trying to keep out of her beloved son Oswald's way.'

'Your half-brother?'

She smiled wryly. 'There was some doubt about that, about Oswald's paternity, I mean. He was older than me and I learnt from an old serving woman who used to attend to my bruises that Lady Adeline had had an affair. Oswald was the result, my father found out, met my mother and had me on the side and that was why the marriage finally ended. When he fell ill and was dying, the result of a chill from a sailing accident, he said that as the only surviving Vantry, it should come to me. I gathered that there was quite a scandal but Lady

Adeline's adultery could not be proved. I was illegitimate and my poor father couldn't even produce my mother, who had abandoned me, gone off and married someone else. So I was out of the running.'

She was silent, biting her lip and I said: 'Tell me about Oswald.'

She sighed. 'Oswald had always hated me, he was cruel, used his hands and feet. One day he went too far, thought he had killed me, ran to her screaming. I was lying still and bleeding on the ground. He had hit me too hard.

'I think she was scared, perhaps she was sorry for me or maybe it was only the family scandal if I had died and Oswald had killed me that worried her. Anyway, I was sent away, to foster parents on the other side of the island, a farm down at St Blane's. They were kind enough and a little girl was useful, as I discovered, an unpaid servant . . .'

(Wait a moment. Kind enough? This was a different story to the one she had always hinted, about being abused by her foster father.)

She went on: 'I was strong enough to work, milking cows and looking after the hens. I even learnt how to wring their necks when required for the pot.' She shuddered. 'My other advantage was that I could read and . . .' pausing, she stretched out long-fingered, elegant hands and regarded them approvingly, 'I could write a very good letter, which was also useful.' She sighed and looked out across the bay. 'I suppose I was happy, we were fairly isolated and the only visitor I remember was a woman – I think they called her Doris – who visited quite often. She always brought a wee present and used to cry over me. She was kind but I found it a bit embarrassing.

'I never thought about the future until the day the farm burnt down four years later, the family decided farming was over for them, they sold the stock and decided they would start again in Glasgow. They were tired of island life. Lady Adeline had heard of the tragedy, of course, and asked me if I wanted to go with them. If not, I could come back to Vantry with her.'

'Did you ever see this woman Doris again?'

She shook her head 'No.'

'You never knew anything more about her? She never got in touch with you?'

'No. I wasn't really all that interested, remembering those tears and the soggy hugs.'

I was well ahead of her, having already decided that Doris was most probably her disgraced mother. Her ladyship had also realised Sadie's potential, as she continued:

'Lady Adeline had a reputation to keep up. She was still a Rothesay worthy, on all the committees, her beloved only child Oswald was at public school and perhaps she was lonely anyway, and I would be useful. As well as my neat handwriting I was good at sewing, and she liked me to read to her in the evenings, she had a taste for romantic stories. I suppose I was happy enough.'

Pausing, a frown darkened her face. 'All this ended when Oswald came back. He was a big, strong lad, bigger than me, and when his mother was absent he was back at his old tricks again, which he was careful to keep from her. However, after a couple of years I had had enough of Oswald and being isolated at Vantry. One of their friends came on a weekend visit, he was very rich and had just taken a house in Wemyss Bay. He seemed to like me and as a promised governess had taken ill and had to return to Glasgow he asked Lady Adeline if I could be spared to come back with them and help to look after their children.'

She stopped, looked at me and sighed. 'You know that part. I stayed with them until I heard that Adeline was ill. She had been in hospital and asked if I would come back to Vantry and look after her while she got her strength back. What I didn't know, and no one told me, was that she was having some sort of mental breakdown – a failed second marriage and that sort of thing.'

A weary shake of her head, remembering. 'That was a fatal mistake. Oswald hated me, now he had me at his mercy, with a sick mother who couldn't intervene. Then one day, he decided to finish me for good. We had a fight and he tried to push me down the stairs. I wriggled free and he missed his footing, down he went . . . broke his neck.'

She looked at me, stretched out her hands dramatically. 'It was a big, sweeping staircase, even grander than the one in the hotel here, but something like it, with steeper steps and a marble floor below. As you might imagine, his mother was out of her mind, she just screamed and screamed, claimed that it was no accident. Her nephew was there. They had heard us quarrelling and me shouting I hated Oswald and wished he was dead.'

She shook her head. 'That was true. I couldn't deny it. You must know yourself, Rose, children do that all the time and don't really mean it. I did mean it and I shouted those words every time he came near me but Adeline said I had deliberately murdered her poor boy. By this time, she had this further axe to grind. She had remarried while I was with the foster parents, a remote Vantry cousin living in the south of England, and although he had left her long before my arrival, their marriage was still valid – he was a philanderer and she had thrown him out, but she reckoned that as I would probably go to prison or hang for murder, legally Vantry would come to him. He had kept in touch and through the years constantly begged to be forgiven. That all fitted with her sighs when I read romances to her and I guessed that she still wanted him.'

She stopped and looked out of the window as if she was seeing it all again. 'After the trial and a not-proven verdict, it was terrible – terrible until Aunt Brook offered me a new life – with her – and I gladly accepted. The past was gone, never mentioned between us.'

I had one question. 'Is Lady Adeline still around?'

She shrugged. 'I don't know, but I expect so.'

'Then why on earth did you want to come here with so many bitter memories? Wouldn't it have been better, especially for you, to forget the past?'

And all the time she had been talking, one other question had been forcing its way into my shocked thoughts, remembering the original story about her foster parents. I already suspected Sadie was somewhat economical with the truth. Were there other lies to be uncovered, but most important of all, what was the truth, the real reason for coming back to Bute and for my presence here with her?

CHAPTER SEVEN

When I put the question to her, she smiled. 'Yes, Rose, there was a reason, a very good one. I have always loved Bute. I was born here and I've always been haunted by the past. Always wanted to prove my innocence and most of all, get the island to acknowledge that I was an honest islander and I hadn't murdered anyone.'

We were both silent for a moment before I said rather awkwardly: 'Well, thank you for telling me all this.'

She gave me one of her intense looks. 'Surely you can guess why I wanted you to know? When I first came to Solomon's Tower as housekeeper to a lady detective, well, meeting you like that was when the idea came to me. I realised that I would never have a better chance, and if I was patient, sometime the perfect opportunity might arise to tell you my story, and you were such a kind, understanding person, I was certain to get your help.

'Then at last the perfect time came, Mr Jack's family wedding anniversary. I had been given a holiday, thought I might go to Oban – I know some folks there. But the real thrill for me, what really changed my mind was when you had to go to Glasgow to the court case and abandon the family visit.' She clapped her hands delightedly. 'It was just like fate had planned it all. We've become real friends lately, we can talk to each other and here was the perfect chance to go back to Bute.'

A little faint light was beginning to filter through. I groaned and she smiled. 'Yes, Rose, now you see why I arranged this holiday and asked you to come with me. Can you blame me? You have solved so many cases, helped so many people who were nothing to you, and I realised as I reorganised your files that you were the one person in this world who could lift this cloud off me for ever.'

'Wait a moment. I'm used to dealing with things in the present.' I stopped and thought of the impossibility – where on earth would I start on a not-proven case where all the clues, if any existed, had been lost and the circumstantial evidence destroyed twenty years ago?

She grinned. 'I take it that means yes, you'll do it? Oh, I'm so glad.'

I shook my head firmly. 'It does not mean yes. Have

you thought what this entails? For heaven's sake, I—we are supposed to be on a week's holiday. What makes you think I can solve your problem in a few days?' I added, swallowing the first bitter realisation about how easily I had been tricked.

Sadie gave one of her brilliant smiles. 'Oh, you're a dab hand at solving mysteries, I'm absolutely sure it will be easy for you.' Her mind was quite settled, her aim achieved. 'Now, shall I ring for another pot of tea?'

I didn't sleep much that night in the splendid frothy white mass of a bed I had been so looking forward to in this luxurious bedroom. Perhaps three courses of a splendid supper with soup, poached salmon and an apple dumpling helped to keep me awake, and when I thought of Sadie in the room next door, in all probability sleeping peacefully, I felt angry and yes, betrayed.

I had been lured here on false pretences – give Sadie her due, she had admitted as much. And the last thing I wanted at this moment was to get involved in a long-dead, not-proven murder case. I realised too that my pride and integrity were hurt most of all. To think that for the past two years I, a respected lady investigator, as well as a senior detective in the Edinburgh Police and a small girl, had been quite unaware that we were living under the same roof as a woman who had once been tried for murder.

Of course, she was probably innocent – if she was telling the truth – but the stigma remained. As for Jack, he would have a fit when he heard about it. For the possible contamination of his innocent little daughter, first of all.

And then his wife, who was always far too trusting, would be his scornful rejoinder.

I had a couple of hours of troubled sleep and when dawn broke I was strong in my resolution that over breakfast I would tell Sadie that having thought her situation over most carefully – which was true, I had hardly slept thinking about it – although I was sympathetic to the plan she had been considering since her arrival at Solomon's Tower as housekeeper to a lady detective, and the possibilities that might be achieved in putting to rights what she had long regarded as an impediment to her reputation, I could not be expected in all truth to spend one week, all that we had, trying to re-establish the past and exorcise the nightmare that had haunted her. I would add that I was sorry to disappoint her but would point out rather sternly that in the circumstances, as I had only been invited on this holiday on false pretences, I would catch the next ferry back to Wemyss Bay and return home.

Of course, I was hoping that she would still consider us as her friends and as our housekeeper, if she was prepared to keep the details of her unfortunate past as confidential between us, and at all costs, endeavour to keep these revelations well away from Jack. I would add that I hoped I had made it clear what his reactions would be. He was a policeman. She would be dismissed, sent off immediately.

With my little speech prepared, I went down to the restaurant, full of firm resolve.

She was already there at the breakfast table, Harry Godwin hovering near.

Not only Harry but an older man introduced as Gerald Thorn. An exceedingly handsome, dark-haired and well-set-up gentleman in an expensive-looking suit, a presence that reduced Harry to the appearance of a gawky schoolboy.

Gerald. He was very tall and as he shook my hand warmly, I realised that he had a charming smile and the kind of face that would inspire all women guests with a feeling of trust – and perhaps even secret dreams.

At his side, Harry beamed on him. 'Gerald is the power behind the throne here.'

So Gerald was the real manager and, as he shook his head modestly, if first appearances were anything to go by I didn't doubt that for a moment.

'Excuse us, ladies. We have the day's business matters to attend,' he said politely and with a bow, the two men left us.

Sadie rose politely as I took my seat opposite and gave me that brilliant smile.

'Well?' she said eagerly. 'What do you think of him?'

I knew she meant Thorn. 'I thought Gerald was going to be the porter,' I said weakly.

She laughed. 'He's Harry's greatest friend.'

'How old is Harry?' I had to ask.

She shrugged. 'Early twenties.' He certainly didn't look it, I thought, as she went on, 'Gerald is a lot older but they've always been quite inseparable. Harry says everything he has learnt about hotel management, he owes to Gerald.'

She was clearly very impressed. And I knew somehow

that the situation had subtly changed and that I would never say a word of what I had rehearsed as I looked at this new Sadie who I had never dreamt existed inside the pleasant, efficient but unassuming housekeeper at Solomon's Tower. Thirty-six years old, never married but with a constant stream of male admirers, that's for sure, and by her happy expression, Harry Godwin – or was it Gerald Thorn? – was about to join the line, next on the list.

And I remembered Jack's words as we met her occasionally on her day off walking in Princes Street Gardens, or encountered her in the Sheep Heid Inn, our local tavern at Duddingston, the end of the street one might say, or having a goodnight conversation at our kitchen door. Always with a man, and seldom the same one twice.

Jack, not usually observant about such matters, had remarked on this before. It was a mystery the way she attracted men and he had even hinted, to put it rather crudely, that she might be making a bit extra cash on the side.

However, when we were alone together I asked her: 'Why have you never married? I mean you seem to have plenty of gentleman friends,' I added delicately.

She sighed, a sad shake of the head. 'I have had plenty of chances, as Aunt Brook would say, but surely you can guess the reason why the men I met remained just friends, why I kept them all at arm's length? They knew nothing about me or my past or that I secretly yearned when I was young – and still do,' she sighed, '– for a husband and children.' She shrugged. 'I'm getting a bit too old for that now.'

'What nonsense,' I said, but realising it was probably true. 'Isn't there anyone?' looking in the direction of the two men who had disappeared into the office, especially Harry who had already indicated that he could hardly keep his eyes off her.

She followed my glance and grinned. 'Harry is really sweet, isn't he?' She was aware of his attentions but I guessed – wrongly as it turned out – that even in his early twenties and looking sixteen, he was far too young for her.

'There has never been anyone,' she was saying. 'I have always told myself firmly that I must never marry.' A pause and a deep sigh. 'That was until Captain Robbie came along – he's very handsome and kind, wants to marry me. He's in the Merchant Navy on short hauls, thankfully, wants an answer when he gets back from Hamburg.' She shrugged. 'I've thought about that and it will have to be no.'

'Why no?'

'Oh, surely you can see the reason, Rose?' she cried. 'Whoever marries me, marries Sadie Brook with no idea of my past, of Sarah Vantry – and what happened. I could never be any man's wife and withhold that dark secret, even presuming I could keep it and that somehow, sometime it would not leak out. And that would be the end of a happy marriage.'

'Not necessarily,' I said. 'Not-proven was the verdict.'

She laughed scornfully. 'And as a policeman's wife and an investigator you know what that means. I quote – "We know you did it, but we can't prove it; go away and don't do it again." I couldn't take that chance, and deceive a good, decent man like Robbie. I would have to tell him the truth.'

'When does he get back?'

'Very soon. They are due in Leith shortly after we get back.' She paused. 'You are my last hope, Rose, my last chance of happiness, if you like. I knew you would help me,' she added bleakly. 'You are a kind woman and I've seen how ready you are to help unhappy clients who have real problems.'

As she spoke, she looked at me intently and the demons clicked in again. Suddenly it was all monstrous, the timing, the way she had planned this: no impromptu holiday but as soon as she knew I was going to Glasgow, all carefully worked out. She would invite me to accompany her to Rothesay with some incredible crazy idea that she could prevail upon me to prove her innocence. What she hadn't worked out, however, was that although I was competent at solving domestic crimes, I could not work miracles.

I did some rapid calculations. We were almost newly arrived at the hotel but from that first moment we stepped into reception, Harry Godwin had shown a great interest in Sadie.

He obviously found her very appealing and despite the absent Robbie away at sea, whose cause I was now learning I had been brought along to support, she was certainly sharing signs that this was a mutual attraction. That was no business of mine, despite the aforesaid Robbie, since there was no commitment there either. It did give me a further sense of the trap that I had fallen into and again revived that sense of having been used. Did she intend telling Harry that she was Sarah Vantry?

She stretched out her hand across the table. 'You will try, won't you?'

The plea wasn't completely wasted. I'm used to listening to clients' sad and complicated histories. I liked Sadie and wanted to believe her story, that as a sixteen-year-old girl, an unwanted step-daughter, she had been framed. But I also knew that I was completely helpless faced with a murder case done and dusted, the page closed on that not-proven verdict twenty years ago.

So where was I expected to find fresh evidence – if any existed – to prove her innocence, when even the police had not been able to find any but circumstantial, not enough to convict and hang her?

I told her so in as many words and she winced visibly. A week, six days was all we had. 'You know Rothesay and as I am a complete stranger, where do you suggest we start?'

Clasping her hands, she looked almost happy, poor girl. She presumed she had won me over. 'Well, at the scene of the crime, of course. That's the procedure, what you do, isn't it, Rose?'

'Where is this place?'

'Just a mile or two away, near the West Island Way. A place called St Colmac, that's where Vantry Castle has been for hundreds of years.'

My heart sank as I pictured another ancient ruin to add to this Gothic horror.

'So how do we get there?'

'There's a horse-drawn tramway from here to Port Bannatyne. Vantry is fairly near.'

I had a sudden, pleasing thought. With my new interest in motor cars, Jack had taught me to drive, I had also seen a notice in reception declaring that this luxury hotel boasted in this age of travel by motor car, the hire of vehicles and a chauffeur, if the gentleman – no mention of a lady – was not himself a qualified driver. And at a price, I suspected.

I mentioned this to Sadie and found that she knew already. She had seen the notice and had worked out that possibility as well. Very thorough she had been, from the moment I imagined her going through my casebooks, on the excuse of providing an updated filing system, but with this idea of returning to Bute always at the front of her mind.

I read her thoughts. Rose McQuinn will prove my innocence. Had it never seemed a forlorn hope, even then?

'Who lives there now? After twenty years, what if it is a deserted ruin?'

'I haven't asked yet. Quite honestly I want to keep a low profile – just in case old Godwin remembered me, I didn't want to seem interested in case that jogged his memory.'

She thought for a moment. 'Maybe we're safe enough with Harry. He won't remember.' She paused. 'But maybe it would be less risky if you made the enquiry about the Vantrys.'

So I took my first cautious step over the threshold

and decided to make what sounded like regular tourist enquiries. But at the back of my mind, struggling and fretful to be recognised, those words – Jack's – as we prepared for the holiday.

Safe enough . . .

CHAPTER EIGHT

Sadie went back upstairs and Gerald drifted over from the reception desk and seemed very eager to resume a conversation regarding the afternoon tea menu. I was surprised to find myself his centre of attraction until it transpired that Harry had told him that I was an authoress, and I was suddenly a person of some importance in Gerald Thorn's orbit. He was eager to wax eloquent on the tourist history.

'The holidaymakers of the last decade arrived as you did, Mrs Macmerry, foot passengers on the steamer, and it was necessary to transport such large crowds as cheaply and quickly as possible to their destinations.

This was done by horse-drawn vehicles. Then five years ago the Rothesay Tramways company opened their electric tramway system from Guildford Square to Port Bannatyne. Last year this was extended to Ettrick Bay and has proved very popular.'

He paused and gave me an encouraging smile. 'Is there any particular part of the island's history you are interested in?'

Not Vantry Castle, in case he remembered Sadie. 'I'd like to know more about St Colmac and St Blane's.'

He nodded. 'Oh, St Colmac isn't difficult, the tramway ride to Bannatyne and then just ten minutes' walk away, there are some interesting standing stones. We believe that St Blane came over from Ireland, one of the earliest saints from that area, but both places are part of the mysterious, unrecorded history of our island.'

Harry had joined us while he was talking and nodded eagerly. 'Mrs Macmerry should be warned that it is more difficult to get to St Blane's, although it's worth seeing for its ruined chapel.'

I thought for a moment and said: 'I noticed that you have motor car hire.'

Gerald laughed, a broad smile. 'We have indeed.'

'That's very up to date and surely still fairly novel on an island?'

He smiled. 'Well, this is a very high-class hotel and so we try to keep everything up to the minute. That is what our wealthier guests, especially foreigners, now expect.'

Harry looked at him and said: 'Although it is costly, many rich folk who pride themselves on being modern like to avail themselves of the unique opportunity of exploring the whole island in comfort.'

Gerald nodded. 'And we also have a couple of sailing boats moored out at Kames Bay and have access to qualified sailors, ready to take guests out round the island or even across to Arran and the outer islands.'

I noticed the use of the proprietory 'we' as he continued, smiling: 'Can I interest you in that, Mrs Macmerry? A great experience and very popular,' and Harry interrupted proudly: 'I'm sure there can't be many such facilities provided by hotels in Edinburgh.'

I murmured vaguely. Although I had got used to the idea of a ferry and felt safe enough, the idea of a sailing boat with the sea lapping at its sides just yards away, bobbing about in the waves and occasionally throwing spray aboard, was terrifying. Persuaded by the family on holiday, I had had a nightmare experience on Loch Muick that I would not care to repeat, not only because of the embarrassment of seasickness but – much worse – the prospect that if the boat capsized I would drown. I can't swim. Even a childhood in Orkney had not encouraged me to go anywhere near the sea and Gran told me when other children went paddling at the water's edge, the touch of a wave on my toes sent me off in screaming terror. Was it an inheritance from my selkie great-grandmother Sibella Scarth, I often wondered, this fear of being reclaimed by the sea?

I had confessed to Sadie my fears as we boarded the ferry. She had found it difficult to understand and laughed. She wasn't afraid of anything except the wrong verdict for Sarah Vantry, but I was sure she had taken into her calculations that I had been so delighted with the Yesnabys' motor car in Orkney this summer that I had persuaded Jack to teach me to drive.

He had frowned a bit over that, the idea of using a police car and so forth, but the roads around us on the southside of Edinburgh were adjacent to the countryside and he was soon satisfied that as well as being a woman who rode a bicycle, once regarded as quite scandalous, I would be competent in charge of a motor car. When he said 'Well done' I was delighted to have his approval, although my achievement was purely superficial in that I had yet to master what happened in the mysterious regions of the engine.

'Your motor car would be excellent. And I can drive.'

'You can, Mrs Macmerry?' Harry's eyebrows shot skywards at my simple statement, surprised but doubtful regarding the mechanical abilities of this small lady with the mass of yellow curls that made her still look quite young. Although Sadie had hinted that she was past forty.

A second's throat clearing from Gerald: 'If you are quite sure, madam.'

'Yes and immediately, if that is possible, Mr Thorn,' I said sternly.

Harry laughed. 'Oh, please call him Gerald.'

A polite smile. 'Very well. In that case . . .' And he drew out a document from under the counter but I suspected with more apprehension than he would have had in dealing with a male customer. Preparing to fill in the details, I was asked searching questions about my abilities, which I listened to with a forbearing smile and prepared to hand over the required fee in a determined fashion. He still looked a trifle uneasy and felt impelled to read me the rather trying instructions, including restrictions on driving any vehicle on any part of a highway less than sixteen feet wide, where motor car traffic would be especially dangerous.

I did a mental calculation that this was fairly narrow and he gave me a hard look before deciding that I was joking when I asked was the driver expected to get out and measure the road.

Harry said briskly: 'I'm sure Mrs Macmerry doesn't need to be bothered with all these tiresome details, Gerry,' and to me a consoling smile, 'I'm sure she'll keep a sharp look out for such things.'

Ignoring Harry and frowning over the document, Gerald gave it a shake. 'There's something else. It says a person shall not drive a motor car at a speed exceeding ten miles per hour within the places specified in these regulations.'

I smiled encouragingly and said I thought it doubtful that I would drive at more than ten. 'So that is settled – when will the motor car be ready?'

'Whenever madam wishes.'

'Tomorrow morning, after breakfast, if you please.'

'Very well. I will have it prepared and provide you with the necessary maps so you won't get lost on the way to St Blane's.'

'You will find the drive quite delightful,' Harry interrupted. 'There are some lovely views across the Firth of Clyde from Kilchattan Bay, aren't there, Gerald?'

Gerald merely nodded. 'Is there anything else I can help you with?'

'There is one more thing. I like old castles too. I know of Kames but I believe there is also one near St Colmac?'

'Indeed and you are fortunate,' he replied. 'There is a special weekend tour to Vantry Castle, a big tourist attraction run by the tramway, which continues from Port Bannatyne and links up with a horse-drawn vehicle from St Colmac, and during the season takes passengers right to the door instead of having to endure a steep walk uphill.'

He looked at us both and smiled. 'But the walk would be no trouble to you two ladies and we are delighted to find out that you are not mere tourists but genuinely interested in the area.'

A tourist attraction with a special tour ominously suggested a historic ruin.

But to my question, Harry said: 'By no means. The original castle is ruinous but Vantry is a splendid mansion, its contents of great historic interest. The family have lived there continually since it was first built in the early eighteenth century. Alas, like many such families there is no direct heir to inherit when Lady Vantry goes. And she must be well past eighty—'

So Lady Adeline was still alive! Sadie will be interested to hear that, I thought, as he went on: 'We see little of her in Rothesay, nowadays. Some years ago she had a riding accident that left her face badly scarred. She was something of a beauty in her day and certainly worthy of the title of the town's lady bountiful, but now only on rare occasions she comes into the town and continues to wear the deep mourning for a family lost long ago.'

Did that indicate she was a widow after all, and what had happened to the absentee husband who had pleaded for his philandering to be forgiven? I asked: 'Who takes care of her?'

Harry thought for a moment. 'No living-in servants any longer. A matter of finances, one gathers – Vantry is expensive to upkeep these days and a couple of relatives, her nephew and niece, came to live with her a few years ago. They take good care of Vantry and look after her well.'

Vantry sounded more and more desolate and less and less the sort of place I wanted to visit. And on what excuse? I couldn't see a reclusive old lady throwing open the door and inviting nosy tourists disguised as archaeologists or writers into her sanctuary.

I knew all about ruinous castles or towers and this was not what I had expected when I left Solomon's Tower. I groaned. How was I to infiltrate Sadie into the scene of the crime? And what was the reality I had let myself in for, with visions of that luxurious holiday in a first-class hotel like a dream fast fading.

On my way to report back to Sadie, I was very impressed by the knowledgeable Gerald Thorn and the responsive and highly intelligent Harry Godwin, mostly because the latter, shaking back that untidy blonde hair from his forehead as he spoke, made him look more than ever like a truculent schoolboy. I wondered how his appearance would strike those wealthy clients from overseas before

Gerald took them over. Sadie had made a casual reference to a fellow she had met in Duddingston, but after seeing them together, I was curious to know more about that and what had led us to the Heights Hotel in Bute.

My account of the present situation at Vantry indicated my thoughts and reservations.

Sadie sighed. 'What a pity. It used to be a pretty place, nice formal gardens and so forth.'

'Mm.' I said. 'That was twenty years ago, remember, and with an invalid owner and no servants, a lot of things can change quite rapidly.'

Fortunately, the hotel also sported a handsome library and reading room. On its shelves were interesting accounts of Bute. I found what I was looking for, a history with an account of Vantry, and what was even better than a line drawing, an oil painting, allegedly by Allan Ramsay. Growing rather dark with neglect and the passing years, this seventeenth-century depiction had the castle as background, banners flying and on a pleasant lawn in the foreground, children playing and grown-ups having a picnic of some sort.

There were to be more surprises that day.

We dined in the early evening and as we were about to leave, Harry rushed over. We were to meet the inhabitants of Vantry, Edgar and Beatrice Worth, the couple who looked after Lady Adeline.

Harry was quite excited and he beamed at us, or more correctly, as usual at Sadie. Turning away from her unwillingly, he became aware of my presence and said, 'As you are so interested in their history, Mrs Macmerry, perhaps I might be allowed the privilege of introducing them. This is an excellent opportunity, well-timed as they only dine with us about once a month.' Leaning over confidentially, he added: 'Usually linked with business matters, running Vantry, bills to pay and so forth. Her ladyship is rather frail and only on rare occasions honours Rothesay with a visit.'

At my side, Sadie's nervous expression as she clutched my arm indicated that she was not impressed at the prospect of meeting some Vantry relatives who might remember her, and relief that Lady Adeline was not with them.

I had my own problems, apprehensive that Harry's introduction would elicit polite but probing questions about this famous authoress Rose Macmerry: What had I written and so forth? Would they have read any of my books? Did I use a pseudonym?

It was going to prove very difficult fielding them off and Sadie whispered that, in the interests of caution, she was off too – a lady's maid wouldn't be expected to put in an appearance surplus to requirements.

I thought otherwise. 'You can't keep running away,' I told her. 'The whole point of this expedition and for you to prove anything is that you must go to Vantry again and this is the perfect opportunity, if we can secure an invitation.'

But she was quite adamant. 'As most of the other guests are dining at this hour, the bathroom on our floor is unlikely to be occupied and it's a great opportunity for me.' She touched her hair with a gesture of distaste. 'Badly needs washing. Hadn't time before we left Edinburgh.'

Her glossy hair was her greatest attribute, one of her only outstanding features, and she was justly proud of it, but so thick and heavy, it needed hours to dry. However, her excuses regarding a dreaded meeting with the couple from Vantry proved unnecessary.

It did not work out that way at all and I was spared the embarrassment of basking in a temporary lie of false glory in my role as an authoress. This was fated to be a very brief introduction to Edgar Worth and his sister Beatrice.

Edgar was, I judged, in his mid forties, medium-tall, thin and balding. If he had ever possessed good looks, then they had already faded, an unprepossessing sallow countenance, sharp-faced and thin-lipped, but it was his expression that intrigued me most. He looked ill at ease, nervous, his eyes darting back and forth. Here was a man who was expecting trouble and Harry had hardly got the words of introduction out of his mouth, bows acknowledged, and I had quickly released his unpleasantly sweating hand when a tall, distinguished-looking elderly man approached. He was obviously their host for the evening. With an apologetic smile in my direction, Harry led them to a table.

I had taken in as much as I could of Edgar's sister, Beatrice. There was no family likeness but she was the same height, elegantly dressed and slim, I presumed, under the hourglass figure, a de rigueur fashion that I personally deplored. She did, however, share a vestige of her brother's nervous disposition but thankfully a firm and mercifully dry handshake.

As important guests, instead of a usual silent waiter, they were taken over by Thorn and ushered to their table where they began at once studying the menus he handed to them. I was curious, I wanted to linger, so I took a seat as near as possible and began studying the history of Bute, while lending an ear to the conversation at the adjacent table. I was to be disappointed: their voices were kept at a very low pitch, but an air of confidentiality and frequent frowns suggested urgency and that business matters were under discussion. Then I had a stroke of luck with the chance to learn more of Beatrice.

Suddenly she leant over and whispered to her brother, both men stood up and watched her leave. I realised she was heading in the direction of the Ladies Room and this was an opportunity not to be missed. I followed her and when she emerged from one of the lavatories I watched her at the washbasin. Gran would have been suitably impressed by those beringed 'lady's hands', long, slim and elegant. She dried them carefully and a moment later we were both side by side looking into a large mirror at our reflections.

She was probably a little younger than Sadie, although there was no comparison in looks. At that first short encounter I felt that Beatrice Worth, setting aside her somewhat forlorn brother, would command immediate attention. A pretty, clever face that caused me to wonder again about that self-inflicted sojourn in Vantry. She must be devoted to Lady Vantry and to her brother to be content with such an existence.

She patted her hair into shape, bit her lips as we all did

to increase the redness, and satisfied with her appearance, turned to leave. I followed, wishing I could think of delaying tactics and strike up more than the polite smile of two women meeting in the Ladies Room.

Clearly she did not intend to further Harry's quick introduction, or, I suspected, had more important things on her mind at that moment. A slight bow as we were leaving, as she held the door for me and walked swiftly to the table where her brother was wearing the rather set smile and making polite gestures, which suggested their host for the evening was someone of importance, most likely a businessman they were anxious to impress with their connections to Lady Adeline, staking out their future if and when they inherited Vantry.

CHAPTER NINE

About to return to my room and heading towards the stairs, I remembered what I had left on the armchair. Returning to the restaurant, Harry approached holding the book.

'I was about to deliver it to your room.'

As I thanked him he said: 'After breakfast in the morning for the motor car – will that be suitable?'

I said yes, and showing a certain reluctance to leave, he turned. 'Am I right in presuming that S—er, your maid will be accompanying you to down to St Blane's? It is quite a long drive for a lady on her own,' he added reflectively.

Again I said yes, my maid would be with me, but in point of fact our planned drive tomorrow was much closer to Rothesay. 'We have decided to explore the area around St Colmac's.'

A moment's hesitation, a frown before he replied: 'If you should have second thoughts about driving, madam, we also provide a chauffeur service.'

At a price, I thought. Maybe he observed that as he grinned, 'Gerry and I both drive. And I particularly enjoy the chance to get behind the wheel again,' he added wistfully.

My curiosity about the Worths still unsatisfied, I had one more question before going upstairs where Sadie was waiting for my report. I wondered how much of Harry's generous offer related to her possible presence in the motor car. And of greater importance, did we really want to have him with us on what might prove to be quite a delicate mission?

'What did you think of those two from Vantry?' she asked, eagerly awaiting descriptions.

This was not a simple question to answer. I told her that I had had little time for a careful assessment of the siblings. They had both had their backs towards me seated at the table and I could hardly spin round my armchair to put into more active operation Pa's well-taught observation and deduction technique. This was based on our early travels by coach or railway train when I was expected to have made an assessment from the appearance of the passengers seated opposite and hazard an accurate account of their occupations, age and circumstances. I had found it an invaluable lesson. Over the years, it became almost an automatic response to meeting strangers – with my assumptions seldom proved wrong, since the odds on a future meeting were highly unlikely.

'The Worths were not in the least alike and there was little to be considered. Edgar was not at all prepossessing, his sister is quite good-looking and obviously keeps up with the Edinburgh fashions, despite being isolated in Bute.'

Sadie looked disappointed, clearly expecting more, so I continued:

'Edgar is the elder, mid to late forties, going bald, average height with no distinguishing features beyond a sharp face . . .' I paused. 'He looked nervous and his expression accounted for those bitten fingernails I could not help noticing when we were introduced.'

Sadie laughed at this piece of observation as I went on: 'He kept glancing anxiously over his shoulder, keeping a good lookout – presumably for the arrival of their important host for the evening. And that set me thinking. Was this a business acquaintance – someone they had just met?'

'Sounds as if they were meeting for the first time and Edgar was anxious to impress him.'

'The same thought had occurred to me and to Gerald. He was in attendance at their table instead of one of the waiters. The pair were both certainly well dressed for the occasion, Beatrice in particular, one might say, overdressed. She had not spared the feathers and flounces.

But after Harry's quick introduction, I got the feeling that both of them were ill at ease as if a great deal hung upon this meeting.'

'Did you observe that she had bitten fingernails too?' Sadie asked mockingly.

Ignoring that I said, 'I got the impression this was not just a casual dinner engagement. There was something more, some important reason for their meeting.'

'Tell me about Beatrice,' Sadie demanded.

'She looked bright and intelligent-looking, but her quick, nervous smiles suggested that this was an important occasion, with more at stake than dining with an old family friend.'

I told her about the encounter in the Ladies Room and what I had observed. 'She was taller than me and slimmer, a good figure, and a closer look confirmed what I expected from their circumstances: they looked well off, well fed. And she's a lot younger than her brother. She was paying particular attention to her hair and I noticed, as always, she has nice hands.'

Sadie sighed. 'Your usual observation point, of course.'

'Hers are long-fingered, slim, like yours, Sadie – not like mine – and I would hazard a guess not much worn by hard work either. She hadn't scrubbed as many floors as I have, so there must be other servants at Vantry who do the heavy work.'

'Any ideas about their mysterious companion?'

'Sitting opposite them at the table and in my line of vision.' I smiled. 'He was no problem for me, Sadie. I meet those who are his very image every day in Edinburgh.'

(And many more during the years of my activities as a private investigator, I thought privately.) 'Everything about him, from well-polished hair to well-polished shoes and in between an immaculate black suit and decorous necktie, proclaimed to all the world that this was a man of substance, most likely a lawyer.'

Pausing, I looked at her and held up the book. 'I had left this on my table and Harry picked it up and was going to bring it up to my room. I think he was hoping for an opportunity of chatting with you, really. He asked if you were accompanying me on the drive down to St Blane's.'

I waited, giving her a chance to comment. She made none, merely shrugged, so I continued: 'He said that Gerald also drives.'

Surely that must arouse a flicker of interest, since it seemed obvious that to any woman offered a choice between the two men, the older one would be much more attractive, and from Sadie's point of view, nearer her own age than the younger man, but she merely shrugged.

Dismissing this speculation, I said: 'I decided to take a chance to find out more about the gentleman with the Vantry couple in the hope that he might be a regular visitor to the hotel. When I said I was almost sure I had met the Worths' guest somewhere before and asked if he was from Bute, Harry said he's a local lawyer, a most esteemed member of the community, much sought after when there are tenant problems with wealthy estate owners.'

'But you were right about him being a business acquaintance,' Sadie said.

'Yes, when I said I must have been mistaken about

thinking I knew him, Harry just grinned and said: "Not at all, madam, gentlemen in his profession tend to look alike." I didn't want to give the impression that I was being nosy so I laughed and said: "Now I know who he reminded me of – he's the very image of an Edinburgh lawyer of my acquaintance."'

Sadie's hair was still drying. She had a book to read but as it was early still and a fine autumn evening with just a hint of a sunset glow over a wine-red sea, I decided to take a walk along the seafront and have a quick look at Rothesay Castle. I had chosen the right time of day with a few rosy clouds floating over its lofty summit. In much the same fashion as an ageing woman, this thirteenth-century castle benefited from the absence of revealing sunlight, giving the appearance of being remarkably well preserved for its age. The gatehouse, I learnt later, had been reconstructed six years ago and the great hall restored for general use. I hoped our time here would allow a closer look.

The shops in the square were closed, all but one, the kind of general store that stays open until all hours in cities and the kind that I find irresistible, enjoying an exploration of the shelves and notices, which give an insight into what is happening in the local and nearby areas.

I was in luck. On the wall a tramways timetable, with a couple for trams to Port Bannatyne, including one each morning and afternoon that travelled the extra distance to St Colmac and back to Guildford Square, presumably for the extra convenience of local travellers with business or shopping in the town.

I heard nine strike on a nearby clock. There weren't many people about; the sea crept towards the shore, transformed by moonlight into a dizzy froth of lacy waves, quite beautiful but devoid of any audience. The only walker was a man with two large dogs. They seemed well behaved enough except that they refused to walk past. Both sat down firmly, staring up at me, and could not be cajoled to proceed on their way.

The walker was exasperated as he had to pull them violently out of my way. He apologised. 'Goodnight, miss. Don't know what's got into them, must be the full moon or something.'

All I could do was smile, shake my head and say: 'Dogs!' Especially when a Yorkshire terrier leapt up into its owner's arms with a shrill yap of terror as we met. 'Silly little thing,' she was saying consolingly as I walked past.

Encountering the dogs, while heading onward to the hotel, made me think of Thane and our close bond through the years. My deerhound was more like a fellow human than, as Jack called him, 'a mere dog'. I missed him on walks, even more than Jack or Meg.

Sadie was still awake, reading in her room, when I returned with the welcome piece of news about the tramway. 'Ten o'clock will be perfect and save the huge expense of the hotel motor car.' I wondered if her accompanying sigh was of approval for my shrewd negotiations regarding our holiday finances, or of relief that I would not be driving her down to Bute.

'We needn't wait until the return journey on the four

o'clock one in the afternoon either,' she added. 'As long as it isn't raining, we can always walk the few miles back. I am sure I can remember a shortcut.'

So it was decided. She would inform Harry, although I was certain from his enquiry as to whether my maid would be travelling with me that any disappointment on his part would be on more grounds than the loss of several pounds.

I had come prepared with my sketchbook. Standing stones and a ruined castle were excellent subjects and offered hopeful opportunities of adding to my pictorial journal of new places visited, which I tried to maintain, not always successfully, on holidays.

After a substantial breakfast served by a silent waiter, with neither Harry nor Gerald in evidence, we walked out to be greeted by a fine, sunny morning and as we reached the tramway terminus, about a dozen other passengers were already assembled. They seemed to know one another, all talking volubly, their English accents giving the hint that they were late tourists in the area.

They greeted us amiably as we waited but even before I had a chance to put my observation and deduction technique into operation, announced that they were, in fact, archaeology students touring Bute and various other islands looking at standing stones.

Sadie, fearless among these harmless strangers at declaring herself a native of Bute, had questions piled her way, to which she was able to contribute little of value. She was quite vague regarding how many standing stones were still intact – four she thought, as well as at least four remains of others.

I realised, as perhaps they did too from their solemn faces, that Sadie had not been particularly interested in this aspect of Bute history. However, our interest quickened when the leader of the group said that they had been invited to Vantry nearby to look at what remained of the ancient castle.

Sadie immediately seized upon this and pushed me forward: 'My friend Mrs Macmerry is an authoress. She is writing a book—'

No more was needed. At once, what she was hoping for, an invitation to join them was forthcoming and I was plied with the usual embarrassing and searching questions about my non-existent writing. Was it fiction, or fact, or fiction based on historic fact? I opted for the latter and as excited interest lurched in the direction of Sir Walter Scott, I hastened to add that I was still at the note-taking and research part.

'That is why we are here,' Sadie put in firmly.

As we boarded the tram, I determined to take a seat well away from my eager questioners. Sadie gripped my arm and whispered: 'This is a great opportunity. What a piece of luck.'

And that was where it ran out for the day. With the suddenness characteristic of the island, within moments the weather had changed dramatically. Rain streamed down the windows even as our journey began. By the time we reached Port Bannatyne and turned west towards St Colmac it was torrential, the standing stones barely visible. The archaeologists did not share our dismay, they merely laughed grimly and said they were well used to digging in all weathers on remote sites and always came prepared and equipped with suitable boots, raincoats and heavy umbrellas.

Sadie and I did not share their enthusiasm, nor were we clad for such an expedition and even that tempting invitation to Vantry was overcome by the prospect of clambering across wet fields. The outing was a time-wasting disaster.

'We can't do anything in this weather,' I told Sadie. 'We will have to delay our exploration of the countryside around Vantry until it clears.'

There was nothing else for it but to remain in our seats, and after the ten-minute wait staring glumly out of the rain-streamed windows into the mists where the archaeologists had cheerfully vanished, we made the return journey to Guildford Square. However, the tramway journey had proved one thing. We now knew that we could take it as far as Port Bannatyne, and it was not impossible to get off at the turning to St Colmac and walk the rest of the way.

Sadie sighed. 'I suppose so. As I remember, it's about ten minutes' walk up quite a steep hill. Vantry is at the top.'

We arrived back at the terminus. Although the first step in any investigation is the scene of the crime, even before that, according to Pa, one must always carefully acquaint oneself and be ready with all information available. So my first port of call, heedless of the weather but with an umbrella purchased at a local store, would be the local library and a look at the old newspapers.

Hopefully they would be stored in the archives.

Sadie wasn't impressed by my decision. She was cold and hungry, her thoughts lingering on the warm hotel lounge.

No, of course. I didn't mind, I told her, hardly wanting her looking over my shoulder, asking endless questions at this particular stage of my investigation. We parted company and in the library I was fortunate, for not only were there available old newspapers relating to the trial but also a file containing reports of each day's activities.

The library assistants were obviously curious about this tourist's particular interest in this piece of old news, so when I mentioned writing a book there was an immediate burst of activity. I was to feel free to come in at any time and consult the file on what had been Rothesay's most stirring and sensational murder case. I was set down at a large table and as I trawled through the yellowing papers there were also drawings made at the trial.

What interested me most was a sketch of the sixteen-year-old girl in the dock who bore not the slightest resemblance to Sadie Brook. With a sigh of relief I realised that was all they had to go by twenty years ago. Unfortunately, taking pictures by camera for newspapers had not reached the level that we now expected and the drawings were only moderately skilful, although the artist had managed to make the suspected murderess look vaguely sinister. It was an ordinary plain face, rather tight-lipped, but there was a certain slyness in that sideways glance that I thought might somehow influence readers as well as a jury to say 'Aye, looks like a killer, that one does'.

I folded the newspapers, closed the file and taking my notebook, thanked the librarians for their co-operation and to their questions added that I would most certainly be returning later and would be most obliged if they would keep the file accessible.

Outside it was still raining, a trial we should have expected as a constant possibility of island weather, and should it worsen, the grim reminder that the Wemyss Bay ferry would be cancelled. Already viewed from the hotel window that smooth-as-glass sea of yesterday had erupted into waves like white horses rearing up and thrashing against the shore.

There was plenty indoors to keep me occupied. The hotel's reading room and library shelves mostly contained novels of romantic fiction left by lady visitors, nudging alongside historic well-worn books of local interest. I also had my notes to reread, and for Sadie this provided an interesting interlude.

She had been spending a lot of idle time closeted with Harry in the office he shared with Gerald next to the reception desk and she came out to me, beaming. Harry was taking her to the local picture house that evening. There was an American film showing and a local pianist played accompanying music.

Of course, she said, I was most welcome to go with them. She was sure Gerald, although not consulted, would come along too. I declined the invitation – issued more out of politeness, I felt, than keenness for my company – with thanks. In fact, I was already beginning to have some doubts about Sadie's sea captain lover, in whose interests this journey to Bute and her conflict with the past had been initiated. Certainly, although first impressions suggested that Harry was young enough to be her son, he was an attractive lad and obviously thought Sadie was a stunner. How fortunate that he had still been an infant at the time of the murder case as I now had reason to wonder how this visit was going to end, and whether proving her innocence was maybe providing a platform for something greater in her life.

As long as she could keep out of Uncle Godwin's way. I gathered that she was learning a great deal about him and the unhappy state of affairs that existed with his nephew. Harry, she said, had told her that approaching age had made him more cantankerous than ever and this included an obsession about having money of his own, constantly asking Harry and Gerald for a few more pounds to spend. Although Harry maintained that he had a good allowance from the hotel's finances, he was extravagant, an inveterate gambler and an alcoholic, constantly slipping down unobserved during the night to the cellars for another bottle of vintage wine and whisky.

I watched Harry and Sadie leave together and as it was pointless retiring at so early an hour, and until I had sorted out my thoughts and my notes, a more agreeable way was to spend the rest of the evening in the lounge with its substantial log fire, relaxing in one of those luxurious armchairs in the shade of a rather exotic and perhaps not real palm tree. I settled down and prepared to dip into the history of Bute from the reading room library after making notes on the day's events.

Engrossed in my activities, I was suddenly conscious of a tall presence hovering above me, a masculine throat clearing. I looked up.

A police uniform.

CHAPTER TEN

A policeman. A moment's panic. Had something happened to Jack and Meg? What had I done amiss? How on earth did he know me?

He bowed, smiling. 'Mrs Macmerry? Chief Inspector Jack Macmerry's wife?' I said yes and he laughed. 'Sorry to disturb you, but you being from Edinburgh, I guessed there must be a connection.' He smiled again. 'It's an unusual name and Jack wasn't married when I left, we used to tease him about it being time he found a wife and got himself out of the bachelor police lodgings. Well, well. Now what a coincidence.' His appraising look said that Jack's choice pleased him. What was this, I thought, some sort of pickup?

He was tall, fair-haired, a good-looking fortyish, I guessed, and as I am slightly under five foot tall, sitting down strained my neck looking up at him. I indicated the seat on the other side of the small table between the deep armchairs.

He sat down still smiling and held out his hand. 'Thank you. I'm Peter Clovis, sergeant here. Jack may have remembered me – we were good pals – when he knew you were coming to Bute.'

What a relief. Seeing that the introduction was involving Jack, it must be respectable. I nodded vaguely, trying to place his name. Jack had probably mentioned him but I had not a clue to his identity. Tactful concealment was indicated and I smiled. 'Am I right in thinking that you were with the police here before coming to Edinburgh?'

He grinned. 'Correct! A born and bred islander, Mrs Macmerry, although I left the force here twenty years ago, often regretted it each time I came back across in the ferry.' He shrugged. 'But I was young then and lured away by the city lights. I thought of Glasgow first of all, but when a vacancy came up with Edinburgh City Police, I took it. No regrets—'

I was no longer listening. Twenty years ago. An ominous thought. While he talked, my rapid calculations did not make good reading. I guessed he was about the same age as Jack and that meant twenty years ago, as a Bute policeman, he must have remembered, if he had not actually been involved in, the murder investigation involving Sarah Vantry. Even if that was not the case, he

101

must have heard all about it, a sensational topic for every conversation and I felt certain that, even now, I could go out on to the high street, just mention Sarah Vantry to anyone of our generation or older, and I would receive a whole rundown on the horrific story.

Rothesay was that sort of place: there was never a lot to report in the local press and events were eagerly seized upon. In particular, scandals or murders, rare as hen's teeth, were highlighted and became a talking point for as long as anyone could remember, destined to play their part in the fabric of local history.

This was bad news, especially for Sadie, despite the consolation that as she had been only sixteen, he would probably not recognise her. But had she changed all that much from girlhood? Most women of thirty-six would have done so, unless she had any distinguishing features that would remain in the minds of those who had known her. I didn't know of any such features except the glorious chestnut hair and at that moment I was again conscious of how very little I really knew about Sadie Brook, either, and could only suppose a natural delicacy or fear of our reactions had prevented her from confiding any of her past during our days in Solomon's Tower.

Mrs Brook was such a trusted family retainer that Jack had never thought – and I would never have dreamt – of asking for something like a reference for her niece as our housekeeper. So there she had established herself with us, on the surface busily taking care of us, cooking excellent meals, taking my bicycle to go shopping or into Edinburgh and collecting Meg from school, I thought grimly – all providing a cloak to examining my records as a lady investigator.

I knew now from her own words that drawing me into proving her innocence was always at the back of her mind. Had it actually only become an urgency after meeting Captain Robbie who had wooed and won what she hoped was a permanent place in her life?

And now sitting opposite in the handsome, well-upholstered, richly carpeted lounge in the Heights Hotel, chatting to Sergeant Clovis about my husband, Chief Inspector Jack Macmerry, and various activities they shared, like golf and so forth, in Edinburgh, I realised this was the man who could put an end to Sadie's plan and destroy all her hopes of having me prove that she didn't push Oswald Vantry down the castle stairs to his death.

'Indeed, I was happy to be home again,' Clovis was saying. 'I decided a few years ago' – his face darkened denoting some personal tragedy – 'that I had had enough of Edinburgh.' He saw me watching him and realised that a reason was required. He said sadly, 'My wife died.' He gulped. 'Childbirth.' He hurried on. 'Suddenly I wanted peace and quiet, I wanted back my old life, what it had been like before I met Jean.' He gave a deep sigh. 'I had been born here and here I would stay until I retired.'

'That must be a very long way off.'

It was even worse than I had thought at first. Alarm bells were ringing. This was not a casual visitor where no one would remind him of twenty years ago. I could hear Jack telling him: Do you remember, Pete, that murder case you were on in Bute, the lassie who got the not-proven verdict?

He was smiling at my remark about retirement. 'I'm forty-six, so it is quite early to make any plans.'

Twenty-six at the time of the case, I was thinking, how much would he remember of Sarah Vantry, aged sixteen, if they were to meet?

'And I look forward to continuing a quiet life here,' he added. 'After Edinburgh, not much happens in Rothesay these days. A small constabulary, just eight of us and that includes Arran. People are very law-abiding – sometimes in summer we have problems with traffic and the tourists, but never anything really bad, like murder.'

I almost jumped. Like murder, he had said the fatal words. He was standing up, holding out his hand, saying how pleasant it had been to meet me. Apologies for interrupting my reading and that sort of thing.

'Are you here alone?'

'No, I'm with a companion, a friend from Edinburgh.'

'Well, I hope you will both enjoy your visit. This is a great hotel, all you need is the blessing of better weather than this morning. Alas, we have no influence with the celestial weatherman. Do you like sailing, by any chance?'

I bit my lip. I wasn't prepared to go into all that with a stranger. A shake of the head and at that moment, the office door opened and Gerald approached. The two men greeted each other, one might add, warily.

Clovis said, 'You have already met Mrs Macmerry, of course.' And to me: 'Gerald is my adopted brother. I bullied him unmercifully but he's too big for that now.'

Gerald smiled. He was certainly at least ten years younger than the policeman, who wasn't inclined to linger.

Giving me a final smile, he bowed over my hand. 'Enjoy your stay, I am sure you will be well looked after. Perhaps we may meet again.'

Not if I can help it, I resolved, watching him with narrowed eyes, walking away, determined to keep him away from meeting Sadie face-to-face at all costs. Bidding Gerald goodnight, I headed for the stairs, wondering if I had stumbled on yet another danger, the possibility that he remembered what had happened in Bute two decades ago. Policemen are trained to have good, solid retentive memories. Observation and deduction, remember – Pa had reared me on those three words.

I had a great deal on my mind and decided to wait up for Sadie, to warn her about Sergeant Clovis and Gerald Thorn. I didn't imagine she would be late and expected to see the door open on her return with Harry at any moment. I was comfortable in the warm lounge with the log fire crackling away, so I went back to my history of Bute, constantly attended by one of the vast but strangely anonymous domestic staff who circulated the hotel. An order for a pot of tea and some biscuits consoled them. However, when the massive and aggressive-sounding grandfather clock boomed through its ritual of Westminster chimes and ponderously chimed eleven, I was yawning and heavy-eyed.

I decided to call it a day, and snuggled down for the night in my warm bed in the cosy bedroom, I didn't open my eyes again until first light streamed through the windows.

Washed and dressed, there was no sound from Sadie, and thinking she had overslept, I knocked on the door. No answer.

Calling: 'Breakfast time. Are you awake?' I opened the door a crack, looked in and saw that the room was empty. Had she gone down already?

Another look revealed that the room was not only empty, her bed had not been slept in. I was somewhat shocked. There was only one conclusion, and that was she had spent the night elsewhere – and with Harry.

Downstairs in the restaurant, she was seated at our table.

Greeting her I said, 'You're early. I looked in, thought you might have overslept.'

I waited a moment, expecting some explanation or excuse. There was none and I told myself that I, respectably married, had no business being judgemental regarding Sadie and her morals. After all, I was not unused to such goings-on, as before returning to Edinburgh, my life for ten years in Arizona's shack towns had included the only female company, that of saloon girls.

Helping herself to a slice of toast, Sadie said: 'Oh, I woke at seven. I was hungry so I came down.' But she avoided my eyes and I knew, even disregarding her empty bed upstairs, that it was a lie.

There was no more conversation. My breakfast arrived and the delicious bacon and egg had my full attention. The maid arrived with tea and toast, and buttering a slice, I asked: 'Did you enjoy the film?'

'Oh yes.' There was nothing more to be said about last night, no question about how I had spent the evening. A quick change of subject as she asked eagerly: 'Are we going to Vantry this morning? The weather looks good.'

I shrugged inwardly. Her behaviour was not my

responsibility, nor was any concern for the absent Robbie. But I did wonder how this was all to end as we walked silently to the terminus, having observed how she and Harry had exchanged secret glances on the way out of the hotel. And the story about waking early had come so smoothly, I began to have doubts and wonder for the first time, was she an accomplished liar in more vital matters, such as our mission in Bute?

I decided to spare her undoubted feelings of panic by keeping to myself the meeting with Peter Clovis, or that he had been a policeman in Rothesay twenty years ago and might well have been involved in the murder investigation, and also that Gerald Thorn, his adopted brother, might have a long memory.

I resolved to do my best to keep Clovis out of Sadie's way and any other policemen who might have long memories. How I was to achieve this I had not the least idea. It was just a further addition to a growing list of those she did not wish to encounter but, mercifully, we were only here for a few more days.

CHAPTER ELEVEN

Armed with a local map, welcomed by a cloudless blue sky that looked as if it had never heard of such a thing as rain, we headed to the tramway terminus in the square. As we stepped aboard, there were other passengers seated, including families with small children.

We were fortunate to get the one tram per day that went on past the Port Bannatyne terminus to St Colmac, a short distance from our destination at Vantry. From the one window seat remaining, the landscape, obscured yesterday by heavy rain, now opened up to a splendid view over garden hedges of various habitations, hills and secret wooded slopes with the backdrop of a horizon of islands, like basking whales resting lazy and peaceful on a bright azure sea.

And across to the east at Kames Bay, an anchored flotilla of sailing boats, bobbing about in the water. 'Aren't they lovely,' Sadie sighed. 'I wonder which are the ones belonging to the hotel. I'd love a trip round the islands, wouldn't you?'

'I'm not a very good sailor.'

'I'd forgotten. What a pity. Anyway, we're in luck today,' she said as we alighted at St Colmac accompanied by the rest of the passengers who had continued the short journey from Port Bannatyne. 'This is the day each month when there is a tour of the house, and this is the last this year.'

This was luck indeed. 'How did you find that out?' I asked.

'Oh, Harry told me.' I noticed that her face had coloured up at the mention of his name, as she went on: 'For a shilling the tour includes tea and scones.'

A look at the family groups suggested that seemed somewhat excessive.

She shrugged. 'I gather that the children get in for nothing.'

I wanted to know more about this proposed visit and when I said surely this was somewhat unusual, opening the doors of a house without historic interest to tourists, she gave me a wry look and sighed. 'Well, it does include a look at . . . at the spot, you know, where it all happened. Isn't it terrible,' she giggled, 'to think they have actually kept that alive as a popular tourist attraction? Bute's one claim to notoriety.'

I thought they weren't the first by any means to take advantage of a long-past murder as a coin-spinner. The King did it regularly by providing the same facility at the palace of Holyroodhouse when royalty was not in residence. Tours arranged with the additional attraction of the bloodstains of David Rizzio, Mary Queen of Scots' ill-fated secretary, pointed out and still remarkably visible, although rumour had it, according to Jack, possibly kept up to date and in good condition by frequent applications of oxblood boot polish.

I felt that the tea would be a good investment. We stepped off at the signpost for St Colmac accompanied by the tourist families and headed past the standing stones, greeted by the children as a fine place for hide-and-seek, despite parental admonishments. As the road climbed the steep hill to Vantry, with a chill wind blowing in our faces I made a mental note that if we were to do this again we would take up the offer of the hotel's motor car hire, with or without Harry or Gerald as chauffeur.

At last the house came into view, before disappearing as we approached to emerge at the end of a long, twisting drive of rhododendrons. There, open gates proclaimed a 'Beware of the Dog' notice, which seemed to belong to a suburban house rather than a stately mansion. A walk across a gravelled forecourt, beyond the sign marked 'Entrance', a sharp ascent of stone steps flanked by two rather time-worn and less than imposing snarling lions, and we stepped inside the massive studded door overlooked by a table where our coins were collected by an elderly man, who proved to also be the guide.

As those ahead of us were being admitted, Sadie touched my arm and whispered, 'He's the gardener. I remember him . . . Oh heavens!' she added, pulling the blue hat's brim well down. 'I hope he doesn't recognise me.'

It was our turn and as he took the money, I felt that he might have washed his hands first – his dirty nails, in particular, were hardly likely to impress tourists – and when I said this to Sadie, she laughed. 'Come on, Rose, you're probably the only one who noticed. You have a positive obsession about such things.' And then she shivered. 'It was really scary seeing him again.'

Over the threshold and into the vast hall with its marble floor, Vantry smelt old. A musty smell I recognised and associated with home at Solomon's Tower; that indefinable yet strangely pungent odour went along with all old castles and had even invaded this solid Queen Anne mansion a short distance from what remained of the medieval castle we had seen on the way in. I suspected from the skeletal, ruinous tower imploringly beseeching the skyline that the present building had been freely constructed from the original stronghold by a liberal use of those thirteenth-century stones.

Now with the guide trotting ahead, our footsteps echoing on the marble floor, we were staring up the oak staircase. Magnificent in structure, but steep, dark and somewhat imposing, my suspicions about the mansion's origins were confirmed by the occasional appearance of ancient doors as well as a dining hall with a magnificent fireplace flanked by two forbidding, bare-breasted ancient goddesses. I wondered how the prim occupants of the late queen's reign managed to digest their bacon and eggs under that fearsome gaze. Wholly out of context, it had doubtless belonged to the original castle, including some rather unexpected items of furnishing, massive ancient and faded tapestries of gruesome events in Greek and Roman mythology that hadn't quite rerooted happily in their new abode and lurked somehow ill at ease in a seventeenth-century building.

We progressed slowly with the guide who did not provide us with his name but had a surprising catalogue of information about the exhibits that he had obviously learnt by heart. The rooms we passed through were large and cold and unprepossessing, and one suspected that occasional empty spaces against walls had once been occupied by *objets d'art* perhaps sacrificed over the years when major repairs to ceilings and roof were required.

The guide now hurried us on, Sadie keeping well away from the surge to the front of the exhibits he was at great pains and at great lengths to explain. Few had any historic interest, beyond the inevitable Jacobite connections. Despite rumour, did Prince Charlie ever set foot in Rothesay during his escape over to Skye? I thought not and regarded one of his gloves, conveniently dropped in his flight, carefully noted and preserved in a glass case, as an unreliable relic.

The door to the library was open, and passing by, we were allowed a mere glimpse inside, perhaps because it was occupied by Edgar Worth sitting at a table intent upon some writing.

He merely glanced up at this interruption and gave us

a polite nod. There was no sign of Beatrice. And no doubt her ladyship also enjoyed sitting at that desk in the library when the doors were closed on the tourists, counting up the day's total of shillings, I thought, as the guide threw up yet another door into yet another unexciting room with portraits of bygone Vantrys staring down resentfully at these intruders in their ancestral home.

I lingered by one portrait for a better look, and seeing what I considered as a fleeting family resemblance to Sadie, I took her arm and whispered: 'That could be you.'

She wasn't flattered and replied: 'She's no beauty.' I could only agree. It had been a tactless remark, a plain rather doughish face, and Sadie was certainly the better-looking. Only the facial contours, the eye shape and the abundant chestnut curls bore any resemblance.

'She has elegant hands.'

Sadie looked again and sighed. 'Well, there's your proof, if you needed any.' As we walked on, Sadie looked at me and laughed. 'You always go on about hands. I never notice them, but you seem quite obsessed.'

There was a reason for that. I had been scared since childhood when I heard that my great-grandmother Sibella Scarth had been taken from the sea as an infant near the shipwreck of a Norwegian merchantman. Although it was stoutly maintained by two surviving sailors that there were no women or children aboard, this had given birth to the rumour that she was a selkie because she had webbed fingers and toes. Despite reassurances from Gran, in childhood I had daily subjected my own rather short fingers and toes to a rigorous examination.

I outgrew that particular terror but it left me very hand-conscious and when I first met Sibella on my visit to Orkney ten years ago, I saw that she wore mittens and sister Emily whispered that no one ever saw her hands, she was shy about having webbed fingers.

As we progressed through the house, staying close to my side Sadie was keeping a very low profile, and in that dreadful hat, looking more like a servant than ever. She had a good reason for that, she said later, terrified that we might go into the library when she glimpsed from the back of the tourists the man sitting there. She wasn't close enough to see his face but guessed it was Edgar.

My brief introduction to the Worths in the hotel the evening before had made her increasingly nervous about coming face-to-face with them. I had laughed away her concern then and she had later said: 'If we had been recognised, they would probably have wanted to talk to us again, you being introduced as an authoress. It would have been awful.'

There were fewer rooms than we expected on display, and we were restricted to ground level. The tour continued duller than ever; we paused in a long corridor leading to the kitchens and were asked to admire large cabinets of china and crystal locked behind glass.

Like ourselves, the guided party was getting restless, especially those with bored young children.

The main attraction for the tourists lay ahead. The one place where they inclined to linger was staring up at that great oak staircase where the murder sensationally described in the press handout, and briefly mentioned by the guide, had occurred. Clutching their offspring to their sides, one could imagine their thoughts: a sixteen-year-old girl, imagine one so young, so ungrateful and evil!

The tour was now almost over. The guide cleared his throat and murmured perhaps we might proceed without him to the gardens.

'There is only one area where visitors are restricted. You will see a locked gate. Behind there are some of our special exotic plants, many are very delicate and poisonous, and were brought home by earlier Vantrys who travelled to exotic places abroad.'

This information was greeted by little interest from the tour, who showed a certain reluctance to leave the one fascinating gruesome spot in the house worthy of their shillings; now satisfied, the tour turned into almost a stampede towards the cafe. This was situated in what must have been the servants' kitchen, lofty-ceilinged with an army of large, imposing bells perched high on one wall near the ceiling awaiting the summons and imperial demands of the long-past Vantrys.

A certain scramble ensued for places at the one long table and the guide regarded the assembly with the stern expression of a teacher overseeing school meals. Once we were seated, he announced that, besides access to the gardens, visitors were also permitted a walk around the terrace close to the house.

There was a question from one of the group, keen to explore the ruined castle, to which he replied, his gaze resting heavily upon the now unruly children, that as this was highly dangerous, it was not permitted except with an experienced guide. He obviously did not include this in the present tour and emphasised that warning notices throughout be carefully observed.

He hoped we had enjoyed our visit to the house with the well-rehearsed parting words, 'We are not the first noble family to open our doors, even royalty do so now, I understand. Our present King is a man of the people.'

With that patriotic flag-waving, the tourists seemed unimpressed, while I thought of Holyroodhouse, including my own personal brief encounters of His Majesty earlier this year at Balmoral Castle as stepsister of Dr Vincent Beaumarcher Laurie, a junior physician to the royal household.

Having consumed a scone less delicious than it appeared under the glass cover, and a cup of somewhat weak and lukewarm tea, our guide lingered to point out the final lap of the tour around the terrace close to the house, with its few ornamental flower beds, all sadly past their seasonal blooms. However, we were permitted a glimpse of Lady Vantry, also known to Sadie as Lady Adeline, leaning heavily on her walking stick.

At my side, Sadie gripped my arm, fearful of being recognised and once more glad of the impulse to bring along her disguise, the close-fitting hat.

Lady Adeline passed close by, and hesitated to stare at us, perhaps resentful of this invasion of her privacy. Her expression was concealed by her veils, the only flesh visible was from a ringed hand, with a flash of jewels, raised against a sudden breeze that threatened her bonnet.

The guide gave her a stylish bow and as she wandered

off in the direction of the servants' entrance, an obvious necessity to avoiding the steep stone steps to the front door, he whispered: 'Her ladyship is very frail now.'

She didn't look frail, she was even a little stout, but that could have been an illusion from the flowing robes, I thought, as he continued: 'She likes to keep up with present day happenings and is very proud of our history. Pleased to open her house to so many visitors from foreign parts who will remember it as part of their visit to the island, and carry away good memories of our heritage.'

Someone asked: 'Who looks after her ladyship now?'

'She has close relatives who live here. Her ladyship never recovered from losing her only son' – a hesitation – 'twenty years ago, as you all are aware, no doubt . . .' Another pause for silent reflection in a nod towards the house with its now infamous staircase . . . 'In such terrible circumstances.'

At the table next to me, a knowledgeable tourist was telling his partner about this brother and sister from a remote branch of the family who had moved up from England near where he lived, and, he understood, leaving a splendid estate, to come and look after her ladyship. The listener was impressed and there were head shakings and murmurs of 'Such devotion'. Personally, I considered that remote branch doubtless had ample rewards for such devotion no doubt provided by a quick scan of Lady Vantry's will.

Keen to hear how Sadie had reacted to this visit, as we left the house I asked what did she think of Lady Vantry.

She shrugged. 'I never would have recognised her again. Didn't look a bit as I remember her. Always thought she was taller and thinner, not so shapeless.'

'That's what time can do. And for all those elaborate precautions, perhaps the same can be said for you,' I added tactfully.

'What do you mean?'

'Well, you've changed a bit, haven't you?'

'I suppose so,' she said and added eagerly: 'That guide, Angus-something-or-other, he must be sixty or more, but he always looked old. Got less hair now, but thankfully he never gave me a second glance. I was quite scared, I can tell you. I'm just thankful that Edgar didn't get a chance to see me.'

'You've certainly made sure of that by keeping out of his way here as well as at the hotel.'

She sighed. 'And with good reason. Edgar Worth was one of the witnesses—er, of the accident.' She thought for a moment and frowned. 'I'm sure he wasn't called Edgar then. Something like Ned, or Teddy.' She shrugged. 'He claimed that he also heard Oswald and I fighting and me shouting that I hated him just . . . just before—'

'What was he doing at Vantry?'

'On holiday from England, I expect.'

'What about the sister, Beatrice?'

Sadie shook her head. 'She wasn't with him then. I never met her. She was maybe too little. I don't recall anything about her or even that he had a sister.'

We were walking down the drive, well ahead of the tourists, and as we turned a sharp corner a man was approaching. He was just yards away, and seeing us, he nearly jumped out of his skin, his anxiety not to be seen reminding me of Sadie as he darted into the rhododendrons.

'Did you see that?' I asked Sadie.

'What?'

'That man. Coming towards us – he didn't want to be seen, just leapt into the bushes.'

Sadie shook her head, she hadn't noticed him, head down, too busy talking, lost in her own anxieties, her Vantry experiences that this visit had reawakened.

But my mind was on that man, his swift movement so furtive it suggested that whatever he was doing on the drive heading towards the house, he was up to no good.

I saw his expression, that startled face. It was not the last we were to hear of him.

CHAPTER TWELVE

We had reached the place where the tram waited, already crowded with noisy, truculent children overcome by boredom, a few of the very small ones now yelling lustily. Sadie and I exchanged looks of resignation. This was not a journey that we cared to contemplate.

A quick decision. Late afternoon and still a pleasant day. Sadie took my arm and whispered: 'Feel like walking back? It isn't far and I think over there is a shortcut.' I was eager to try it and we followed the path she had pointed out between the fields. On high ground, we were soon in sight of Ardbeg and emerged from the wooded slope on to the road to Rothesay.

'Tell me about Edgar. You're quite sure it was him?' I asked Sadie.

She nodded. 'Yes. He was older than me, past forty now, I would guess, and I do remember that Adeline seemed very fond of him on that last holiday.'

'What about her son, this Oswald? How did the two boys get along?'

She thought for a moment, frowning. 'Oswald was the young one, but they played together, card games, cricket, that sort of thing, very boisterous and often fighting over trifles the way all young lads do.' She paused thoughtfully. 'Harry says that Gerald never got along with Peter, his adopted brother, either. There was too much difference in their ages. They still haven't much in common, which is a shame.'

'Age doesn't always matter. Tell me about Harry and Gerald.'

'Maybe it's different with friends and Harry says they have always been close, more like brothers, really, and Gerald came to live in the hotel a couple of years ago.'

'What do you think of him?'

Suddenly I wanted to know. He had shown not even that solitary gleam of interest I had observed in every man meeting Sadie for the first time.

Now she shrugged. 'He's all right, I suppose.' That seemed inadequate, incredible to any observer that a woman like Sadie could prefer the boy-like Harry to the more mature, and although it was a moot point, also better-looking, Gerald.

'What did you think of Edgar?' she asked.

'Not a great deal. But then I hardly had time to make an assessment.' However, the remark set me off on an interesting but alarming train of thought. Despite Sadie's account of the accident, what if, on that fatal day, it had been Edgar and Oswald fighting on the stairs? Suppose Lady Adeline had seen it, but with reasons for wanting rid of Sarah, did she persuade Edgar to blame her, turn that accident into murder? I realised again that I needed to read a full account of that trial. But how?

And I had it. Sergeant Clovis, off duty, was in the hotel lounge. So much for my resolution to keep him out of Sadie's way.

He stood up, put aside the newspaper he had been reading, and smiled: 'I was waiting for you, Mrs Macmerry. Have you had a good day? Harry said you were going to Vantry.'

I said it had been enjoyable and he continued eagerly: 'It's my father's eightieth birthday and we are having a wee party this evening. My folks would love to meet you and we wondered if you would care to join us?'

I was conscious of Sadie lingering in the background. As we entered the hotel she had said she was exhausted and intended going upstairs to have a rest before dinner. 'And do bring this young lady with you,' he added, with a bow in her direction.

I had hoped to avoid this meeting with Clovis, but it was too late now. She had removed the hat, revealing her best feature – that cascade of chestnut waves. She smiled, came forward and shyly thanked him.

That was good, he was politely treating her as a

stranger, asking her how she liked Bute. I sighed with relief as moments later they were discussing Edinburgh and how lucky she was living and working in that great city. And suddenly I was an observer only, listening to a repeat of his conversation with me – born and bred islander, served with the Bute police twenty years ago – but he obviously had not the least notion that this was Sarah Vantry he was talking to. My presence was forgotten and Sadie Brook was working her charm on the policeman. How did she do it?

Following her upstairs, the coquettish manner faded like a light switched off. She frowned. 'I don't know about that party, Rose, there might be unseen hazards.'

I agreed with her. Even if Peter had not worked on the case, the elder members of the Clovis family would certainly have memories of the trial. What if someone at the party had reasons for recognising Miss Brook as Sarah Vantry? She had been fortunate so far, since Gerald had not realised her true identity, which was just as well for her association with Harry.

When I put it to her, she agreed and said the thought of meeting the Clovis family made her nervous and that I would be better going on my own. Besides, she had a better excuse.

Harry was taking her to the pictures again. 'He's delighted to have someone to go with. Gerald can't abide these moving pictures. He's a bit of a snob and thinks the stories are silly.' She sighed. 'Anyway, we couldn't get in the other evening, the tickets were sold out.'

I gave her a hard look.

She had lied about that. When I asked her had she

enjoyed the film, her answer clearly indicated that they had been at the picture house. 'It has been very popular. As well as the main film, they have been showing the fourth Marquess of Bute's wedding last year and all the local folk are thrilled with Mount Stuart being local and so near. It's been a great draw—'

Returning to the lounge, Sadie's story was interrupted by Harry with a message from Sergeant Clovis that the party would begin shortly.

'They live in one of the big houses up the hill, quite near at hand, just five minutes' walk away.'

Gerald came forward, smiled. As I was a stranger to the area, he would be delighted to personally escort me there.

Sadie and Harry watched us leave. 'We're looking forward to the films,' Sadie said and I observed those warm glances exchanged between the pair.

Climbing the hill with Gerald, I had to tell myself firmly that although it was now obvious that a love affair was in bloom, it was no business of mine and if I hoped to fathom the enigmatic Gerald walking firmly by my side, I was to be disappointed.

I received nothing more personal than a warm hand gripping my arm crossing the road and on a treacherous piece of pavement. His only conversation was an extended version of the tourists' guide to Bute and what was important not to miss.

The approach to the Clovis house had a sensational view over the river and inside it was most attractively furnished, enhanced by the candlelight from the drawing room's large bow windows and rivalling the town's lights twinkling far below. Appropriate for such an occasion, moonlight obligingly sparkled on a smooth sea.

When I arrived, the rooms and the hall were already crowded with guests. Peter's mother Jane came forward and greeted Gerald with a kiss. She was obviously delighted to see him and said so. I thought that odd considering that he now lived a mere five minutes away.

James Clovis made his way through the crowd, was introduced and smiled wryly at his adopted son, hoping that he was happy and that the hotel was not working him too hard. A nice piece of sarcasm, I thought, wondering what this family scene would be like when they gathered together behind closed doors.

Drinks were being passed around, and aware of my poor head for alcohol, I accepted an orange juice.

Peter rushed forward to greet me, his eyes searching I realised for Sadie as he said: 'You are alone?'

I told him that Gerald, who had drifted off to greet other guests, had escorted me and added that my companion sent her apologies, she already had a previous engagement. I could see by his expression that this was a disappointment, but taking my arm he said: 'There is someone who is anxious to meet you.'

And there was Lady Vantry. I spotted her immediately, an unmistakable figure from the gardens at Vantry that afternoon, wearing the same attire complete with mourning veils and seated in an armchair in a corner of the vast drawing room.

Peter was saying: 'She doesn't go out except on rare

occasions and it is an honour to have her with us.' He smiled. 'As our lady bountiful, it would have been considered an insult not to invite her to such an occasion since Father has been an honoured member of the community all these years, a lawyer of some standing.'

A lawyer, indeed. How fortunate Sadie had made the right decision not to come, I thought, as Peter took my arm and whispered: 'I must introduce you to her ladyship, Mrs Macmerry. She is just looking in for a short while, out of politeness. She won't be staying for the meal. She never eats in public now. Her scarred face, you know.'

Introduced as the authoress – to my embarrassment – who was also the famous Inspector Faro's daughter, Lady Vantry offered an elegant hand: 'I once had the pleasure of meeting your father on a visit here, long ago. We entertained him at Vantry and I am delighted to meet his daughter.' That was quite a speech considering the throaty quality of her voice, perhaps with age, hardly above a whisper.

I was conscious of a figure looming in our direction. It was Edgar Worth, regarding his aunt and patroness with anxious eyes. Apparently, he never relaxed even at parties, the hand holding the glass tightly with those bitten fingernails was a sure sign of nervousness.

As Lady Vantry murmured an introduction, he bowed in my direction. 'Mrs Macmerry and I have already met at the hotel, Aunt Adeline. Beatrice and I, the other evening – a dinner engagement,' he reminded her rather loudly. So age had also contributed deafness.

Edgar turned to me and shook his head: 'Beatrice

cannot be with us this evening, alas, she has one of her migraines.' A somewhat twisted and reluctant smile. 'Unfortunately, they are quite frequent at this time of the year.' Another bow. 'She will be sorry to miss the party and the chance of meeting you here, Mrs Macmerry. She is a keen reader.'

Oh dear, the false authoress persona again. I smiled in polite acknowledgement. I looked at Lady Vantry and hoped she wasn't also a keen reader armed with the usual questions as Peter was carried off to welcome another newcomer. Thankfully, she merely nodded and Edgar put in quickly: 'How long are you staying, Mrs Macmerry?'

'Just for a week.'

A deep sigh from Edgar registered polite disappointment, or could it have been relief?

'Perhaps you might visit Vantry,' said Lady Adeline.

Edgar gave her a sharp look for that throaty invitation and added quickly: 'Indeed, yes, and Beatrice would like that.'

The rattle of glasses heralded the approaching drinks tray. I shook my head while Edgar seized one and offered it to his aunt.

She took it eagerly enough, and shielding her face from our direct gaze, turned her head away to lift a corner of the veil. I felt a moment's compassion, so much else destroyed by age and a tragic accident, but those elegant beringed hands had been spared.

Edgar was watching her. The sonorous note of a gong from the hallway indicated that dinner was about to be served.

'We must leave, Aunt,' Edgar said loudly. 'The carriage is waiting.'

Eager to depart, he helped her to her feet, stick in hand. He remembered a bow in my direction as they disappeared among the guests now heading downstairs.

Peter came across with Gerald and as neither had partners I walked arm in arm with both men as they led the way into the large candlelit dining room. There I discovered that I was an honoured guest, seated between Peter and Gerald, opposite their parents, James and Jane, on one of the long, white covered tables provided for the occasion, all richly decorated with flowers and candles and, I suspected, the meal provided by the Heights Hotel's very best and most expensive menu.

The Clovis family were long-established members of the Rothesay community; Peter's father bore the weight of his eighty years exceedingly well, rosy-cheeked and healthy-looking, his only failing apparently being short-sighted and having to ask his wife several times to read what was on the menu.

She smiled at me and whispered: 'He won't wear his glasses.' She laughed. 'I thought it was only ladies, but men are so vain sometimes.'

Leaning across, he said he had met Chief Inspector Jeremy Faro on a visit to Rothesay long ago and what did I write?

I was spared an answer due to the noisy conversations nearby, particularly a woman with a strident voice and shrill laugh – I suspected a relentless application to that frequently passing drinks tray on arrival. I missed some of Mr Clovis's remarks but he was most eager for news of my father.

Peter had inherited his looks from his mother who was keen to hear all about Edinburgh, particularly the fashions and whether I had ever been to Holyroodhouse. They seemed anxious to include Gerald in the conversation.

'We were very keen that he should do law,' said his mother, glancing at him fondly, 'but he had no inclination for that kind of study. Has he mentioned his travels in Europe and that he was very good at languages?'

Gerald sat through all this silently, offering no comment, and I had a distinct feeling that he would rather be anywhere than at this family gathering. Certainly, the animation he showed in the hotel was sadly missing in this display of forbearance.

Leaning across, Mr Clovis said he had met Chief Inspector Jeremy Faro on a visit to Rothesay long ago. He smiled. 'What kind of books do you write?'

He had accepted my fictional identity as an authoress and although Peter Clovis had been an Edinburgh policeman, he had returned to Bute before I arrived back from America, and two years later, believing that Danny McQuinn was dead, I married Jack Macmerry. So although Peter was aware that I was Jack's wife he had no means of knowing about my career as a lady investigator and I suspected that his wife's notorious occupation was not one Jack cared to boast about to his colleagues.

I was thinking of something suitable about just doing research when danger was averted by the arrival of the next course while one of the Clovis's friends from Arran came over to offer congratulations.

I sat back. Sadie could have been here in safety. It was unlikely that the short-sighted James might have recognised Sarah in the thirty-six-year-old woman, and Gerald had had every chance of doing so, seeing her regularly in Harry's company at the hotel.

I might well sigh with relief that there were pleasanter topics for discussion and presumably Rothesay's twenty-year-old murder had been forgotten or had no particular interest for the Clovis family. Perhaps Sadie was getting unnecessarily concerned and I had been in danger of allowing that to influence me. Two hours later, the remains of an excellent four-course meal transported to the kitchen with more bottles of wine passed round, glasses were raised for toasts and speeches applauded.

At last the evening was over and having thanked my hosts, I found Peter at my side. Gerald had already left to return to the hotel, he said, and insisted on seeing me safely back. On the way, he introduced a few casual-seeming references to my companion. They did not fool me. Peter Clovis was very taken at his first meeting with Miss Brook and I saw looming on the horizon another possible hazard, as well as an opportunity I had not expected to gather useful information.

I said she was very good as my secretary too. He was suitably impressed and I dropped into the conversation that murders always intrigued me, to which he said jokingly that they were his bread and butter, after all. We had a good laugh at that and I said as we had been at Vantry, and being on the spot as it were, here in Rothesay,

I was particularly interested and would very much like to read an account of the Sarah Vantry trial. Would the police files still be available?

He frowned. 'As an authoress, I could get you access to a complete verbatim account if you like. Couldn't let you take it out, of course, such files are confidential reports, but if you'd like to come into the station you could read it there.'

And that was exactly what I wanted.

He asked if I had enjoyed seeing Vantry and I said I thought the house was splendid, especially since it had also become a tourist attraction.

He smiled. 'Edgar Worth is very proud of his heritage and not ashamed to bring in a little extra money from our one sensational murder case. He knows a good thing and Vantry must be expensive to run. They have far fewer servants than the usual landowners.' He looked thoughtful. 'An odd sort of chap, in many ways, can't make him out personally, especially as he doesn't seem to want to fit in with the community, the way Lady Vantry did before her accident, and they've lived here since then, when they moved in to take care of her.'

He paused, frowning. 'Although he and his sister Beatrice – Miss Worth – are devoted to Lady Vantry, which must take up a lot of their time, it surprises me that neither of them ask anything more of life than looking after an aged relative. There is always a lot going on here in Rothesay, something for everyone, whatever their age, young and old,' he added enthusiastically, 'but the Worths hardly ever leave the castle, as they still like to call it. Strange, it seems to me, for a youngish, active couple – Edgar is over forty but Beatrice is quite a bit younger – living like that, very independent, without living-in servants. They make do with a daily maid, which must be difficult in that size of house. There's a gardener, of course, Angus Betts' – he shook his head – 'a right odd cove: served the Vantrys all his life, like his father before him, frequents the local pub but never has a word to say for himself.'

I laughed. 'We met him. Probably exhausts all his supply of words as the tour guide. He was certainly voluble enough conducting us round.'

Peter looked surprised. 'Maybe Vantry is his only interest, then. I've only ever him with the Worths when they come in to do their shopping – pony and trap once a week into the town and that's about it. Keep themselves to themselves, all right.'

There was a pause and I said delicately: 'I presume they will inherit Vantry when the old lady goes, and she looks quite frail. We saw her on the terrace, walking with a stick.'

He smiled. 'I gather that is her only exercise these days. Hard on someone who was a great horsewoman in her day as well as being so active in the community. Oh, they look after her exceedingly well, certainly aren't in any great hurry to lose her. They will want to keep her alive and well as long as they can. You see, there is a clause in the Vantry deed of inheritance established by an ancient trust, that entitles her ladyship to receive a substantial annual income.'

He paused and smiled. 'And that obviously also helps

to keep the place going, but when she dies that money goes with her and with no direct heir the house will go back to the trust to dispose of it as they wish. Hard lines for Edgar and his sister. Remote branches are not considered, so they will be thrown out, penniless.'

It sounded a heartless arrangement as he went on: 'No repayment for their wasted years of devotion to her ladyship. If you study ancient laws, some of them dating back to the Middle Ages and never updated, they are very complicated.' He smiled. 'If you are a fan of Mr Dickens, he knew all about the unfairness involved in tontines, and how they could ruin a family and cause generations of embitterment.'

We had reached the hotel, and saying goodnight to Peter, I was going over what he had told me and, reading between the lines, I realised that life at Vantry was not exactly a bed of roses for the Worths.

CHAPTER THIRTEEN

Sadie was waiting for me in my room. She seemed troubled. Was she concerned about my late arrival back from the Clovis party?

'How did it go? Were the Vantrys there? Harry said they would be invited. Did you talk to them?'

'Not much more than an introduction—' I was saying more but stopped.

Sadie wasn't listening. She was shaking her head, looking scared, sitting on the edge of my bed. What was it, a quarrel with Harry, I wondered?

'What's wrong, Sadie?'

She shivered and took my hand. 'I'm scared, Rose.

Something awful happened. You remember I thought old Uncle Godwin might have recognised me? Well, I was right about that. When I was a maid here before the accident, he was the owner of the hotel and he kept making up to me with lewd suggestions and roving hands. As I told you, once I hit him with a saucepan.' She smiled wryly. 'I was rather pleased to see that his face *does* still bear the scar.'

Sighing, she got up and walked over to the window. 'I decided not to wait up for you and as I was going up I met him, he seemed to be waiting for me at the top of the stairs, blocking my way. He grinned and said: "The little scared girl, is it? I thought it was you and you still look scared after all these years." I pretended to be indignant, said I didn't know what he was talking about, but he grabbed my arm and said, "I've a long memory for faces and I'm amazed that you have the nerve to come back here after what you got away with. What will your fine lady say if I tell her the truth about her fine companion, that she was a murderess who escaped the gallows on a very thin not-proven verdict?"'

She sighed miserably. 'I knew it was no use denying it, Rose. I was in a panic, I said I had a different life now, and he said: "Very well, if you want to keep it, I'll do a deal with you." I didn't know what he wanted but he said: "You can keep your virtue, Miss Vantry, that no longer interests me. However, your fine lady authoress looks as if she has plenty of money. I could do with a bit of that myself, if I am to keep our secret." I asked him what he meant by that and he grinned. "Oh, word might get around. Not only your fine lady will dismiss you, but Mr

135

Edgar Worth will be very interested to know why you've come back when you got off with murder last time you were here."'

Sadie sat down again. 'He wanted twenty pounds. Twenty pounds, Rose.' She groaned. 'What on earth am I to do now?'

I would have given her that to get rid of him, but I knew better. 'Twenty pounds, Sadie. That's just for starters.'

'What do you mean?'

'I mean that blackmailers don't stop at first asking.'

Wringing her hands, in tears now, she said: 'What can I do, then?'

This was the most frequent problem I encountered as an investigator and I always told my clients that the usual procedure, as advised by the police when threatened by a blackmailer, was to inform them – but most victims were so terrified of the truth being made public that they came to me instead. And Sadie almost certainly also fell into this category, so I said:

'Do nothing. Think about it, Sadie. Time is on your side. As for Edgar spreading the word, well, that hardly matters since we will be gone in a couple of days. He could always try sending you threatening letters to Solomon's Tower, which will go straight into the fire, harmless squibs seeing that I know all about what happened. So what else are you worried about?'

She was biting her lip, shaking her head miserably. I looked at her and asked the question foremost in my mind.

'Has he told Harry?'

She shook her head. 'No. But that is part of the deal.

He knows that we are . . .' she hesitated a moment, 'well, friends. He's been watching us.'

We were both silent. Then I said: 'Perhaps you should tell him yourself.' I felt, but did not add: depending on how far you have travelled in this affair. If it is merely a passing holiday romance holiday then the consequences as far as you are concerned do not matter. You go back leaving a disillusioned Harry Godwin. He's very young and inexperienced, he'll get over first love, we all do! Meanwhile you marry your devoted Captain Robbie and live happy ever after.

I waited for her reactions about telling him, hoping that this was her chance to confide in me. Her silence indicated that she was not ready to do so and I felt rather saddened that with such an overwhelming personal crisis she either did not trust me with the truth about her relationship with Harry Godwin, or decided that I would be shocked and that would make us both uncomfortable and perhaps even destroy my readiness to help prove her innocence.

She stood up and said: 'I'm going to bed. Thanks for your advice, I'll give it consideration.' Saying goodnight, I told her to cheer up, try not to worry and sleep well, but I was aware of her disappointment, her feeling that I had let her down somehow, having always suspected that Sadie's plan was irrational and, indeed, beyond belief and had plenty of flaws. They were already becoming evident: her urgency to prove her innocence in order to marry one man while she was fast falling in love with another. It just didn't make sense. Uncle

Godwin recognising her and demanding his silence for a price was merely one more flaw and I knew that what was happening now was just the beginning – as her relationship with Harry evolved, the situation could certainly get worse.

Perhaps I should have insisted that we left then, but I recognised that was not for me. True, I had been reluctant at first, but having now set foot in the labyrinth, I was determined to see it through.

In less than a week. It seemed impossible.

When we met at breakfast she looked tired but was smiling gallantly. Harry was beside her, his fond looks suggesting that Sadie Brook's identity as the notorious Sarah Vantry and Uncle Godwin's threat had not yet been revealed to him.

Gerald was hovering in the reception area, that enigmatic look revealing nothing of his thoughts.

Sadie followed my glance in his direction, and as if aware of what was in my mind, she smiled wryly. 'Doesn't have much to say for himself, does he? The world's most silent man.' And with a shrug: 'According to Harry, he can talk a lot on things that interest him.'

Our porridge arrived and no further mention was made of Sadie's encounter with Uncle Godwin as we ate together. It was as if the revelations of last night and her terrible anxiety had never happened as she asked brightly: 'Well, where do we go today?'

When I told her that I was going to the police station as Peter had promised me a look at the trial papers, she demanded angrily: 'And what am I supposed to do meanwhile?'

'I'll only be gone for a couple of hours.'

She leant across the table, her face contorted. 'The trial papers. Is that really your only reason for going there? Nothing to do with what I told you?' she hissed and it was only then that I realised she believed I intended reporting the blackmailing threat.

'Of course not, Sadie. That is something you must decide for yourself. Looking at the trial papers is a great opportunity to fully acquaint myself with all the details—'

She stared at me angrily and said coldly: 'You surely haven't told him who I am?'

'Calm down, Sadie. He knows nothing about you, only my interest as an authoress – thanks to you inflicting this new role on me. He accepts that but has no idea that I am an investigator, and he left Edinburgh before I married Jack Macmerry.'

Quite unrepentant, she said: 'I'm glad of that.' But she didn't look convinced. 'After your promise about the blackmail, I mean.' She shrugged and said resignedly: 'Anyway, seeing papers of the trial won't do much to help. I could tell you every detail, word for word. And it may be too late now, anyway.'

It was useless to argue and my attempts fell on deaf ears trying to make her understand that police reports often contain additional information that is not available for newspaper reports, information that might in fact hold vital clues for this investigation and a situation that got more ridiculous every day. And hardly an hour passed that I did not blame myself for getting involved when there were so many more important issues that I should be dealing with than a twenty-year-old not-proven murder. There was so much going on in the world beyond this tiny island.

1906 had been a momentous year, nationally and personally. In April, the earthquake in San Francisco had reached worldwide headlines. Visiting the city during Danny McQuinn's work with Pinkerton's Detective Agency, I had been delighted with its handsome buildings and warm-hearted residents. We had made friends there and its destruction touched a personal sense of grief.

But of great importance to me this year, nearer home, was the Women's Suffrage Movement plan for a protest procession in London in 1907. There was considerable organisation needed and as chairman of the Movement's Edinburgh branch, I should have taken the chance to remain at home this week alone instead of embarking on this fool's errand with Sadie, and used the valuable bonus time to get in touch with the various people involved, to arrange meetings with fellow members and together make lists of sympathisers for our cause to approach, who might be prepared to assist with donations towards our London visit to take part in this most important march.

Full of very disagreeable thoughts, I left Sadie and shortly afterwards presented myself at the police station where Sergeant Clovis had told them to expect the authoress Mrs Rose Macmerry. They were obviously impressed and the file of Vantry versus the Crown was set out ready on a table.

The witness statements were of particular interest.

Nothing from Sarah Vantry's former employer and new tormentor Uncle Godwin, who had clearly found the sixteen-year-old kitchen maid memorable enough to be worthy of his amorous attentions and had a scar to prove it. In the circumstances, I didn't expect to find him mentioned anywhere in her defence, but I carefully read and reread the evidence of Edgar Worth, who had witnessed the attack.

The lawyer defending Sadie took the stand, asked the young Edgar if he actually saw the attack and the exact place where he was standing at that precise moment. So saying, he produced a map of the house, to which Edgar pointed to the foot of the stairs.

The lawyer was triumphant: 'Then I am afraid your statement is invalid. As anyone can tell you who has been to Vantry, it would be impossible for any person of average height, unless they were a giant twelve foot tall' (this drew a laugh) 'standing at the foot of the stairs, to look up and see whether in the struggle of the two young people one, in this case the unfortunate victim Oswald Vantry, fell or was deliberately pushed down and tumbled from the head of the stairs to his death on the marble floor below.'

Reading on through the lawyer's testimony, there were other witnesses called, servants who knew allegedly of the fights and arguments between the two cousins and confirmed the bad feeling that had existed between them. One said it was common knowledge that they were always hitting each other, she had seen them in the garden arguing, and fighting. Another had actually seen

Oswald strike Sadie, and although they had been alerted to the noise of a violent dispute on the landing that night, this was a regular daily occurrence that servants kept well out of. What went on 'upstairs', as they called it, concerning the family, was ignored by them as none of their business, unless they wished to interfere and be dismissed by Lady Vantry.

At the time of the fatal attack, none of the servants had been near enough, although they heard the two youngsters shouting on the stairs, their voices quite audible from the kitchens. The only ones who were on the scene and claimed to have actually seen what was taking place, heard us quarrelling and me shouting I hated him and wished he was dead were Lady Vantry and Edgar Worth, visiting at the time.

Curiously enough it was the servant witnesses who made the most impression and saved Sarah from being hanged. Most of the jury were working-class folk, not the upper crust of Bute society, and well aware of what went on amongst those they had been reared to regard as their betters. They were clearly sympathetic: this was a young lass and reading between the lines they all knew from personal experience that she had a troubled existence at Vantry. Many of them had worked in big houses like Vantry and knew perfectly well how poor relations were treated – as little more than unpaid servants by the aristocracy or the wealthy members of society.

As I read, I had a feeling that had they been asked, they could have provided the court with stories of many similar incidents related to bullying – and worse, but with

142

less fatal consequences – in their own lives by sons and daughters of the aristocracy. Regarding their testimonies, I suspected that their validity as witnesses was also doubtful. Even those who might have seen what happened realised what was at stake if Lady Vantry was offended by their testimonies and were fearful of losing their jobs and being dismissed without a reference. It did not take long for this jury to make up their minds. They weren't inclined to give a guilty verdict and sentence an ill-used young lass to the gallows on such evidence as existed. Hence the accusation of murder received the not-proven verdict.

Before returning the file, I made a note of two sisters, Mavis and Ellen Boyd, scared servants whose testimonies had varied and whose tears had irritated the judge. Both were young and it seemed that they were upset because they were fond of Sarah, who in their own words: 'was always nice to us'. They lived at Kilchattan and although it was doubtful if they were still at the same address twenty years later, it might be worth investigating.

Heading back to the hotel, I met Sadie, who said she had needed a few things and had decided to do some shopping, remembering the old shops, all of which had changed hands over the years, or, their owners deceased, had passed to their children.

'Thank goodness,' she added, 'they all took it that I was on holiday, or a tourist and this was my first visit.' She laughed bitterly. 'Some of them were younger than me and had probably never heard of Sarah Vantry. I was quite safe and they were all very nice and hoped I would enjoy my stay.'

We were passing by the picture house and hoping to lead her into more cheerful subjects, I asked: 'What was the film like, did you enjoy it?'

She looked at me blankly. I thought obviously the horrendous encounter with Uncle Godwin had eradicated it from her mind. Then she smiled, remembering.

'Oh yes, it was delightful. *Rescued by Rover*, all about a dog, and it was the director Cecil Hepworth who also acted in it with his entire family, his wife and baby daughter, as well as the wee dog that made it all the more exciting, as if it was really happening. You would love it, Rose, it would remind you of Thane. I was glad we didn't miss it.'

'What happened the other night, the first time?' I didn't want to remind her that she hadn't told me then about the sold-out tickets and let me believe she and Harry had been at the cinema. A lie, in fact, or an evasion of the truth. Again, it wasn't my business, she was a woman, and Harry was a single man too, but on this so-called holiday and for the task she had set me, I realised I was taking on her actions as my responsibility.

She thought for a moment, then said glibly: 'We had a good long walk and stopped off at a cafe for ice cream. I thought I told you.'

I shook my head. 'I'm glad it wasn't a completely wasted evening.'

She gave me an anxious look. 'He has promised to have Gerald take me out sailing in one of their boats. I'd like that, if we have time to spare, I mean.' A pause. 'It would be such a treat.'

I said I was sure it could be arranged.

The hotel was in sight and although pleased with the morning's work on the police file, I had a strange feeling that I was missing something and that Sadie was telling me more than one white lie.

A pony and trap was parked outside. I had noticed it outside the stables during our Vantry visit and its presence indicated that Edgar and Beatrice had been shopping, otherwise they would have used the carriage. Presumably they were being considerate and saving Angus, who was also the coachman, having to wait for them as they had lunch in the restaurant.

Sadie didn't want to meet them. She whispered: 'I'll get something later when they've gone.' She was heading towards Harry's office. 'I bought him a little gift, he has been so good to us.'

To you, not us, I thought, as I went upstairs to the bathroom. From my bedroom window, I noticed a man walking back and forth beside the parked pony and trap. His vigilant manner suggested impatience and determination and I realised he had been there when we came in, standing by the entrance, his face concealed as he read a newspaper.

Now he was looking up at the hotel. The adjacent pony and trap meant only one thing: that he was waiting for the Worths to emerge. And there they were, being served by a waiter as I walked through the restaurant. They nodded politely, greetings were exchanged but I was not ready to take a seat at their table. I would wait for Sadie, who would certainly have no wish to join them.

As I went back upstairs to my room, I thought about the man outside. Perhaps he was a servant, but he was too well dressed for that, and looking out of my window overlooking the entrance, even from a distance with his face no longer kept hidden by that concealing newspaper, I knew I had seen him before.

CHAPTER FOURTEEN

This was the man we had met on the Vantry drive, the visitor who had no wish to be seen and had leapt into the shelter of the rhododendron bushes. After washing my hands, I went to summon Sadie, but her room was empty. Back at the window, I looked out again, but he had vanished, and so had the Worths and their pony and trap.

If only I had kept watch. I was furious that I had missed those last few moments and their encounter with this waiting man. Now I would never know the reason why such a well-dressed man had not gone into the hotel to talk to them and why he had wanted to keep his presence secret.

With an exasperated sigh, I swore and picked up my notes from the police file on Sarah Vantry's trial. I remembered and had noted in particular the reported behaviour of the Boyd sisters, whose testimony the police had found unsatisfactory. The elder, Mavis, had been lady's maid to Lady Vantry, and their home at Kilchattan, I discovered from the large map in the hotel's reception, was in the south of the island near St Blane's.

I already had a curious feeling about that area, and remembering Sadie's childhood, a kind of intuition that it might hold useful information or even dark secrets. At the back of my mind I was hoping the sisters might remember something, provide some clue from Sadie's past.

I dined alone that evening and after a solitary breakfast, with ominous feelings regarding Sadie's absence from both meals, went into the hotel library. Gerald came in while I was studying the wall map. He said cautiously that Sadie had not been down yet and although he did not mention it, because Harry was also absent I could not help considering that the two were together.

Gerald was asking cheerfully where I was thinking of going today. When I said St Blane's, he shook his head and said that some of the approach roads were poor and others almost non-existent.

His worried frown suggested that his main worry was concern at the prospect of a lady guest driving the hotel motor car I had booked for hire that day. He said rather weakly with little enthusiasm: 'I could drive you there.' And with a glance skyward: 'The weather is looking none too promising. Unfortunately, there are urgent matters I have to attend to this morning.'

That was fine by me. I wanted to go alone, the last thing I wanted was to have Gerald's company and his curiosity about my own behaviour as to why I wished to search out Vantry former servants.

When I thanked him politely for his offer, he became very businesslike and leading me over to the map, pointed out the easiest route to take.

I had rather fancied the road down the coast, with maybe a glimpse of Mount Stuart, but he hastened to say that route would not be pleasant as the wind, which was strong, would be in my face all the way. I would be advised to take the more sheltered inland road down through Townhead and branching off at Kingarth. He assured me that there were plenty of signposts but not all the roads were easily negotiable for drivers new to the island.

I decided to put his fears at rest.

'I have had a splendid idea. There are other means and much more negotiable on doubtful roads than a motor car.' I smiled reassuringly. 'A means of transport that I am familiar with every day of my life in Edinburgh. Bicycles!'

Ignoring his raised eyebrows and look of mild amusement, I said I had seen a shop with bicycles for hire when I was exploring the area last night and had even then considered it would be an alternative way to travel around Bute.

I thanked him for his help, said I would not be needing

the motor car and went in search of Sadie for her reactions to this new plan. She was upstairs and said yes, she had breakfast early.

'I think we might have a look at St Blane's today.'

'You mean just because I lived there as a child?'

'Yes, that's a good reason and don't you think it would be pleasant to see it again?' But my thoughts were focused on those two Boyd servants who had been witnesses at her trial.

She ignored the reason I gave her, a weary sigh indicating complete disinterest.

I said: 'Gerald warns me that the roads are bad where they exist at all and as it's not suitable for the motor car, I thought we might hire bicycles – there's a place in the high street.'

Sadie continued saying nothing, just staring at me. 'Bicycles, no motor car?'

'Yes. It would be easy and rather nice to get some fresh air, don't you think? You like bicycling in Edinburgh,' I added encouragingly. 'It's a good day, that is if the wind is behind us.' I smiled hopefully.

She gave me one of her intent looks and sighed deeply. 'You're wasting your time, Rose.'

Taken aback by this remark, I found her sudden lack of enthusiasm infuriating and bit back asking whose fault was that indeed, the idea of coming here had been hers in the first place, had it not, as she went on: 'We're almost running out of days, and we haven't had any luck so far, no clues to follow, absolutely nothing. We might as well give up, Rose. It seemed such a good idea at the time, now

I'm truly sorry to have wasted your holiday,' she added apologetically.

I noticed that I had interrupted her writing a letter. There were several pages and indicating them, she said: 'If you're determined to go, you can post this. I was going to ask Harry but you are sure to be passing a postbox close by.' She folded the letter carefully and I watched her seal the envelope. She must have been aware of my curiosity regarding its contents and said: 'To Robbie, at the shipping office in Leith, they'll forward it to him.'

She sighed again but I had a strange feeling as I left her that she had suddenly also lost all interest in her sea captain and the urgent matter of proving her innocence in order to marry him, once her pressing reason for this visit to Bute and dragging me with her.

I gave her a hard look. Something much more important had taken over her original wild plan, something that she was not prepared to confide in me, but I was certain concerned Harry Godwin and his obsession with her company.

A complete volte-face, now so indifferent, she was saying we might as well give up. She might give up, but that was not for me. She didn't really know that side of my character and realise that all my early reluctance for a seemingly lost cause had vanished. I had the investigator's bit between my teeth now and I was determined to continue. To be honest, I now considered this as a mystery, and I was in the business of solving mysteries, even the hopeless challenge of this particular not-proven case.

I looked at her, unable to find the appropriate words,

seeing and hearing her lose heart, her enthusiasm evaporated. Indeed, she looked paler than usual this morning and said she had slept badly and had a bit of a sore throat.

I had heard her coughing during the night and hoped she wasn't going to be ill for the journey home.

'I'm sorry, Rose,' she said again. 'I really don't feel like bicycling all that way.'

The prospect of sitting around the hotel, wasting another day doing nothing, appalled me. It had become important that although I had known right from the outset that this was a fool's errand with the remotest chance of success, it was not in my nature to admit defeat so readily, especially when I had already a few startling theories about the Worths taking root, vague suspicions based on what I had heard and seen, that I wanted to put to the test.

'You don't mind if I don't come with you?' Sadie said anxiously. 'I don't want you to feel that I am letting you down when you are so keen to go. But I am a bit off colour today and I think I should stay indoors. I didn't sleep much last night,' she repeated and, shivering, gave me a look of appeal. 'It's not like me, but I'm really not very well, Rose.'

This surprised me. It certainly wasn't like the Sadie we knew in Edinburgh, always so strong and robust and reliable. I had never known her to suffer from even a head cold, ready to nurse Meg as well as Jack and me through a few minor indispositions during the time she had been with us, always prepared with a shelf of soothing remedies at hand.

True, she seemed unwell, but my demons were whispering and feeling unworthily suspicious: conscious that we were running out of time, I wondered if this had something to do with Harry and the progress of whatever was going on between them. Was this sudden imaginary indisposition maybe just an excuse, a plan to spend another day with him?

I prepared for my journey. Fortunately, the style of clothes I usually wore were suitable for bicycling and when I went downstairs, Harry was waiting.

Smiling, he handed me a lunch package. He smiled. 'When Gerald told me of your plan, I had this made up for you. It's quite a long way and not many places where you might get refreshments en route. Here's the map. I marked directions for the more direct route. And a rain cape. I hope you won't need it, but just in case . . .'

It was such a kind thing to do, I thanked him, and said I was really looking forward to this excursion.

He frowned and looked seaward. 'I would strongly advise against it, Mrs Macmerry. The barometer is low and I think we are in for a storm.'

I looked at the cloudless sky, a faint mist over the sea. 'Really?'

'Yes, really. I've lived here all my life and you can trust me where the weather is concerned. Later today, or tomorrow, it will break over the island.'

I had to take his word for that as he continued: 'If you are absolutely intent on this journey, as Gerald told you neither of us can manage this morning – we have business meetings and we must go to Bannatyne – but I will be back in time to drive you down to St Blane's this afternoon.'

'That is most kind but I am used to bicycling. I enjoy it.'

He regarded me wide-eyed. 'With all those hills in Edinburgh, you are a brave woman.'

'I never notice them. It's something one gets used to.' I thanked him again and looking skyward, he frowned: 'I think you will be safe enough for daylight, but if the wind increases and we have squally winds,' he added firmly, 'I will bring the motor car and fetch you and the bicycle back myself.'

'That is very good of you, Harry.' I thought, here is a nice, caring lad, with the welfare of his guests at heart, although he seemed still so young for such responsibilities. As well as keeping a watchful eye on his spendthrift uncle, who was still the legal owner, the Heights Hotel was undoubtedly flourishing, with the support and guidance of Gerald Thorn.

As I was leaving, he walked to the door with me and pointed to the sea, no longer smooth as glass, its mirror image shattered by angry-looking waves.

'If it stays rough over to Wemyss Bay, the ferries will be cancelled and you may have to extend your stay with us,' he warned. 'That sometimes happens.'

'How long would it last?' I was thinking of Jack and Meg returning home with his parents looking forward to their long-promised holiday in Solomon's Tower. Aware that there was much work and cooking for Sadie and me in preparation for this visit, it was also essential that I make a good impression on Jess Macmerry, who I could already see in my mind's eye casting a critical glance upon her son's wife's methods of housekeeping, so very much inferior to her own.

Harry was saying: 'Depends on the intensity of the storm – they usually only last a day or two.' He was smiling, with a rather faraway look that suggested he would not be too disappointed if Sadie were to be kept here for an extended visit.

I emerged from the hotel and made my way along the main street, looking for a postbox for Sadie's long letter to Robbie, very curious about its contents. Although only minutes had passed since my conversation with Harry, it seemed that the weather had already worsened and I observed with some misgivings the waves like monstrous white horses creeping up to the shore under a heavy grey sky.

I allowed myself some second thoughts. Perhaps it was madness to choose such a day, but as Sadie had warned me as if I didn't know, time was running out for us, and I couldn't afford the luxury of wasting a day.

At the bicycle hiring shop there seemed doubt in the assistant's attitude towards a lady hiring such a machine, and I realised immediately that all these questions he put to me regarding my experience and ability before releasing into my care one of his precious machines would never have been uttered to a man. He also added to Gerald's instructions about keeping to the inland roads and I headed up the high street past Rothesay Castle and the High Kirk, another place of interest on my list yet to be explored, on and on through Townhead, then an easy downhill road with Loch Fad on one side and Loch Ascog on the other. Both were imposing stretches of water, even on a rather dismal day, and I thought how they would transform for a delightful summer's day picnic.

Reaching Ambrismore, I got my first glimpse of the Sound of Bute across to Kintyre, and in the far distance, Arran. I followed the twisting road south and eastward through a rural landscape, with moors stretching to the horizon broken by the shapes of a few farms and a thriving population of sheep; some of which settled on the road in front of this woman on a bicycle, quite unwilling to move over or take the slightest notice of her. They weren't afraid and I might well have been invisible. As shouting and gesticulating were of no avail, I had several times to dismount and shoo them away bodily, ignoring indignant baas.

At the sign just before Kingarth, I noticed a track leading past a group of standing stones. As I wobbled along, deciding this was a mistake and I would have to go back, at last I caught a glimpse of the sea. As I rode down the track that led down to the shore at Kilchattan Bay, I expected to be in the full force of the wind, but the inland bay provided protection and I eventually came to a signpost, which I welcomed: St Blane's. Down another twisting track past ruined, roofless cottages, and as threatening clouds now erupted into fine rain, I decided I was hungry and this seemed the appropriate time to find shelter, however inadequate, don the rain cape and eat the hotel's no doubt delicious sandwiches.

On closer inspection, the houses were sad indeed, with the ghost of a lost race of crofters who had been born, lived all their lives and died here. At last, I found one that had survived with the remnants of a roof. I pushed open the door to find myself in the ruins of a once proud room with tattered rags of a curtain fluttering pathetically on the paneless window, a chair with a leg missing, a shattered table, and in the fireplace, ashes as if someone before me had sought shelter here.

Consuming my sandwiches and the small bottle of milk thoughtfully provided by Harry, as the rain had momentarily ceased I did not linger: my ruined shelter was too depressing.

Onward to St Blane's. A long track and through the trees a church spire visible against the sky. Parking the bicycle I climbed the steep hill, a pathway well worn by the feet of pilgrims through the ages, and found myself in a peaceful, rocky hollow with fine views out towards the sea and Arran. Once a monastery, the site about which I had read in the library last night was reputed to have been founded by Blane, who had come across from Ireland in the sixth century when Bute may have been as important as Iona in its earliest days.

My footsteps echoing loudly, I walked across old paving stones and, surrounded by an enclosure wall, in its midst sat the twelfth-century church built by the Fitz-Alan or Stewart family who had gained control of Bute at that time and had also built or rebuilt Rothesay Castle.

Strange, as if in welcome, as I stared up at the finely decorated Romanesque chancel arch, the clouds momentarily parted. A shaft of sunlight swiftly came. A moment of warmth and illumination, then as swiftly gone, but somehow I felt heartened by its brief presence. In that holy place, if I had been of a religious disposition I might have concluded that it had brought a message of faith and hope.

On the way down to collect the bicycle, I noticed that the graveyard held some interesting medieval stones, but with a cold wind stirring last year's autumn leaves about my feet, I reckoned that I had had sufficient melancholy for the day.

CHAPTER FIFTEEN

There was now little human habitation in the area and I turned my thoughts to Kilchattan, fully aware that with not even a certain name I could hardly knock at the doors of the scattered houses in the hope of finding the one where Lady Vantry had deposited a small girl who could not even remember her foster parents' surname. Sadie thought it might be Brown, but wasn't sure. Her recollections of that particular period of her life were vague in the extreme, one was her father's occasional smiling presence. It was not at all unusual that in common with so many others, her childhood unhappy memories had been safely buried. The chances of anyone knowing the present whereabouts of those foster parents believed to have gone to Glasgow were doubtful in the extreme. And I couldn't quite see myself asking for Doris, who I suspected was her real mother, bringing her sweeties and sobbing over her more than thirty years ago.

Heading towards Kilchattan Bay, with no plausible excuse for my visit without revealing the true reason, as the wind would now be behind me and heedless of warning, I decided to take the coast road back towards Rothesay.

As I rode, again struck by the insanity of my mission, depressed by the cold, grey day that had sunk its melancholy deep into my bones with enough rain to dampen any enthusiasm, I realised the utmost hopelessness of ever finding the mysterious Doris, or the Boyd sisters still at their address of two decades ago – said vaguely to be in Kilchattan Bay. As it drew nearer, the fact that islanders often spent their entire lives, from birth to death, in the same house gave me little heart, and if by some miracle the sisters opened their door, my presence still needed a lot of explaining, providing a logical reason for delving into their unhappy past.

I was within sight of the little township when I felt an ominous drag on my pedalling. A sound I knew only too well. The rough tracks to which I should have had more sense than to subject the machine's wheels had caused a slow puncture. This was disaster indeed. However, in the small cluster of houses, there was a general store and it was open. Behind the counter stood a white-haired woman, fresh-faced, stout and friendly.

She seemed surprised to see a stranger. 'What an awful day. Have you come far?' I told her from Rothesay. She smiled. 'On holiday, are you, from Glasgow?' I said Edinburgh.

'This your first visit? How long are you staying?'

I told her it was supposed to be until the weekend and looking towards the window, she sighed. 'Oh, I've no doubt you'll be with us in Rothesay for a day or two longer once this storm gets under way and the ferries are cancelled.'

I said at this moment I was even more likely to be remaining in Kilchattan as I had travelled all the way to St Blane's on a bicycle.

'Riding a bicycle, were you?' In an amazed glance she took in my small frame and my unruly yellow curls to which the rain had done no favours. A female bicyclist, and obviously the first of this new breed she had ever encountered. Her eyebrows raised as I said:

'Yes, and I have had a puncture.'

'Oh, you poor lass.'

'Is there anyone who could mend it?' I asked desperately. 'It's a long walk back to Rothesay.'

She tut-tutted sympathetically. 'The blacksmith down the road. Bill – I'm sure he'll be able to do something. Excuse me a moment.' She lifted a curtain behind her and called, 'Albert!'

A bespectacled, studious-looking young lad appeared, book in his hand, frowning, obviously not happy at being interrupted. She quickly explained the situation and Albert followed us outside and, without a word, seized the

161

bicycle and departed, pushing it down the road. Watching him, she smiled at me.

'This won't take long, I'm sure.' And she ushered me indoors again: 'Now, I know what you would like, miss. A nice cup of tea.'

'More than anything. Thank you,' I sighed. Back in the shop, pulling aside a curtain, she said: 'Come along, this is where we live.'

Following her, I was in a large room, comfortably furnished with bookshelves on one wall, and a window overlooking the sea. There were more premises to be revealed, a door leading into two bedrooms and what I needed most, a washroom.

'We had that put in after a wee holiday in Glasgow,' she said proudly. 'They were all the rage, height of fashion. Not many of those around in Bute, or even on the mainland, those days.'

I made good use of it and returned to a table spread with teapot, pretty china and a tray of freshly baked scones with jam and cream to go with them.

'Awful weather, raining again,' she said, while I sighed contentedly over my second scone. Introductions over, I was interested in Mrs Forsyth and busy with my observation and deduction. She didn't sound local, and from the line of books, here was a cultured, well-educated woman, isolated in the depths of Bute.

I had to know more. 'You are not from these parts, are you?'

She smiled. 'Well, after twenty-five years, I feel like a native.'

My spirits rose. Here was a shred of hope as she said: 'I'm from Edinburgh originally, met my husband on a holiday here in Bute.' Pausing, she shook her head sadly and I knew what the next words would be. 'He died ten years ago, but I decided to stay. We had the little shop, you know. We had both been teachers and fell in love with Bute, we didn't mind the isolation.' She sighed. 'We were happy and content here. Never had any children, but after a while, that's something you accept. "The good Lord's will", my man used to say. It's a funny thing, isn't it? Folk either have great big families these days or none at all.'

I was smiling, listening to her while trying to frame words by which I might introduce the Browns and the Boyd sisters into the conversation. I could think of nothing adequate and Albert came back, rather wet, but with the bicycle repaired. He handed me back my coin: 'Bill said he didn't want the young lady's money. It was a pleasure to help a stranger,' and with a glance at me, he added embarrassedly, 'especially a young lady in distress.'

I smiled. 'Then you can keep the coin. As a thank you for taking my bicycle down the road and back.'

The coin was gratefully acknowledged while he gave the machine a wistful look and sighed. 'I want one of those someday, Aunty.'

Mrs Forsyth laughed. 'When you are a bit older and a bit bigger, Albert, we'll see about that.'

About to leave, making it look like an afterthought, I said: 'A friend of mine in Edinburgh once stayed here, years ago, with some folk called Brown, near St Blane's. I think it was Kilchattan.'

She thought for a moment and shook her head. 'There were Browns but they left before my time, I only heard of them. I didn't know they took in boarders.' She laughed. 'D'you know, I'd be surprised if they were the same folk. You see, they had connections with the Vantrys up at St Colmac, you know, upper-class folk.'

'Oh, Brown is a common name,' I said, but Vantry was a thread I didn't want to lose. 'But my friend used to get Christmas cards from two sisters she had met during her stay, Mavis and Ellen Boyd.'

It was a long shot, but it paid.

She sighed. 'Oh yes, the poor Miss Boyds. One of them died suddenly. They were very devoted, more like twins, really. Never married and poor Ellen never got over losing Mavis, who had always taken care of her. They were in service together and Ellen was never very strong herself, took depression after her sister died and couldn't live here alone any longer. Wasn't able to look after herself, her mind just went all to pieces. She's in a home in Rothesay.'

Rothesay, I thought. And I had come all this way. 'When did this happen?'

She frowned. 'Mavis took heart failure and died on a visit to Vantry with Ellen. Both had been maids there once and hearing about her ladyship's accident, were determined to go and see her again.'

She frowned. 'The sisters were having a rough time here, no work and no money. We all hoped that having been devoted to Lady Vantry, now that she was disabled, she might take Mavis back as her lady's maid and take on Ellen too.'

She looked sad. 'Such a tragedy, it was. Poor Ellen was heartbroken, used to say she wished she was dead too, that she had nothing to live for with Mavis gone.' She shook her head. 'She wasn't all that old, just in her late forties, but it was the finish of her too.'

Time to leave, and giving my thanks, Albert came to the door. 'I'll just see the lady away, Aunty, see she gets on the right road.'

'You're a good lad,' Mrs Forsyth shouted and waved goodbye.

'Watch your step, miss, the roads are very bad and you don't want another puncture. Can I push your bicycle?' he added wistfully.

'Of course you can.' He took it from me and said: 'One day I will have one of these, Aunty Doris has promised – for my fourteenth birthday.'

I wondered if I had heard right. 'Aunty Doris, is that her name?'

He grinned. 'She's a kind lady, miss. More like a mother. I lost my own when I was little and she's always taken care of me.'

I looked back at the house. Doris, indeed. Was she the one I had been looking for? I went over our conversation but decided there had been no clue that this could be the same woman who had wept over Sadie and brought her sweeties.

As I followed the signpost's directions and took the

road north to Rothesay, the sad story of the Boyd sisters had me feeling that my visit hadn't been a complete waste of time. Even the punctured wheel had been a blessing in disguise, leading me to the kindly Mrs Forsyth. Doris was a common enough name, another coincidence, and Sadie, I resolved, would have no reason to wonder if I had stumbled on her real mother.

That fund of local information was an unexpected boon, but although Mrs Forsyth had been somewhat vague about the Browns, knowing that Ellen Boyd was in a nursing home in Rothesay was very useful indeed, and made the cycle ride all the way in rather foul weather very rewarding. There wouldn't be many such homes in Rothesay and I would search out Ellen for a visit.

I now had the wind behind me; a glimpse of the beach at Strathvallan, so bleak and unappealing, menaced by the waves of an angry sea that looked even more threatening than when I left this morning, brought anxious thoughts about the weather. Would it have cleared and the ferries be running to Wemyss Bay when we were due to take our departure?

I dismounted at the crossroads and considering the black clouds heralded another bout of rain, decided to head back as quickly as possible and abandon my original plan of taking the attractive coastal road, especially as there was little to consider scenic on a day like this and it was too late for a look at Mount Stuart. So I turned west, took the inland route to Kerrycroy, where according to the hotel map there was a road from Ascog Bridge to Rothesay.

Returning the bicycle to the shop, the owner gave my bedraggled appearance a sympathetic grin. 'You could have chosen a better day, missus.'

I was inclined to agree, but there was another crisis waiting for me. In reception, a notice saying the ferries to Wemyss Bay had been cancelled for the meantime because of the high winds.

That was bad enough, but there was another crisis for which I was completely unprepared.

Sadie was ill.

CHAPTER SIXTEEN

Sadie was still in bed where I had left her that morning. She opened her eyes as if it was too much of an effort:

'Had a good day?' Any further questions and my reply were cut short by a bout of coughing. When that subsided she smiled weakly, but said she was still feeling quite poorly.

I looked at a tray of untouched food. 'Have you eaten anything today?'

She shook her head. 'Don't feel like eating, my throat's too sore. Harry brought this and said bed was the best place for me. I should stay here until I felt better. And the rest would do me good,' she added forlornly. 'Harry is so concerned, he was so anxious—'

The rest was lost in another coughing bout. 'Oh dear, Rose, I don't know what's wrong with me,' she wailed. 'I'm really feeling so awful, I'm not well.' She looked far from well, and when I touched her forehead, it was hot.

She had a temperature. Harry had been right and I realised she had better remain where she was and hope that it would not get any worse.

In despair as I retreated to my own room to change out of my damp clothes, I had to face the fact that, in addition to the cancelled ferries, the possibility that Sadie was quite ill might conspire to make us remain in Bute, on an enforced stay longer than we intended.

I certainly couldn't leave her here, and all thoughts of tracking down Ellen Boyd and those other loose ends regarding the Worths and Vantry, all ideas of solving a mystery disappeared rapidly from my mind, substituted by a grimmer picture. Jack and his parents arriving in an empty house, and Meg not prepared for school after the break.

I was hungry after my day's activities. In the restaurant as I ordered supper, Harry came over. Gerald was at his side and regarded my damp curls ruefully.

'A successful day?' he said. 'Did you enjoy St Blane's despite the weather?'

Harry looked anxious and interrupted to ask: 'Is Sadie feeling any better? I've looked in once or twice but she was sleeping and I didn't want to disturb her. Sleep is the best cure for all ills. What did you think? Is she still feeling poorly?'

'She is a bit under the weather.' At this stage I preferred

not to put into words my suspicions that she had a fever.

He nodded and said firmly: 'You are not to worry, Mrs Macmerry. She can stay here until she's feeling fitter.' A glance at Gerald. 'We will look after her. It need not change your plans to go home, as soon as the ferries are running again. Rest assured, we will take good care of her.'

I did not doubt that Harry would take care of her personally. He added that they had given her some medicine from the cupboard kept in the hotel for emergencies, powders for guests with bad colds and sore throats.

'We'll see how she is in the morning,' he added consolingly.

I had nightmares that night and even wondered if I was coming down with some illness myself. At dawn I crept into her bedroom. She was asleep, moving restlessly and sweating, she seemed much worse.

What a time to take ill, always so healthy and robust, never even a headache much less a head cold in the two years she had been with us at Solomon's Tower, so how on earth had she taken a feverish illness?

When I went down to breakfast, Harry was talking to Dr Wills who I had met briefly at the Clovis party. He had been doing his weekly visit to Uncle Godwin so I asked him to have a look at Sadie.

Harry had already done so. He sounded worried, whether on behalf of his uncle, who was always complaining, or Sadie, who was really unwell, as I followed them upstairs.

I waited in my room until Dr Wills emerged. His examination was brief. Putting away his stethoscope he shook his head and said: 'I am afraid she has all the symptoms of influenza and she will certainly have to stay in bed until we get her temperature down. I have left a prescription of powders for her, not that it will help much, these things take their own time. The body works it out better than any doctor's medicine,' he said by way of consolation. 'No need for anxiety, Mrs Macmerry. Miss Brook is a strong young woman, she will survive. She couldn't go anywhere at the moment, anyway, with the ferries being cancelled. I'll look in when I'm passing later and check her temperature.'

With a sigh he picked up his bag. 'Now I must rush to my next patients. I have had three calls this morning, more than I get in a whole week normally. They are usually a healthy lot here.'

He frowned and added: 'I am just hoping there will not be more in the course of the day.' A weak smile. 'Alas, Mrs Macmerry, a bad time to make your visit to the island when we might be on the threshold of an influenza epidemic. No need to worry, merely a question of rest and care for the young and healthy, like Miss Brook and yourself.' He shook his head. 'It is most serious, and indeed often proves fatal, only for the very young and the very old.'

Harry was waiting downstairs obviously anxious for the verdict. Dr Wills said: 'I am afraid you will have one of your guests for a little while longer. I think Miss Brook may have influenza and it will be a week at least before she is fit enough to travel back to Edinburgh.'

Watching him leave, Harry slumped down at one of the tables, looked up at me and groaned. 'This is all my fault,

Mrs Macmerry, if I hadn't taken her to the film the other night she would have escaped this. I know when there is influenza about on the island we should avoid crowded places, but it is my fault,' he repeated. 'I just love going to the pictures.'

Sadie had told me that was his favourite pastime, twice a week if the programme changed on a Wednesday. She had smiled. 'He would love to be a film star, and he certainly has the looks, although the only acting he has done is in the local drama group. He's got all the young people interested and even tried to get the Worths involved, particularly Beatrice.'

Harry was saying: 'That evening we were packed in like sardines, lucky to get the last seats. A young boy with his parents squeezed in beside us and all three of them seemed to be sniffling and blowing their noses, the lad sitting next to Sadie worst of the lot, coughing and sneezing all through the film.' He looked at me despairingly. 'We are always warned that the influenza is highly infectious. Poor Sadie, she must have got it from them. I am so sorry.'

I tried to reassure him that he could hardly be blamed when the doctor had said there was a possible epidemic brewing up on the island. 'But what will you do, Mrs Macmerry?' he asked. 'This is a setback to your plans. I know you won't want to leave her, but I can assure you Gerald and I will look after her, and when she is fit again, we'll make all the arrangements for her to travel back to Edinburgh.'

I shook my head. 'That's very good of you but no,

thanks. I must stay here until she is well enough for us to travel back together.'

He opened his mouth to protest, but I cut short his words. 'You are very kind, but taking care of Sadie is my responsibility.'

As I said the words, I thought again quite desperately of Jack and Meg with Thane and the elder Macmerrys preparing to leave the farm and heading homewards to Solomon's Tower, expecting to see me waiting to welcome them and, I was sure, looking forward to Sadie's excellent cooking.

'I must let my husband know,' I said to Harry. 'Have you a telephone?' Telephones were a rare luxury, still a novelty confined to big businesses that only the wealthy could afford.

With all their modern installations, of course, The Heights had a telephone. My problem was how to get a connection to Jack at a remote farm like Eildon.

The Macmerrys looked in awe upon telephones, considering them an unnecessary extravagance that they wanted none of. Farmers had horses to ride and carry messages as they had always done. There seemed no need to make such a radical change in the manner of country life that had lasted for generations past.

I didn't quite see the significance of horses and telephones in emergencies as I told Harry I had no idea of the name of anyone near the Macmerry farm.

'Then the local police station will send someone to the farm.'

I would have to seek their help, and heading in the

direction of the Rothesay police station, with a fierce wind now blowing from the unruly sea, I could just imagine Jack and his father watching a strange policeman coming up the path – fortunately neither of them were subject to panic attacks.

Sergeant Clovis was at his desk. He looked up and greeted me with a wan smile. 'Sorry about the ferries.'

'That's not my only problem.' I went on to tell him about Miss Brook taking ill and ignoring his look of concern explained the situation as briefly as I could while he opened up a drawer and searched through some sheets of paper. A moment later he was dialling a number on the telephone and handing me the instrument. The person at the other end asked for the address of the Macmerrys' farm and the telephone number at the hotel where I was to be contacted. Sounding very competent, he said they would get in touch immediately.

Aware of my anxiety, Peter said consolingly. 'It shouldn't take very long. They are quite efficient,' and while my imagination still wrestled with this marvel of our modern age, he continued, 'I'm sorry to hear that Bute has let you down on your holiday. Not only our weather and the cancelled ferries, but now the added complication of Miss Brook taking ill.' He frowned. 'There is a lot of this influenza strain about. Hardly to be described as an epidemic, though, more of a seasonal outburst, but very inconvenient.' He looked at me. 'And you must take care to avoid it.'

There was nothing more to be said except to thank him once again for his help in this emergency. He saw me to the door and said: 'If you are to be around for a day or two, perhaps we might meet again.' I said I would like that and he asked: 'Have you any plans?'

'I haven't had much time to make plans. Miss Brook being ill came as something of a shock when I returned from St Blane's.'

He gave me a quizzical look. 'The authoress at work, doing research?'

This gave me an idea. As that was the generally accepted reason for my visit to Bute, it might provide a good excuse for appearing at Vantry and being accepted, even welcomed, calling informally on Edgar and Beatrice Worth. After all, writers did that sort of thing, at least male writers did but I was not sure how far this concession applied to females.

However, I had no idea how long the police station would take to reach Jack and with neither the wish nor the patience to sit around the hotel waiting for a call from the far distant Borders, I decided to leave a message with Harry. If Jack should telephone in my absence, he was to be briefly told of my possible delayed return, the cancelled ferries, that Miss Brook had a chill but I was well, and this change of plans was a mere inconvenience and no cause for anxiety.

Leaving the police station I had already the beginning of a plan in mind: my present circumstances of an enforced stay provided the perfect opportunity to meet Lady Adeline and see if any clues still existed that might be used to prove Sarah Vantry's innocence, for although I had a strange feeling, based on observation, that her future with Captain Robbie was no longer uppermost in her thoughts, I had my own reasons now for wishing to solve this mystery. After all, as Peter Clovis had once pointed out unknowingly, crime was a policeman's bread and butter, but it was more than that: for me it was the very air I breathed every day, my *raison d'être*.

As I walked back to the hotel, the weather had improved slightly, with even a hint of blue in the sky. A sudden shaft of sunlight on the mainland far across the bay touching those wild waters brought hope that they might soon be stilled enough for the ferry services to resume.

But whatever tomorrow brought, it was still too early for Sadie to be fit enough to travel to Edinburgh.

With the probability of a few more days of freedom, my feelings of anxiety suddenly vanished in a cloud of elation, the challenge of solving a mystery.

It was as well I did not know at that moment what dangers were hidden in the future or I might have decided on an immediate retreat with a book to one of the hotel's luxurious armchairs, beside the potted palm.

Safe enough there, to quote those words that haunted me.

CHAPTER SEVENTEEN

My first thoughts on returning to the hotel were of Sadie. Harry was in reception and he looked grave. When I asked how she was, he looked worried, and said she stayed about the same, with no improvement in her condition.

'Dr Wills is going to keep an eye on her. There don't seem any new cases of the influenza so far, so we're hopeful that this is a minor outbreak, not an epidemic, which would be very bad for the tourist trade. Even late in the season, we expect visitors from abroad,' he smiled wryly, 'trying to escape from hot weather, like those from the Antipodes. Many of them have ancestral connections with the Hebrides.'

I went upstairs and looked in on Sadie. She seemed to be asleep and I didn't want to disturb her, so I left a note that I was going out to Vantry and would see her later, hoping she felt better.

Ready to leave, I met Harry in the corridor outside, he was carrying a tray and said: 'A few goodies for her and some milk, when she wakes up. She has eaten so little, I really despair. She needs to keep her strength up.'

He seemed very awkward, and I realised that he had little experience in taking care of the sick when I reminded him of the old adage: 'They say feed a cold and starve a fever.'

With an anxious glance at the tray, he frowned: 'Is that so?'

I opened the door of Sadie's room for him and passed on my instructions. Should Jack telephone, I would be out for the next few hours. 'What is the weather going to be like?' I added.

'It's not good. Where are you heading?'

When I told him I was going to visit Vantry, he frowned again. 'I'm not sure about the tramways today. You have missed the morning one and that's quite a walk from Bannatyne. Have you seen the timetable?'

'I have. But I don't need it. I'll get a bicycle again.'

'It's a long way and a lot of it uphill. Besides, you might get very wet. Best take a rain cape – we keep one hanging behind the door in the reception office.' He raised his eyebrows, a clear indication that he thought this woman was mad, and with a despairing shake of his head he vanished inside with the tray.

I wasted no more time. The man in the bicycle hire shop seemed surprised to see me again and issued the usual warnings about the weather and so forth, which I ignored. Soon I was on my way, up the road through Ardbeg, then Port Bannatyne. As I wasn't sure of that shortcut, and there were no visible pathways, I didn't want to risk another puncture, for there would be no obliging Mrs Forsyth with a blacksmith on hand this time, so I rode on along the tramway route to the terminus at St Colmac and followed the steep hill up to Vantry. It was hard going on the bicycle and I had to get off and push most of the way, a cold, strong wind hampering my progress and adding to my problems. Was this perhaps an omen regarding the kind of welcome awaiting this alleged and, from the Worths' point of view, presumptuous authoress?

By the time I reached the gates and started down the rhododendron drive, which at least was decently paved for carriages, my confidence was ebbing. I had a bad feeling about this place as I remembered the frightened man not wanting to be seen and darting into the bushes on the drive as Sadie and I approached. The same man, I was certain, who had lingered outside the hotel by the pony cart while the Worths had lunch in the restaurant.

What had become of him, I wondered? If his business was legitimate, then he would certainly have gone into the hotel, but even at a distance there was something furtive about his behaviour that suggested he was not expecting a warm welcome from the Worths. I was still cross at not having watched their departure from my window. Had they taken him with them in the pony cart rather than risk an argument or a confrontation in public?

At last I reached the gravelled entrance to Vantry, propped up the bicycle, climbed the stone steps and raised the brass knocker on the ancient door. Although it reverberated loudly through the house, apparently no one else heard it. Perhaps there was no one at home, but even if the Worths were absent, surely Lady Adeline who didn't get around much would have heard the sound? As she moved slowly I gave her a few minutes. Still no response, so I decided to try the servants' entrance.

The house seemed to watch me as I pushed my bicycle round to the back premises. I was conscious of that strange deserted feeling and the back door was ajar. I knocked again, called loudly: 'Anyone at home?'

Another wait, still no response.

Behind me, a scraping on the gravel and I turned to see a huge black and tan dog rushing towards me, snarling. I remembered too late the Beware of the Dog sign and now I was face-to-face with the fiercest dog I had ever met. No gladiator in the Roman arena facing lions could have been more scared, for I had always been terrified of big dogs until Thane came into my life. But strange ones still have that effect. Now I stood paralysed, could think of nothing. He had a savage, wicked look suggesting that kind words would not deter him.

And then, when he was two yards away, he stopped dead. He lay down, rested his head on his paws, stared up at me. I went forward boldly now, stroked his head and said: 'Nice dog.' At that he seemed satisfied, leapt off and disappeared again from the same direction he had appeared.

Very odd, I thought, as pushing the door open I found myself in a very untidy scullery that smelt of dust and stale food, beyond it a glimpse into an equally unkempt small kitchen. The grimy state of affairs, the unwashed dishes in the sink, made the absence of servants apparent and I began to have misgivings about the food they served in the huge room now furnished as a cafe for the tourist excursions. I was glad I had not seen the premises where the tea was prepared on that first visit.

Even as I thought of it, I knew it was wildest folly but the house was empty and a glimpse of that corridor ahead leading into the main rooms was very tempting.

There were three doors ahead of me, one leading directly into the reception area at the entrance, and my footsteps echoed on its marble floor overshadowed by the great oak staircase, gloomy even in the morning light, the sun not having yet travelled round to the south of the house.

I stood and listened to the silence. The house was definitely empty. Not only empty but there was a faintly sinister feeling, the kind one might feel in an allegedly haunted house, and my voice sounded unnaturally loud and echoing as I called out: 'Hello! Anyone there?' I was not expecting an answer and there were no footsteps from above.

I looked around, wondering what to do next, and a little demon whispered: having come this far, why not explore? Here's a great chance, you can look around at your leisure and be off before anyone appears.

Sniffing the air, I was remembering my first visit.

Vantry smelt old. Like all ancient buildings, the strange medieval smell of age called up in me a sudden homesickness, a longing to be back home in Solomon's Tower. I allowed myself a moment's hope that Jack would have been in touch with the hotel before I returned, as I wandered from room to room, followed by the remembered and now ghostly voice of Angus, the tour guide.

I would have been happy with some of those people at my side now. The rooms were dull and uninspired, a strange combination of furniture that was merely old rather than antique, with the occasional *objet d'art* that had been removed from the original castle and now sat ill at ease at the side of shapeless, misshapen and shabby armchairs with squashed seats and once handsome Aubusson carpets now dirty and threadbare. Family portraits glared down at me, and once again I was looking at the one reminding me of Sadie.

Back in the reception area, my footsteps unnecessarily loud on the marble floor, the *pièce de résistance*, the great oak staircase, looming above me. The tour had been restricted to the ground area. We had not set foot in the upper regions and I lacked courage to wander upstairs, open doors, although I was certain the house was empty and Lady Vantry was not at home. From outside, the guide had indicated her massive bay window, the best room in the house he had called it, looking down over the drive, with horizons stretching way beyond Bannatyne to Kames Bay and the sea.

I was tempted. At the foot of the staircase, I shook my head. Should anyone return it would be easier to explain my presence on the ground floor than in the upper regions of the house. I had been fortunate thus far, better not stretch my luck, so I retreated back the way I had come.

Once again opening the door to the kitchen regions, there were three doors, two of which were cupboards. Opening the third, I realised that this must have once been the gunroom, for there were rifles on shelves and a dazzling and rather horrid display of disembodied animal heads: stags, foxes, wildcats and other animals, small and large, including a tiger, all grinning glassily down at me from the walls.

The room had been turned into a kind of museum, for there were other displays of animals, some of them quite huge in glass cases, and the curious rather acidic chemical smell of animals long stuffed that no amount of glass casing can conceal. I seemed to be allergic and whatever it was resulted in a violent bout of sneezing surrounded by this panorama of the jungle, with here and there a nod toward civilisation. That was achieved, also confined to glass cases, by various robes and costumes, worn by ancestral Vantrys at celebrations over the passing centuries. Some models were seated in armchairs, the robes spread about them realistically but rather weird *sans* heads.

The collection was brought up to date by robes plus an elaborate wig and headdress worn by Lady Adeline at the coronation of King Edward in 1902, according to the photograph on the wall alongside. That must have been just before her accident.

Suddenly I heard footsteps. I panicked, but it was useless to hide. I was trapped and about to be discovered, nothing for it but to make a bold appearance.

When I opened the door, I don't know who was most scared, Edgar and Beatrice, or me. The big dog was at their side.

'I do apologise—' I began but I got no further.

'What on earth are you doing here? You are trespassing, that's why we have a guard dog.' She gave him a bewildered look. 'Boxer, Boxer! Really!' she said reproachfully but he ignored her, staring at the ground.

Edgar said: 'He is very savage, that's why we warn people. We have to keep him chained up when we have tourists.'

Beatrice was staring at me, and she cut in: 'How on earth did you get past him?' A pause. 'Mrs . . . Mrs Macmerry, isn't it?'

'Indeed yes, and I'm terribly sorry. Research, you know. I so wanted to meet you again and learn something of the history of Vantry. I was just looking at your museum . . .' Embarrassed, I trailed into silence.

Beatrice was clutching a basket of flowers and wearing gardening gloves. She gave me a shocked glance while Edgar stood at her side, wide-eyed, biting his lip and speechless. She took his arm and looked me over: 'Ah, the authoress?'

I nodded and took refuge in the lie. 'Yes, indeed. I knocked at the front door, and then I came round the back. The door was open so I thought someone must be at home . . .' I gabbled on, all the while realising how dreadful and improbable it sounded. A pause for breath with an attempt at an apologetic smile. 'Oh dear, I am so sorry to have come at such an inconvenient time.'

Beatrice was watching me, listening with a look that clearly said she didn't believe a word of it. Indicating the basket, she said: 'We were in the garden. You would have found us there,' she added accusingly. 'We are not prepared for visitors just now.'

'Perhaps some other day?' I added weakly but hopefully.

Beatrice nodded vigorously. She exchanged a glance with Edgar. They had both recovered. 'You would be most welcome, for your research, Mrs Macmerry, but not today,' she added firmly. 'Today is most inconvenient.'

'Of course, of course. You are most kind,' and as I prepared to depart, she added: 'We are at home most afternoons.'

I hoped my smile was grateful enough. 'Perhaps I could have a word with Lady Vantry next time, you know – the history of the family and that sort of thing.'

Beatrice nodded. 'I'm sure that can be arranged. She rarely leaves the house these days but like all old people, she enjoys the occasional visitor.'

A pause and then from Edgar: 'The bicycle? Is it yours?'

I nodded. 'My favoured form of transport, very useful in Edinburgh. I hired this one in Rothesay.'

Edgar nodded. 'The hills must be something of a trial. Even to walk,' and he gave the nearest he could manage to a sympathetic smile. 'Perhaps tomorrow for your visit?' A quick look at Beatrice. 'Are we doing anything?'

A shake of the head.

I was hovering near the back door, preparing to depart as quickly as possible. Edgar followed me, making certain that I left. Boxer joined him, sat down and sighed in dog-like weariness. I found it unbelievable that this could be a fierce guard dog. The gardener-cum-tour guide Angus had also appeared on the scene and was subjecting the parked bicycle to a careful scrutiny.

He looked at me. 'I remember you,' he said accusingly. And to Edgar: 'She was on the tour the other day.'

I managed a smile. 'Yes, and most enjoyable it was,' I added patronisingly. 'You did it so splendidly.' As I was extolling the tour's virtues as well as giving a kindly mention to the rather deplorable cream scones, Beatrice had disappeared. I heard a loud bell ring, one of those on the kitchen wall summoning servants. She reappeared, looking flustered.

'That was Aunty. She's awake now and waiting for her tea.'

All three watched me as I mounted the bicycle and rode away. I had an odd feeling they were making sure that I left.

Where the gravel forefront joined the rhododendron drive, I turned and looked back at the upstairs window that Angus had said was Lady Vantry's room. But no face watched me, no curtain twitched from that great window.

I was now feeling embarrassed and chastened by my illicit visit, for although I could have sworn the house was empty, I had been wrong and I decided that her ladyship must sleep very deeply or be very deaf not to have heard me calling. However, I was glad indeed that I had not ventured beyond the ground floor and shuddered at my narrow escape from an outraged encounter with the reclusive Lady Vantry or a savage attack from Boxer, who for a fierce and dangerous guard dog had been remarkably friendly.

I remembered the evening I was exploring Rothesay and the odd behaviour of the dogs I had met. All dogs behaved like that when they met Thane.

I shook my head. I refused to even try to work that one out.

Anyway, I had tomorrow afternoon to look forward to another visit to Vantry, by invitation this time, a legitimate visit.

CHAPTER EIGHTEEN

Aware that Jack might be on the telephone at any time, I thought it wise to stay in the vicinity of the hotel. My ride back from Vantry had been cold and windy, but thankfully the wind was behind me on that steep hill back towards St Colmac and I was grateful for good brakes. On the way I had a fit of sneezing, but searching for a missing handkerchief, I remembered the gunroom at Vantry and hoped I had not dropped it there.

As I sat by the hotel's cheerful log fire, with a pot of tea delivered by one of the immaculate but silent servants, the rain clouds moved in again. It was not a good day for exploring, although there were several places I was tempted to visit, especially the High Kirk and the picturesque ruin of Rothesay Castle.

My visit to Miss Boyd would have to wait until later and a warm seat in a comfortable armchair fulfilled my immediate needs, the continued reading of Bute's history a pleasant companion. What did a few hours matter, even if the ferries were running again tomorrow, as Harry had now predicted, I was a prisoner, even a welcome prisoner, until Sadie had fully recovered.

Dr Wills came to where I was sitting. Having seen Sadie again he believed there was a slight improvement. 'At least she is no worse,' and I felt his words were merely to comfort when he added: 'I gather from Harry that this is all very inconvenient for you, but by next week she should be fit enough to travel back to Edinburgh.'

He smiled. 'Meanwhile, I dare say you will find plenty to keep you occupied.'

And glancing down at my reading matter, he added: 'Perhaps you will get inspiration for a new book.'

For a moment I wondered what he was talking about and then the authoress kicked in. I smiled and said: 'Maybe you are right.' And I had a sudden idea: 'There is so much in Bute for a visitor to enjoy, and as a matter of fact, a friend of mine asked me to look up an old acquaintance from Kilchattan, a Miss Ellen Boyd, who I gather is now in a home here in Rothesay.' When I gave him the name that Mrs Forsyth had supplied, he frowned and looked at me sharply.

'Chanonry is not a nursing home, Miss Macmerry. I think I should warn you it is an asylum.'

'Asylum?'

'Yes, for the insane. The inmates, or patients as they prefer to be called, can be quite violent and we do not encourage visitors, except, of course, near relatives.'

A hard look making it clear that I fell into the former category, he went on: 'I take it that some time has elapsed since this lady you know, saw Miss Boyd?'

'I haven't any idea, but I was given to understand that Miss Boyd was suffering from depression after the death of her sister.'

Dr Wills snapped his fingers. 'Ah, now I remember. That's Miss Ellen Boyd. Of course, it was a tragedy. They had been servants at Vantry . . .' and I was hearing again the story Mrs Forsyth had told me about Mavis Boyd's devotion to Lady Adeline and the tragic consequences of her visit.

He shook his head sadly. 'Such an appalling thing to happen. According to Mr Worth, her ladyship was delighted to see her old servant again. They were having a cup of tea together, sister Ellen was outside looking at the flower beds with the gardener. She had been promised some plants to take back to their garden at Kilchattan when they heard shouts and ran inside.'

He paused and raised his eyes skyward. 'What a scene. Her ladyship and Edgar were bending over Mavis who was lying on the floor, still clutching the cup of tea. They were horrified, said there was no warning, she had just suddenly reeled over and collapsed. When she saw Ellen she tried to speak to her, but it was too late. Her ladyship was terribly distressed, as you can imagine, and so were the Worths.'

He sighed. 'I was sent for immediately, but I was away in Glasgow at my son's wedding at the time and our locum signed the death certificate and gave Miss Ellen a sedative. I got the whole story from him. Poor Ellen had fainted clean away and was sent home in the Vantry carriage where it was hoped their kind neighbours would look after her.'

He sighed again. 'A heart attack, I've seen it so often. Alive and kicking, laughing and not a care in the world one moment, and the next – dead and gone. When I got back, the funeral was over and I thought I would go out and see Ellen, give her my condolences, but it was obvious that she was in a very bad way. I've heard of people going mad with grief, mostly in grand opera, but I never expected to see it in real life. Well, here it was, Ellen was already way beyond the normal emotions of a bereaved sibling, maintaining that Mavis had never had a day's illness in her whole life and that she hadn't just collapsed and died. She had been murdered.'

He smiled wryly. 'Of course, it was ridiculous. Those caring, friendly neighbours had done everything they could to console and reassure her but they couldn't deal with this kind of situation. It seemed that even before the funeral she was back at the police station here, demanding that they make enquiries and find out who killed her sister Mavis. All very sad but she started making such a nuisance of herself, going out to Vantry as well and threatening Edgar, that with no one to restrain her or to take care of her, I was consulted and we decided that she should go into a home. They tried the regular nursing home at St Colmac, but that didn't restrict her. It was too near Vantry and as she made life hell for everyone, it was realised that she would have to go to the asylum.'

'When did all this happen, Doctor?'

'Just after her ladyship's accident, four years ago. She had been visiting friends near Glasgow for a local horse show. She was an excellent rider, but unfortunately this animal from her friends' stable was still rather wild. It threw her, her left leg was injured in the fall, she still walks with a limp, but worst of all, her face hit a tree and she was badly scarred.'

He thought for a moment. 'Perhaps it was seeing her former employer, who was a great beauty in her day, so changed that gave Miss Boyd a heart attack. She was devoted to her ladyship and must have been terribly shocked.'

He stood up, looked at the clock and smiled. 'Off for a game of golf,' he said cheerfully. This was his weekly relaxation when patients and influenza spared him. He had left me with some interesting thoughts. Four years ago would be 1902 and this accident must have happened very soon after Lady Adeline was at King Edward's coronation, her robes now in the Vantry gunroom museum.

Despite the doctor's warning, I was determined to see Miss Ellen Boyd, who I was almost certain had been wrongly incarcerated in an asylum for what should have been normal grief at losing a beloved sister. She already had my sympathy and my keenness to hear her story, as I had listened to so many other strange cases from people wrongly accused and desperately needing help in my years as a lady investigator.

Believing that her sister had been murdered was what really intrigued me. Such suspicions were often why clients came to me and in most cases, I was well-equipped to solving. Here was a problem, perhaps more than a problem, and any mystery was an irresistible challenge.

I had been faced with a similar situation regarding Sadie's problem, basically stemming from the same root of mismanagement, and again I had no idea where to begin. However, if I could sort it out, find a solution and prove that this poor unfortunate woman was not mad, the reward would be in restoring her to a normal life again outside the asylum's walls.

Laying aside the history of Bute, it suddenly struck me as rather odd that I had been brought to the island to solve one woman's innocence and perhaps destiny had decided that I was to remain to discover another mystery to be solved, another woman's apparently mad behaviour, and at the back of both stories hovered the sinister shadow of Vantry.

I sighed, aware that again time was not on my side as I recognised the folly of this particular challenge, a mere few days in which to prove Ellen Boyd's accusations were not merely the wild derangements of a disordered mind but had a firm link in reality. But how on earth did I start to prove that her accusations were justified and that her sister had indeed been murdered?

And as always, bearing in mind the motive: what possible reason could Edgar Worth have for murdering his aunt's former servant? And by what means? The only obvious one was poison, but this never occurred to a visiting locum, who had diagnosed the cause of death as heart failure. The inescapable question remained: what had Edgar Worth to gain?

Hospitals, and I presumed asylums, had regular visiting hours and much to my disappointment my desire to strike while the iron was hot, so to speak, with Dr Wills' revelations still churning over in my mind, was thwarted as there were none available until tomorrow.

I had a word with Harry, explained to him about Miss Boyd and the imaginary Edinburgh friend. He looked faintly alarmed at my idea of visiting Chanonry House Asylum, but I assured him that this was just a sick old lady who wasn't likely to fall upon me with violence. I owed it to my friend, I said, and as they had been close, perhaps someone thinking of her would give her a little stability.

He sounded doubtful but he smiled. 'You are good to your friends, they are lucky to have you.' He sighed deeply. 'There's Sadie, what would she have done without you at this time?' I was unable to answer that as Gerald signalled from the office that someone was waiting to see him. Leaving apologetically, he called:

'Look, I'll go with you – to the asylum, tomorrow, just in case.'

I declined with thanks. Here I thought was another person whose friends were lucky to have him.

At last, after hours of waiting, Harry said excitedly. 'Your husband is waiting to speak to you, Mrs Macmerry.'

I ran into the reception office, sat down and suddenly across the miles of sea and land, from the far distant Border country, I was hearing Jack's voice in a panic –

unusual for him – asking: 'What on earth has happened, love? Are you all right?'

'Yes. I'm fine, but Sadie's not well.'

A querulous voice at his side, his patient response. 'Yes, Meg, Mam's all right – you can speak to her in a minute.' Then to me: 'I thought it was just this damned weather, we've got some of it here. Pretty stormy and I thought about those ferries. They always get cancelled . . .'

'You're right about that, but there's another problem, Jack. Sadie has apparently gone down with influenza and the doctor tells me it might be at least a week until she can leave her bed and travel back to Edinburgh.'

I heard his deep sigh, perhaps more of exasperation and inconvenience than mere sympathy, as I said: 'The thing is, Jack, I must stay with her, surely you realise that? I can't leave her to make that journey back alone, if she isn't up to it. I'd never forgive myself—'

He interrupted: 'Of course not, of course not, love. I understand. Oh, poor Sadie – and poor you. How awful. This is a miserable state of affairs. You must stay. It is a damned nuisance but we can cope, meantime. You being absent will be all right for Meg and me – and Thane. But as you know this is Pa's retirement holiday. They have been looking forward to it for months now. The chance for Ma to see Edinburgh and stay in the Tower.' He sighed again. 'They will be so disappointed, you not being there. Let's hope the delay is just a day or two—'

An urgent whisper at his side. 'Yes, Meg, of course you can.'

A shuffle as the instrument was handed over. Meg's

shrill: 'Mam, is that really you?' An excited laugh. 'Wonderful to talk to you and you so far away. I can't believe it. Like magic, isn't it? You sound as if you're just next door. As if I could look out of the door and see you.'

Suddenly, just hearing her voice made the tears well. 'Oh darling, it is so good to hear you. Have you been having a lovely time?'

'Oh yes. I've been riding a pony too. And Thane has loved being here. Does Sadie being ill mean you aren't coming back right now, after all?' She had been listening to the conversation. A wail: 'Oh, Mam, I miss you awfully.' She sounded tearful now. 'Please – please come – soon.'

A buzz on the line indicated that our time was up. Jack's voice, urgent. 'I'll call you again, have the hotel's number. Bye, love.'

A voice choked with tears: 'Oh, bye, Mam!'

They were gone. And I had never even asked about the Macmerry's golden wedding party. I felt ready to cry too, like Meg. That wasn't like me at all. So marvellous and really quite emotional hearing their disembodied voices across all that distance, separated from them by hundreds of miles of sea and land. At least they would be well looked after by Jess Macmerry, but the thought of her going through my untidy cupboards and finding dusty corners, spiders and perhaps even mice, as well as other signs of neglect that even Sadie had not noticed! I would never live this down. I could almost hear those sighs of resignation.

I looked in on Sadie before I went to bed. She opened her eyes, gave me a weak smile and groaned, tried to ask me something, but was interrupted by a bout of coughing. No, there wasn't anything I could bring her. Harry was so good . . .

There our conversation ended. Feeling miserable and disorientated, I prepared for bed. Talking to Jack and Meg on the telephone had made me miss them terribly, and on top of that I was plagued with uneasy thoughts about their return home without me, as well as our domestic life in Solomon's Tower being subjected to my mother-in-law's sharp eyes. Then there was Meg's preparation for school and the special things she liked, a piece of chocolate at bedtime before she cleaned her teeth. I was sure that indulgence would be frowned upon.

I pulled myself up sharply. I had to stop this, feeling sorry for myself wasn't on my agenda. Tomorrow morning I would, from all accounts, need to be vigilant and not expect too much from that visit to the asylum for the insane and an encounter with Miss Ellen Boyd. Meanwhile in preparation for tomorrow before retiring to bed, I got out my notebook and made careful and exact notes of what Dr Wills told me.

CHAPTER NINETEEN

Chanonry House Asylum did not advertise itself. Indeed, it seemed eager to keep its presence as secret as possible as I soon discovered to my cost when I went in search of it, as I had been directed, in the wooded area beyond Ardbeg. There was a morning visiting hour and that meant I would also be able to visit Vantry in the afternoon, glad that I would not have to waste another of the next few days, when hopefully Sadie might be well enough to travel. Thankfully, the ferries had taken to the water again, back on their daily schedule, with the storm clouds brushed momentarily aside.

Once more the tramway had been useful but I was

experiencing problems with persuading the conductor – who was either deaf or, by his expression of amazement, taken aback, looking at me wide-eyed – to please set me at the stop for Chanonry House.

He frowned, regarded me anxiously and asked was I sure, then in a whisper so that the other occupants might not overhear, he leant over: 'The asylum, is that what you are wanting, miss?'

I said yes, definitely, and with a clanging of bells the tramway vehicle duly stopped and he pointed: 'There's a path up there, across a field.'

And on foot was presumably the only access for visitors. Without a roadway, any carriages would have to be parked where I left the main road, before setting off in the direction of a building hidden by trees and invisible from the junction. Fortunately, the weather was reasonable in that it was not raining, otherwise a cold, windy and unwelcoming walk to a cold, unwelcoming house might have put off all but the stout-hearted.

At least the gates were unguarded with a short walk up to the front door of an unimposing building, once a handsome private residence but now appearing much the worse for wear after many years of neglect. There was a garden of sorts, thinly planted with a few shrubs, and with a sprinkling of rickety tables and chairs, sadly in need of paint and sprawling in disorder close to the walls, as if the residents had just left or had been called inside, or abandoned them in a hurry to escape a shower of rain.

I rang the bell on a door that had seen better times and waited with some unease, wondering what I might expect to find inside. At last there were footsteps, the door opened and a uniformed maid, neat and tidy, appeared. When I asked to see Miss Ellen Boyd, her surprised expression and repeated question suggested Miss Boyd had few visitors, and nodding vaguely, she indicated that I enter and take a seat.

I found myself in a dark room with a dozen chairs thrust back against one wall, opposite a window that shed little light into the gloom. There were no other visitors, only an ominous silence reminiscent of a doctor's waiting room.

The footsteps returned. This time a large lady appeared in the uniform of a senior nurse and, with a brisk manner combined with an air of authority, declared herself the matron of Chanonry House Asylum.

'Is it Ellen Boyd you wish to see?' she asked sharply and as she said the words she frowned, her expression as surprised as the maid who had opened the door.

I stood up. 'If that is possible, yes,' I said, already dreading what those words were to bring forth and with a confidence long since evaporated. I was not feeling at all competent about dealing with a woman reputedly mad and inclined to violence.

The matron nodded and indicated that I should follow her.

'Are you a relative or a friend?'

I smiled. 'Friend of a friend. I'm visiting Rothesay and I promised to look in and see her.'

The matron nodded again. The explanation seemed to satisfy her. 'I merely wondered. Ellen does not have any relatives or many visitors.'

From the warnings I had received, I felt she might have conveniently substituted 'any' for 'many', as I followed her from the main reception area through a door and down a narrow, tile-lined corridor with a somewhat forbidding, prison-like atmosphere.

I wondered in alarm if this was where the inmates were kept securely in locked cells, when the matron said: 'In here, miss,' and opened a door out of the gloom and into a blaze of sunlight.

I blinked. Here was a large kitchen, with a few servants scurrying about and a rich smell of baking.

Ushering me inside, the matron shouted: 'Ellen, a visitor for you!'

From the furthest table, a woman looked up, stared towards us short-sightedly, and laying aside a rolling pin, dusted her hands on her apron and came briskly across.

At first glance, she did not look mad or violent, no more demented than a shop assistant overburdened by customers on a busy Saturday morning. I guessed she would be fiftyish but looked older, her hair streaked with white, an amiable and polite, but rather surprised expression, understandable since we had never met before. She looked pleased, a warm, shy smile, a welcoming hand.

Looking over her shoulder to one of the other kitchen women, similarly clad in caps and aprons, she called: 'Watch that oven, Betty. They'll be ready in five minutes. I shan't be long.' And touching my arm: 'We can talk in the sitting room.'

The sitting room turned out to be the gloomy place

with those vacant chairs. Indicating one, she sat down beside me, turned with a smile and said: 'So good to see you, miss.'

I said, 'Mrs Macmerry.' She smiled again and waited, obviously for some explanation. I began rather awkwardly, saying that I was on holiday in Rothesay.

To my relief, without waiting for any further explanation as to how I had come to visit her, she said eagerly: 'And how do you like it? Have you seen the castle?'

The next minute I was listening to all the glories of Bute that were not to be missed. Had I seen this and that? Had I been here or there? And all the time I was thinking this conversation was like meeting a stranger on a train journey, skimming across the surface of polite acquaintanceship with never a hint of anything personal. And in Ellen Boyd's case, not even a question or at least a curious enquiry as to why I had come to visit her in Chanonry Asylum.

I felt I knew the answer. The sad, sad reason being – and the matron had provided the clue – Ellen Boyd had no visitors, and she was so glad to see even a stranger that she asked no questions of who or why.

I also thought I had found another grim answer. This pleasant, friendly woman had been falsely incarcerated in an asylum. She was as sane as I was.

A lull in the conversation. Weather had been discussed, suggesting the finality of topics. The moment I dreaded. In the silence that followed, she was smiling politely, doubtless waiting for some further explanation regarding this unexpected and surprise visit.

I could tell her a lie, about some mutual friend, or get up and go, but I would leave with an unsolved mystery, the main reason I had come to the asylum to further Sadie's cause and unearth more revelations about the tragic events at Vantry twenty years ago. The two sisters' strange behaviour as witnesses at the murder trial was why I had been sitting here talking to Ellen Boyd, all part of that deeper reason, to prove Sarah Vantry's innocence. How wild and even curiously unimportant that was becoming, I thought, as I stood up and said that I must be going now. She looked disappointed and nodded. 'I suppose you must, but it has been so good to meet you. Thank you for coming.'

It was then I took a deep breath and blurted it out. 'I was so sorry to hear about your trouble – the sad business about your sister Mavis.'

For a moment she stared at me wide-eyed, not understanding, and then she said quickly. 'I can never forget her last words, before . . . before she died. She said to me it wasn't her ladyship. So it was Edgar Worth who killed her.' And then as this sudden realisation unlocked some forbidden chamber in her mind, like a blast of lightning it struck her.

She leapt to her feet, threw her arms above her head and screamed: 'Get away from me. They sent you – I know who you are. You came here to kill me!'

I staggered back as her screams rocked the room.

The door opened and the matron came running in, followed by two muscular-looking nurses who went swiftly to Ellen and got her to sit down again, holding her and stroking her arms gently, trying to placate her until her screams changed into heart-wrenching sobs. Gently they whispered, raising her to her feet and leading her towards the door, darting bitter, accusing looks in my direction.

The door closed, leaving me with the matron. She looked at me silently for a moment. 'What have you done? Do you know what you have done?' she added sternly.

I merely shook my head, bewildered and too shocked to find any appropriate excuse or answer, sickened by how a few ill-chosen words could transform this gentle-seeming woman into a screaming madwoman.

The matron was leading me firmly towards the entrance while I stammered apologies, saying I had no idea.

The matron shook her head sadly. 'No, you had no idea, how could you have any idea? How the mention of her sister could still have this effect. We have to be very careful never to mention her sister Mavis, that still does the damage. Otherwise, she is just a nice, kindly, normal person.' She sighed. 'She believes that Mavis was murdered. It has obsessed her whole life, destroyed her. I expect you know the story, madam – or was it idle curiosity that brought you here?' she added bitterly.

I could think of nothing, no excuse. She opened the front door, touched the flaking paintwork. 'We do not have an easy life, money is scarce. There is no income. We have to rely on charity – in this case, Lady Vantry gives us what she can, helps us to stay open to offer shelter to those whose afflicted minds, if unrestrained, might damage the fabric of our society.'

She gave me a hard look. 'Something you might bear

in mind, madam, regarding the nature of asylums. The description, the very word frightens people, they avoid them, think of them as prisons.' She shook her head and added sadly: 'Not all are mad people, some, like Ellen Boyd, are brought here for their own protection.'

The door closed behind me and I was faced with the long, bleak walk back across the field once more.

CHAPTER TWENTY

I had plenty to think about heading back through the trees along past Ardbeg to the hotel. I was still shocked by what I had witnessed and now it seemed that all roads led back to Vantry. To Sadie's false accusation of murder, there was now added Ellen Boyd's incarceration at Chanonry Asylum, its doors kept open by the charity of Lady Vantry, Bute's lady bountiful, and I remembered the matron's ominous warning, that perhaps Ellen Boyd was there to keep her safe.

Safe from whom or what! At every turning Vantry was there in some shape or form and it was there, I was sure, I might find the answer.

There were so many threads in this sinister web, for the moment I was dismissing Sadie's original problem regarding her reply to Captain Robbie's proposal that she should marry him, which I now had reason to suspect had been overwhelmed and cast into the shadows by a newer problem, her affair with Harry. That was something she had to work out for herself, but I was now in the grip of mysteries surrounding Vantry. I had little time left but as I reached the hotel, I resolved to hire the bicycle again and visit Lady Vantry as planned.

Dr Wills was just leaving. He was in reception talking to Harry and had been to see Sadie. He saw me arriving and said there had been an improvement.

Smiling he added, 'She is a strong, healthy, young woman and I am hopeful that by next week she should be fit to travel back to Edinburgh with you.'

Although I responded with relief to Dr Wills, I felt guilty that I was now the one who was reluctant to leave with yet another unsolved mystery. I hated the questions burrowing into my mind, questions that gave me nightmares and kept me awake half the night when I was on a case, despite Jack's assurance that I slept like a log.

Dr Wills had a companion. Perhaps I had interrupted some important conversation, as in the pause that followed, I thought I detected a reluctance to introduce me. 'This is Dr Richards, Mrs Macmerry.' As we shook hands, Dr Wills said: 'Tom is just here visiting friends. His mother lives in Wemyss Bay.'

This was greeted by a smile. 'And don't forget my

esteemed relative in Rothesay. My cousin is with the police, an inspector, no less.' His dry laugh and the doctor's frown indicated that there was not much love lost in that relationship. 'But the doctor and I worked together. I was his junior, before I moved over to Glasgow. I am a Bute man too, but I succumbed to the mainland's attractions – I like the bright lights and high life, unlike some I could name.'

An attractive man, some twenty years younger than Dr Wills, with a charming smile hinting at a bedside manner that must be most agreeable to his women patients. And then I remembered the name. Dr Richards was the young locum who had been summoned to Vantry, signed the death certificate for Mavis Boyd's death and attended her hysterical grieving sister.

From my point of view this was a piece of unexpected luck. He was the very man I wanted to talk to as I wondered if his had also been one of the signatures on the certificate declaring Ellen Boyd insane and committing her to Chanonry Asylum.

Dr Wills was saying: 'I have some patients to see still, but if you'd like to stay here we can meet for lunch.'

'I'd be delighted, Ambrose.' A beaming smile. 'Perhaps Mrs Macmerry would like to join us.'

Dr Wills did not quite conceal a slight frown but the polite invitation was the perfect opportunity. Vantry could wait. How much would Dr Tom Richards remember? There was only one way to find out. In Ambrose Wills' absence – odd I had never thought of him having a first name – I would broach the subject of Ellen Boyd.

First of all, I went up to see Sadie, who was sitting up in bed. She looked much better and said although she still felt weak, her old self was emerging. She greeted me cheerfully and said that she was sure she was on the mend. I said that was good news but when I told her I had seen the doctor and he thought she might be well enough to travel back to Edinburgh next week, her smile faded.

'I thought you would be pleased, Sadie.'

'Yes, of course,' but she didn't seem convinced. She shook her head. 'I'm rather worried, Rose. That awful Uncle Godwin looked in this morning – I don't know how he dared – said he had heard I was ill and so forth and hoped I hadn't spread my infection round the hotel. So bad for their reputation and their takings. He was just checking.

'Cheeky old devil! Then he got to the point, said he wanted another twenty pounds as money didn't go far when you were a man with expensive tastes. I was taken aback. How dare he—'

I stopped her. 'Wait a moment, Sadie, you said another twenty pounds. Don't tell me after all my warnings about blackmailers and going to the police that you actually gave him money the first time.'

She sighed deeply. 'Yes, I did, Rose. I shouldn't have and I know now that you were right. But I was scared, really scared that he'd spread it around that he knew who I really was – and that he'd tell Harry.'

It was on the tip of my tongue to say that if they were as close as appearances indicated, then she should tell

Harry herself, but I said: 'That was a lot of money. And have you given him another twenty?'

She shook her head vigorously. 'Of course not. I haven't that much on me any longer. I told him that he'd have to wait until I was on my feet again and able to go to the bank,' She paused and looked at me. 'He said I could get it from my rich lady. Meaning you, of course. And I said no, I couldn't without telling you and I certainly wasn't going to steal it.'

I gave an exasperated sigh. 'Why didn't you just tell him to bugger off!'

She looked tearful, shook her head. 'I'm scared of him, Rose. He frightens me and he is horrid about Gerald too, saying such malicious things when he knows he is Harry's closest friend and such an asset to the hotel.'

I could understand her being scared of Godwin: just seeing him slinking about the hotel, appearing unexpectedly in his carpet slippers, I found quite unnerving, but there was one consolation. 'You don't need to worry about Uncle Godwin and his blackmail. We'll be leaving in a few days and he can't touch you in Edinburgh.'

She didn't look as relieved as I'd hoped by that observation.

Downstairs, Tom Richards was seated at a window table overlooking the sea. He stood up, bowed and seated me opposite.

Looking again at the sea, he pointed. 'Great day

for a sail while I'm here. Might take one of Harry's boats out.' Again the beaming smile that crinkled his eyes in a very charming way. 'Care to join me, Mrs Macmerry?'

I thanked him but said hastily that I had an engagement. He shook his head, looked me over rather candidly and drawled: 'Another time, perhaps?'

I nodded vaguely while we considered the menu that appeared as usual handed over by an enigmatic and expressionless waiter.

Richards said: 'I'm starving. Shall we give Ambrose a couple of minutes before we order?'

I agreed and there followed some polite preliminaries regarding Edinburgh, Glasgow and inevitably the weather. Then, with a show of anxiety, whether I had enjoyed my holiday.

This was my chance, at last. I said I had met a former patient of his.

He looked surprised, until I added that it was a Miss Ellen Boyd and once more produced the fictional mutual friend in Edinburgh – I was beginning to believe in her myself – who had asked me to visit her.

He thought for a moment. 'Ah yes. She is still at Chanonry?'

'She is indeed, and I am rather hoping that I can set some wheels in motion to procure her release.'

His well-shaped eyebrows rose at that. A rather cynical smile. 'As a danger to the community, that would hardly be wise, Mrs Macmerry. Or was your visit merely related to your professional requirements?'

I stared at him in astonishment. How on earth did he know that? Who had told him? But he was shaking an admonishing finger. 'I know why you are here. Harry tells me that you are an authoress. Asylums are always good for a chapter or two in novels. We need look no further than Mr Dickens.'

I sighed with relief: 'I assure you, Doctor—'

He held up a hand. 'Please – please call me Tom.'

I nodded. 'My visit to Chanonry was merely of polite interest for news to pass on to my Edinburgh friend. But now that I have met you, I would be most interested to hear how Miss Boyd's incarceration as an inmate came about. She seemed so reasonable. Quite normal,' I added, omitting the last painful scene. 'I believe as Dr Wills' locum you attended her after her sister's unfortunate death.'

'Indeed. A heart attack. Sad business, quite tragic. . .'

And I was hearing the same story, word by word, nothing new or varying it seemed from the account I had heard from Dr Wills. Every detail intact, from finding Ellen screaming spreadeagled over her sister's body. The only omission was her claim that Mavis had been murdered.

As he paused for breath, I supplied that.

'Murdered,' he repeated, shaking his head sadly. 'Ah yes, my dear, there is a very plausible reason for that, one we are very aware of in our profession. People suffering from the shock of grief, suffer great delusions. They need someone to blame for this cruel blow, the unexpected death that has removed a loved one, who only minutes ago was laughing, happy and alive.'

He sighed. 'And sometimes, or in most cases, I am reluctant to have to admit, it is the doctor's misfortune to be blamed. For a variety of reasons: the wrong treatment, the wrong medicine being administered, or in the case of young children, frequently not getting there in time. We get a lot of that.'

He looked thoughtful. 'Ellen had to accuse someone. In this case it was poor Mr Worth.' He sighed. 'You were extremely fortunate to encounter her in one of her more lucid moments.'

We got no further. Dr Wills arrived and took his place beside us at the table. The menus were once again produced and our orders taken.

The doctor seemed a little strained, perhaps he had had a gruelling morning and he was tired, but I had an odd feeling that he was uncomfortable in the presence of his fellow doctor, as any conversation ground to a dead end, leaving an absence of topics worthy of discussion. Soup came and was consumed, followed by a main course and a dessert.

All were suitably commended and removed. Then at last it was over, we were released.

There had been no further mention of my visit to Chanonry. As we parted, I said to Dr Wills that I had seen Ellen Boyd that morning. A sharp look was exchanged with Dr Richards, who said rather weakly, 'One of our unfortunate cases, Ambrose.'

'Indeed it was,' Dr Wills responded.

I nodded. 'And still is, gentlemen. I think there is a mite

of injustice to be sorted out there,' I said, and thanking them for lunch, I headed off.

It had been an interesting encounter. I had learnt something. Dr Wills did not greatly care for his one-time locum. We had that in common. Neither did I.

CHAPTER TWENTY-ONE

The storm had been more severe than usual and had wreaked havoc beyond Bute. Although the hotel boats were safe, Gerald had just heard that a boatload of tourists caught on the Kyles had been swept out to sea. Mainland police were still trying to recover bodies.

'We were lucky not to be caught in the eye of the storm,' said Harry. 'A terrible thing to happen . . .'

'Terrible indeed,' Gerald nodded. 'But strangers to the area on holiday are determined to enjoy themselves despite the weather forecasts and will put out to sea regardless of the danger, insisting that they know best and will be all right.'

'The coastguards are out searching,' said Harry.

Gerald was silent for a moment. 'Tragic news for the families involved.'

Harry gave him a quick glance and I remembered Sadie saying he had told her that when Gerald's parents drowned he, their only child, was left orphaned, and the Clovises adopted him.

With a complete change of subject, Harry said: 'Sadie is looking much better, isn't she?' He smiled. 'You might not be delayed as long as you feared if she keeps on improving.'

Now with our stay in Bute drawing to its close, I knew I had to get in touch with Jack by telephone again. It would be relatively easy once they had left Eildon and were back in Edinburgh, when I could call and leave a message at the police's Central Office for him to call the hotel.

Harry asked me what I had planned for the rest of the day and I told him a bit of exploring, a bicycle ride out past St Colmac. He wished me well and off I went to keep that afternoon appointment with Lady Adeline. First down to the square and the shop where I was becoming a regular customer, to be treated with a friendly greeting by the shop owner, a discussion on the day's weather and how I was enjoying my holiday, as well as a careful repeat of the solemn instructions to be given to a complete beginner who had just learnt to ride a bicycle.

A pleasant, windless day, I enjoyed the exercise and although the last stretch of the steep hill defeated my bicycling abilities, I reached Vantry without further incident, my thoughts on what the interview with Lady Adeline might reveal.

There was no sign of the fierce guard dog today as I bicycled up to the front door. Angus was at one of the flower beds. He watched me as I dismounted and indicated the steps. 'Just go ahead, ring the bell.'

This time it was answered immediately by Beatrice, smiling pleasantly. I was made to feel welcome, although Edgar looked solemn, lurking nervously in the background.

Beatrice said she would go upstairs and tell her ladyship that I had arrived. Perhaps I would care for a cup of tea while I waited. Gesturing towards the tray set with its delicate china, she said they had just had theirs.

Watching her elegant right hand with its handsome antique ring hovering above the teapot, I declined politely. Was I sure? She seemed disappointed and, departing, left me with Edgar, who remained locked in heavy silence. No attempt was made by him to start a conversation while the minutes ticked away on the rather asthmatic grandfather clock, and strangely enough I found myself remembering Ellen Boyd's words. Had he indeed murdered her sister four years ago? Surly indeed, often speechless and nervous, he didn't look like a murderer, but then they never did, according to Pa's vast experience. At last, Beatrice called:

'Edgar!'

Excusing himself, he left me. The distant murmur

of voices indicated that Beatrice was calling him from upstairs.

When he reappeared it was to apologise for the delay. 'Her ladyship is having one of her bad days and that means it takes my sister more time than usual to prepare her to receive a visitor.' With an ominous feeling that this was going to be another useless effort, I stood up, started to say I was sorry and perhaps I could call at a more convenient time, but Edgar held up his hand.

'No, Mrs Macmerry, she is very keen to see you. I am only warning you that she is rather frail, so do not ply her with too many questions. Allow her to do the talking, if you please,' he added, quite a speech for him. 'Some days she has little strength and tires easily.' So saying, he opened the door and ushered me up the notorious great staircase to Lady Vantry's apartments.

He knocked on the door and a faint voice called: 'Enter.'

'Mrs Macmerry to see you, Aunt.' Pushing the door open, he whispered to me: 'My sister will see you before you leave, she has an urgent domestic problem about her ladyship's chimney smoking – the cause of the delay – to discuss with Angus.' With a sigh, he tut-tutted and went downstairs again.

Lady Vantry was seated back in one of the deep armchairs by the great window, swathed in shawls, veiled as usual. The room was cold, the fire long turned to ashes. She seemed exceedingly frail and hardly raised her head, merely nodded but did not invite me to take the seat opposite.

I said good afternoon and waited for her response.

'What is it you wish to know, Mrs Macmerry?'

Had she been misinformed regarding the nature of my visit? As this opening gambit without any preliminaries was in the form of a question, I realised this was going to be in the nature of interviewing a possible servant, rather than an informal, meaningful chat.

'Well?' Although the note was impatient and imperious, her voice was thin and weak.

I stated my case briefly, that I was interested in the history of the Vantry family.

'And for what purpose?'

'For a book I am writing.'

'Ah yes, the authoress.' She made it sound somewhat contemptuous: I detected a sneer in that faint voice.

I dreaded the next question and the authoress lie about what did I write and so forth but I need not have feared.

'There is a book in the library, which you may borrow. Edgar has instructions and you may return it via the hotel.' A pause. 'That is all.'

She stretched out a long slender hand from the shawls and tried to reach the bell rope. She couldn't quite make it unaided.

As I rushed forward to help her, she did not thank me and I noticed she was wearing only one ring today, a large handsome ruby similar to Beatrice's. Presumably Lady Adeline was liberal with the contents of her jewel box.

I went towards the door and turned. She seemed to have already forgotten my presence as the sound of the bell echoed through the house, then she dismissed me with a mere: 'Good day, Mrs Macmerry.'

Footsteps on the stairs and there was Edgar. He had no words, merely led the way downstairs and ushered me towards the front door, where he handed the book presumably from the library.

'My sister has been delayed.' It was then I noticed the handkerchief on the hall table. Edgar pointed to it. 'Presumably yours, Mrs Macmerry? The initial R? You must have dropped it on your last visit.'

It was mine, lovingly embroidered by Meg. As I had feared, I had dropped it in the gunroom after my sneezing bout. They must have found it there, my snooping activities reported to Lady Vantry, that accounted for my hostile reception by her. Now whatever might have been embarrassment was replaced by indignation, that I had been invited back not to a cordial or at least a polite reception, merely to stand before her in the manner of a prospective servant being interviewed for a job – not even offered a seat. I was angry.

Angus looked contemptuous too as he watched me mount the bicycle and start down the drive. I glanced up at Lady Adeline's window, but she wasn't watching me leave. What a disagreeable lot these Vantrys were and I came very close to certainty that they were the kind of people who would stick rigidly together, be it truth or lies. I was convinced at that moment that Sarah Vantry's story about being framed was absolutely true, although neither she nor I had the time or means to prove it. I had a low opinion of Edgar, a weak character who was only too eager to do anything that his aunt suggested. And with a sudden enlightenment, I now decided that might well include murder.

Absorbed and propelled forward by angry feelings I rode fast, hurtling down the steep hill. Aware suddenly that I was going uncontrollably and dangerously fast on a narrow road, I put on the brakes to slow down. Nothing happened. I tried again, something was wrong. Alarmed, I tried to stop, but merely gathered speed, on and on, uncontrollable . . .

A motor car was approaching just yards away, driven fast, sounding its horn, and I was heading straight for it. I steered violently to the right, towards the margin of the road, and the force of hitting the raised edge had me catapulted into the air.

The bicycle went one way and I the other. I crashed to the ground and literally saw stars, stunned by the impact. My face burrowed in the grassy verge, I opened my eyes, dazedly wondering what was broken, and how was I to get back to the hotel pushing a wounded bicycle.

Bruised and shaken, wondering if any bones had been broken, I heard the motor car brakes and the next moment footsteps and the now familiar face of Dr Richards looking down and asking was I all right.

'I think so,' I said shakily and he gently helped me to my feet.

'Are you sure you aren't hurt? Nothing broken? Sure?' he added, looking me over in his best consulting manner.

I shook my head and it remained attached. I was still in one piece, my bruised limbs and grazed knees would hurt later.

'You were very lucky,' said the doctor. 'What on earth did you think you were doing hurtling down the road like a bat out of hell? You can't ride like that on these narrow roads,' he added sternly.

'So I gather,' I said. 'I was riding at a moderate speed when the brakes failed.' He didn't seem impressed, sighed and said: 'We must get you back to the hotel. You can't walk all the way back pushing that.'

Walking over to where the bicycle lay, its wheels still whirring gently, he added:

'I'll put it in the car and take you back.'

Still shaken, I accepted, and glad of his arm, limped to the motor car. 'No damage as far as I can see,' he said, helping me into the passenger seat and settling the bicycle behind us.

We started off with my apologies for delaying him.

'Don't mention it. I was just going to Vantry, as a matter of fact. I know the Worths and I believe her ladyship was once a patient at my hospital. I wanted to see how she was getting along, although I doubt there will be much improvement.'

I refrained from telling him of my experience and that he would be fortunate to get more than half a dozen words from her.

He said: 'This is a hotel motor car, thought it would help getting around my visiting quota.' And giving me one of his looks of concern: 'Thankfully, I was on the hill at the right time to rescue you. Just sit back and relax, we'll be there in five minutes.'

Apart from occasionally glancing at me anxiously, he did not try to make conversation. I was glad of that: beginning to feel the delayed effects of my fall, bruises were making themselves felt and it was a relief when I directed him to the bicycle shop. There was a young lad lounging at the door who watched our activities with considerable interest as Richards handed the bicycle over and I stepped down from the motor car.

I had obviously had an accident and the lad asked: 'What happened?'

I said the brakes had failed.

Pushing the bicycle inside the shop, he said: 'Boss's out just now. I'll tell him when he gets back. They're good machines.' And with a solemn shake of his head: 'He'll not be pleased.'

'I wasn't particularly pleased either. But tell him I'll be back later.'

Richards helped me back into the car and drove the short distance to the hotel. Escorting me firmly up the steps, before relinquishing my arm at the door, he said anxiously: 'Are you sure you will be all right?'

'Perfectly sure, thank you,' I said. 'And thanks anyway for seeing me back safely.'

I apologised again for delaying him. He bowed. 'Think nothing of it, my dear. Glad to have been of help. Any time.' There wasn't much a doctor could do for my grazed knees.

Harry had seen us arrive, and taking in my dishevelled

appearance, he said: 'What on earth happened to you?'

Wearily I told him about the failed brakes and gave the standard assurances that I wasn't hurt, just a few bruises that I'd attend to.

'Your husband telephoned when you were out. Left a message that he was back in Edinburgh and would call again at six o'clock.'

CHAPTER TWENTY-TWO

Sadie was sitting up in bed with a heap of magazines and what looked like a box of chocolates, presumably courtesy of Harry. Obviously recovering, she gave me a startled look. 'Gosh! You've been in the wars. What happened?'

With a sigh I repeated how the brakes had failed on the steep hill and of my rescue by Dr Richards.

She gave a shocked exclamation. 'That was a narrow escape. If he hadn't stopped like that, you might have been killed. And you wanted us both to bicycle there! I'm not as experienced or as confident as you are.'

I hadn't a reply to that and she went on eagerly: 'How

was Vantry? Did you see Lady Adeline – and what did you make of her?'

'Not a lot. I was pretty cross, Sadie. She treated me like a servant coming for an interview. A few questions and I was dismissed.'

She looked surprised. 'Gracious! She must have changed. She used to talk all the time.'

'People do change in twenty years,' I reminded her.

She nodded. 'How did she look?'

'Frail.' And I told her Jack had telephoned.

'Yes, Harry came in search of you, said he's calling again this evening.'

'Good. He'll want to know if you'll be well enough to go back to Edinburgh at the beginning of the week.'

She frowned, looked thoughtful and then stretched her arms above her head. 'Well, I'm feeling so much better today. And I'm hungry, first time in ages. Think I might pop down to the restaurant, have some tea. What about you?'

'I have to attend to my wounds,' I said lightly. 'Some soap and water and sticking plaster should do the trick. Then I must go to the bicycle shop.'

'Yes, indeed you must. Give that man a right telling-off for his rotten machines. He should be giving you compensation. You might have been killed.'

As she spoke, she jumped out of bed. 'See you later, then.'

'Don't overdo it,' I warned. Having made myself presentable once more I went downstairs. Peter Clovis was talking to Harry and Gerald. They turned when I approached, their expressions serious.

'You missed our moment of big drama,' Harry said.

'Yes, a body was discovered on the beach near Kames Bay, must have been washed up and lay there when the sea went out at low tide,' said Peter.

'How awful. Do they know who it was?'

'No idea, as yet,' he replied.

Gerald said: 'I've told him it is most likely one of the passengers from that sailing boat wrecked in the storm the other night.'

'I expect you're right. They were still searching for bodies, so this is probably one of them.'

'Surely it's a long way from the Kyles, though,' Harry said.

'That's the way with drowned bodies, especially with island currents.'

And I remembered Orkney and how corpses from wrecked boats could be washed ashore as far away as Norway. I felt very sorry for that family who had gone out on a day's pleasure trip from Glasgow. After the agonising wait for news, an even greater ordeal lay ahead, dreadful for some family member to come to Rothesay, identify and collect the body.

A silent servant hovered, Harry excused himself and Peter said to Gerald: 'Call at the house tonight if you can manage, will you? It would make Mother happy, she hasn't seen you for a while, always asking, you know.'

The way he said it held reproach and Gerald's sigh of resignation indicated that he was well aware of his shortcomings as the adopted son who lived just minutes away but seriously neglected his parents.

I saw Peter's expression as he watched Gerald leave without a word. He sighed deeply and I suddenly wanted to know more about his enigmatic foster brother.

'There's quite a big age gap between you, isn't there? That can't have always been easy.'

He nodded. 'Ten years and that doesn't make for the best relationship between siblings. He was seven years old, I was seventeen, keen on the girls. Very full of myself, I was, and fed up at being expected to take him everywhere with me.' He paused and then said: 'I wasn't the perfect elder brother model and to be honest I resented sharing my father and mother, who were pretty indulgent, with this new member of the family, but they had been close to his parents, and after their tragic accident and knowing I was keen to leave home and join the police in Edinburgh anyway, and being their only child, I suppose they wanted to fill the empty space.'

He shook his head. 'I'm sure he was grateful enough, glad to have a home with us, but there was always from my point of view something missing. Even then Gerald was always his own person, he treated Mother and Father with the proper respect, but I don't think he ever cared deeply for any of us, or anyone.'

With a sigh, he continued: 'Until he met Harry. And then the whole scene changed. They would have liked him to go to university and study law – disappointed that I had refused, now Gerald also declined. He seemed very lacking in any sort of ambition and content with an assortment of office jobs through the years. He even moved to Glasgow for a while. Then, like I said, a couple of years ago he got to know Harry Godwin and, despite having always had his own place at home – our house which was far too big for the parents, anyway – he decided to move into the hotel. I think the parents were pretty miserable and Mother still misses him.'

'I can understand that, but surely a fellow past thirty needs to feel independent of the family home and have a place of his own?'

I had sat down while he was speaking and in the short silence he looked at me quickly. 'Are you all right? You look a bit done in.'

He didn't know about my accident and I said: 'Fell off the bicycle. But nothing to get alarmed about.'

'Sure?'

'Just a few bruises – nothing a bit of sticking plaster couldn't deal with,' I said lightly. 'Dr Richards came to my rescue in the hotel motor car.' Suddenly Peter's remarks about Gerald touched hints of another troubled family relationship.

'Richards' cousin is my boss,' he sighed and added rather wearily, 'Inspector Rudd doesn't particularly like being reminded of Tom, some sort of family feud, I believe.' I had one more urgent question. 'Has your inspector been in Rothesay long?'

'Just a couple of years, promoted from Dundee.' That was a relief from the Sarah Vantry angle and if Peter thought my interest was odd, his face didn't show it.

He said: 'When Jack telephoned I was chatting to Harry and my name being mentioned, Jack immediately

229

asked if he could have a word.' He nodded eagerly. 'It was great to talk again after all this long time.'

I wondered about that. Jack was normally very uncommunicative on the telephone and seemed to treat talking to someone he couldn't see with suspicion.

'I told him how nice it had been meeting you,' Peter was regarding me intently, smiling. 'I had to tell him all about that. He was very interested.'

I was certain he would be and asking some anxious questions about our departure. I had guessed right as Peter went on: 'When are you leaving, by the way? I wondered if you might have a chance to visit the parents before you go. They enjoyed meeting you at the party but you know what it's like, small chance with all that crowd for a proper conversation.'

With one eye on Sadie, who gave us both a cheery wave as she flounced into the restaurant, I said it depended on whether she was fit enough to travel. Following my glance, he smiled. 'Looks as if she's made a good recovery. Of course, bring her along with you. She would be most welcome.'

I smiled secretly. I didn't doubt that. Peter was captivated by Sadie and obviously did not know that his rival was his friend Harry Godwin. The only one she had failed to impress so far was the enigmatic Gerald.

I guessed it would be too late for the bicycle shop and thought I had better wait until Jack telephoned. He would expect me to be sitting around waiting. I didn't mind, I was looking forward to speaking to him again. Meanwhile I'd enjoy a leisurely dinner with Sadie.

However, I was to have it alone: she did not appear and neither did Harry. I watched Gerald leave with Peter, no doubt returning home to the Clovis house to spend the evening with their parents.

I had just finished my last course and was having coffee when the telephone rang in reception. Harry wasn't in the office, but I guessed it was for me. I picked up the instrument and heard Jack's voice asking for Mrs Macmerry.

It was such a delight to know it was him, and as always I was momentarily overcome by the magic of it all, the strangeness of hearing his voice as if he was sitting opposite me in the kitchen in Solomon's Tower and not miles and miles away across sea and land.

'Are you well, love?' he asked. 'You've escaped this infection? How is Sadie? When will you be home?'

We both had a riot of questions and I could hear background noises. 'Is Meg with you?'

'No, I'm at the station. We got back yesterday, settling in nicely. Ma is making herself at home, finding out where everything is.' I could just imagine. I thought guiltily of those dusty neglected areas as he went on: 'Pa has already climbed to the top of the hill with Meg and Thane. I think he's glad to be home, back to his usual disappearing tricks. Vanishes all day on the hill. Ma gets worried about him, thinks all dogs are pets who should sit by the fire and wait to be taken for walks every day. I've told her not to worry. She's getting Meg ready for school again. We're all fine . . .' And so it went on, the minutes ticking away.

'We miss you. When will you be back?'

I said I hoped early next week.

'Good, telephone the station. If I'm not around, leave a message . . .'

A click and he was gone, I looked at the black instrument resentfully as if it was to blame that we had been cut off with still so much unsaid. I knew how much talking to Jack had made me long to be safe home again with Sadie, this new and very different Sadie from the one who was our housekeeper. Even though I had failed to solve her mystery, I felt that the visit to Bute had laid the ghost of Sarah Vantry to rest and proved that the past was no longer of great importance. She would probably marry the besotted Robbie and forget about the whole thing, put it down to experience.

How wrong could I be? Sadie and I were not finished yet, nor was Harry.

I spent the rest of the evening reading by the log fire and decided to have an early night as I was beginning to ache, the aftermath of the accident.

Sadie always had home remedies for everything, pills, potions and ointments, so I looked in to also tell her about Jack's call. Her room was empty. As she was feeling so much better, I guessed she and Harry were spending one of their few remaining evenings together. Soon they would have to part and as she had never confided her feelings for Harry and had been quite secretive, I was glad that offering advice on her future was not one of my problems. The Sarah Vantry episode had been more than enough for me.

* * *

I slept well enough and although my bruises had me feeling a bit sore and somewhat stiffer than usual, I was grateful to be none the worse for the accident.

Sadie was already at breakfast, looking rather tired but I made no comment. Dr Wills would be coming in to see her for the last time before we departed. She didn't seem very interested as I outlined plans for the return journey on the ferry to Wemyss Bay and back to Edinburgh via Glasgow.

She looked so sad, very different from the Sadie who had such boundless enthusiasm for our outward journey across on the ferry. I felt sorry for her, guessing that so much of her life had changed unexpectedly with the advent of Harry Godwin into her world.

A pity he was so much younger.

She asked me rather diffidently what were my plans for the day? I hadn't any really since she seemed no longer concerned with her original idea, her obsession that had inspired this visit to Bute. I suggested that we might go for a bicycle ride, do a bit of exploring, if she felt up to it.

She shuddered 'You must be joking! After what happened to you with that bicycle, no thank you.' A sigh. 'And I'm still not feeling particularly energetic.'

'In that case, how would you like to take up Harry's offer of the motor car and I'll drive you round the island. We can stop somewhere for lunch.'

This suggestion was met by a blank stare. She didn't want a drive round the island – at least, I thought, not with me.

'I have things of my own I'd like to do before we leave, a bit of shopping, you know.' She stood up and said: 'See you later,' as she wandered off towards Harry's office.

I set off for the bicycle shop. Although I had paid for the hire I knew I could not leave it at that. I must warn the owner how the brakes had failed on the steep hill from Vantry. Not only for myself, but for any future bicyclists.

The owner, Mr Craig, did not look glad to see me. He scowled as I went into the shop. 'First time I let you hire one of our machines, you had a puncture. The next time, the brakes failed. You don't have much luck with bicycles, do you?'

That remark made me furious, as if everything that happened was all my fault.

'I could have been seriously injured yesterday. Faulty brakes on a steep hill are a dangerous matter.'

He thumped his hands on the counter, his face scarlet. 'Faulty brakes! Faulty, is that what you are calling them?' I thought he was about to explode. He leant over and shouted in my face. 'I'll have you know, madam, I supply only the very best machines, the most expensive, and they are also the most up to date on the market. You couldn't get any better in any of your big cities like Glasgow or Edinburgh – or down in England.'

I realised he was sincere. I had hurt his pride and I apologised: 'If you know the area, it was a very steep hill from Vantry,' I repeated, 'as well as a poor road surface.'

'I know that area well,' he snapped. 'It's not popular with bicyclists but we've never had any problems before. I'll have you know this was not the fault of the machine.' He stood up straight and said calmly: 'After the lad told me, I carefully examined it.' Taking a deep breath he looked at me gravely. 'This wasn't wear and tear, madam, it's a brand-new machine. And it looked to me as if . . . as if, well, that brake cable had been tampered with.'

'How could that be?'

'It was in perfect condition when you left the shop . . .'

A slow and terrible realisation was dawning. 'You can't mean someone deliberately cut the cable?'

He shook his head. 'That is exactly what I mean. On their return to the shop, I examine each machine after it has been hired. You had the same bicycle on each occasion, the other day when you had the puncture and again yesterday. There was no other hiring in between.'

'But that is impossible.' Even as I said the words, I realised the implications, what was involved.

Mr Craig obviously believed me. He had calmed down and said: 'I will need to provide new brake cables before this machine can be used again.'

'In that case, as I am responsible, I will pay for them.'

And I immediately handed over and paid for what he told me the cost would be. We parted on polite terms, although I knew he would be more than reluctant to see me again in his shop. Putting the few pounds in the till, he was satisfied.

I left the shop but I wasn't satisfied. I had a growing undeniable realisation that if those brakes had been cut, someone had tried to kill me. And that could only have happened while I was in Vantry visiting Lady Adeline.

CHAPTER TWENTY-THREE

Someone had tried to scare me off, perhaps even kill me.

I was stunned by the enormity of what I now knew – that the brakes cable had been deliberately cut. But why, what was the possible reason for such an act?

With no one to confide in, I felt terribly vulnerable, as if my potential assassin having failed once was lurking near at hand and ready to strike again. Still wrestling with my horror as I reached the hotel, I was going upstairs to see Sadie when Peter Clovis rushed in.

'We have an emergency,' he said, and to Harry: 'Can I use your telephone? Something wrong with ours at the station. Seems out of action, it's always happening.'

Peter looked at me and gave me a brief nod. As both men disappeared into the reception office, I could hear voices and was curious about this emergency.

At last they emerged, Peter saying to Harry: 'They will notify him at once and he'll come across from Glasgow, but these things take a little time.'

Thanking Harry for the use of the phone, he seemed to notice me again, and taking my arm he led me over to one of the quiet corners. 'We have a problem, Rose,' he said, his face grave. 'Not only the influenza, the severe storm and people drowned down the coast. Now we have a dead body.'

'Yes, so I heard, one of the men from the sailing ship.'

He shook his head firmly. 'No, not from the sailing ship. We thought that too. It seemed the obvious thing to have happened. But no, they have recovered all the bodies, and this one at Kames Bay – well, it definitely isn't one of theirs.'

'From another ship?'

He sighed. 'There were no other wrecks or accidents reported. How are your bruises this morning?' Without waiting for an answer – perhaps my shocked expression, resulting from my having just discovered what looked like an attempt on my life, suggested a different source of pain – he led me to one of the armchairs. 'Let's sit down and I'll tell you about it. A man discovered this body at low tide – thought from a distance that it was a dead seal washed up.'

'Could it be a local man?'

'No, we are pretty sure of that. Not even a wallet to

identify him. We have no information as yet.' He looked very worried.

'How did he drown? Was it an accident?'

'We don't know for sure. Dr Wills has had a look at the body but we need the procurator fiscal. That's what I was telephoning about. It's the usual thing in accidents but it can take a little time for him to be notified and get here from the mainland.'

'What did Dr Wills think? Was it . . . a heart attack? Some visitor to the island, perhaps a tourist staying in a guest house?'

'We have no idea. Of course the man's details – what we know of them – will all be circulated.' He sighed. 'The body was discovered by a St Colmac man out walking his dog. He's very short-sighted, wears thick spectacles and his dog had rushed across to inspect what looked like a dead seal washed up and left by the ebb tide. He called his dog but it was excited and wouldn't come to heel, so he went down to the sand to have a look. The dog was scratching at seaweed covering his find. When he saw a hand and realised it was attached to a human body, the man ran for Dr Wills who raised the alarm. Before rushing to the scene the doctor alerted the hospital, although, following the dog owner to the shore, he knew what to expect – a dead man, probably drowned in the night.

'Wills couldn't make more than a rough examination. He had another problem too: the dog owner who had made this gruesome discovery, one of his patients, had insisted on coming with him. He was very distressed and almost had a heart attack. Got a dreadful shock – he's quite elderly and all that rushing about hadn't helped. Wills had already attended him earlier in the week, in a panic about his invalid wife taking this influenza.'

He paused. 'We were summoned at the station and I went in the hospital ambulance down to the shore. I had a bad feeling that this was no accidental death, no body from the wrecked sailing boat. On the beach, when the doctor turned the man over, his head had been bleeding and he had what looked like a fractured skull. I suspected that he was already dead before he was put in the water. That head injury hadn't been caused by a fall on the shore, there was nothing but wet sand, nothing that could account for the severity of the blow on the back of his head. He had been attacked.' He paused and looked at me. 'This was murder.'

I must have looked concerned and as I listened, and made occasional comments, I could not help wondering why Peter was telling me all this. I think he read my mind for he smiled wryly.

'I know what you are thinking. But you haven't been completely honest with us, have you, Rose? Pretending to be an authoress?'

'That wasn't my idea,' I protested. 'It was a misunderstanding.'

'I'm not blaming you, don't think that. Pretence isn't a punishable offence, unless you are using it intending to cheat someone. And you are quite at liberty to be an authoress as well in your real profession – as a detective.'

I stared at him. How did he know? He smiled. 'Your husband gave the game away. As I told you, I happened to be in the office when he telephoned and we had the opportunity for a wee chat. When I said I had the pleasure of meeting you, Jack groaned. "For God's sake don't have any murders up there while she's staying on the island," he said. And out it came, that you were in fact a lady investigator – quite famous, he said, in Edinburgh – having a holiday up there with your housekeeper as companion. He laughed, and although he hated to mention it, he said they do follow you, knowing your profession – murders, I mean.'

I felt cross about Jack not minding his own business, as Peter continued: 'This is our first murder in twenty years and the last one had a not-proven verdict.' Thankfully he hadn't recognised Sadie, I thought, as he sighed: 'To be honest, I am right out of my depth. Not only do I not have a clue about the corpse, or to put it more bluntly the victim, lying in the hospital mortuary, but I doubt whether Inspector Rudd has any idea, either, on how to conduct a murder investigation. We've done nothing here but investigate poachers, petty thefts, lost dogs and cats and a very occasional violent drunk, and unless we had some definite proof that this is murder, I could hardly approach Rudd with it. He is a stickler for facts, keeps us all up to scratch. He'd just laugh and say I had been reading too many crime stories, and real life in Bute wasn't like that.'

I had a feeling that Rudd wasn't the most popular and well-liked inspector as Peter gave a bewildered sigh: 'I can't even rely on my Edinburgh training manual. That was for detectives and I was just a beat policeman.'

'Well,' I said consolingly, 'not to worry. I expect it will be handled by the lads from Glasgow.'

He looked at me, seemed about to say something and changed his mind. We were silent for a moment, then he grinned weakly. 'However, once the word gets around there will be general consternation. First an influenza epidemic – that turned out to be premature – and now murder. Panic all round.'

Another deep sigh. 'This is the year that will go down in the island's history. Folks here like to boast that we are a law-abiding community, and have even said they didn't need a police force and it was a waste of money. Now, if we don't produce the killer, they will believe that they are not safe in their beds, and we have a murderer on the loose.'

He regarded me sadly. 'I'm a novice at this game. I just wish I had your experience – you must have solved a lot of crimes as a lady investigator.'

I said hastily: 'Most of my cases have always been domestic matters, fraud, thieving servants, adultery or blackmail, rather than murders.'

'So maybe you can give me an idea from your greater experience in Edinburgh where one starts searching for clues,' he said mockingly, but the remark had a serious implication as, frowning, he added: 'There will still be a day or two before you leave the Glasgow lads and the procurator arrive, and we might have some evidence to present to Rudd.'

Suddenly I knew what he had in mind. Clouds cleared from my mind. With Sadie's illness, perhaps fate was taking a hand. The plan to prove her innocence had never been feasible, just a dream, and now since she seemed no longer particularly interested in anything but Harry – in less than a week the whole situation had changed.

And until we left I could lend my experience to help Peter solve his first murder, especially as he knew Bute well and I might need assistance in discovering why someone wanted to kill me. There had to be a motive.

What did I know of vital importance that had scared or driven someone at Vantry into the role of my would-be killer? Main suspects were Edgar and Beatrice – surely not Lady Adeline, but what about Angus? He had easy access to the bicycle to cut that brake cable while I was indoors. Did he have a secret history, perhaps a police record?

Peter was waiting for me to say something. I nodded and said: 'Very well, I'll do what I can, though I should warn you, that might not be much—'

He jumped to his feet. For a moment I thought he was about to hug me. 'You will?'

'What else am I to do until we leave? Sadie isn't well enough to go gallivanting about the island, so I might as well make myself useful. Where do we begin?'

Peter had taken out a notebook and was gathering his thoughts when I said: 'First of all, I need to speak to Jack, tell him as little as possible, just that I may have to stay a little longer – until Sadie is completely recovered.'

Peter was pleased and I was glad that he had asked for my help and that I was back in business, instead of sitting around trying to work out who had tried to kill me and watching over Sadie, I was free to do what I loved most.

Peter had called it my bread and butter, and so it was, solving a mystery.

'What was this man like?' I asked.

'Would you like to come and have a look at him?' Peter said eagerly. 'He is in the hospital mortuary,' he added with an anxious frown. 'Maybe you wouldn't—'

He wasn't the first to feel doubtful regarding the abilities of this under-five-foot, fortyish woman with the mass of unruly yellow curls. For a detective, mine was not an appearance most likely to inspire confidence.

I said quickly: 'I've seen many corpses in my career. I lived in Arizona in the Wild West with my first husband who worked with Pinkerton's Detective Agency. We were on both sides of the bullets from marauding bandits – and Indian arrows, Peter. I assure you, I'm not at all squeamish.'

He sighed. 'That would be a help.'

That settled, I went on: 'First of all, I'd like to see the exact spot where the body was found.'

'The usual procedure in Edinburgh, I seem to remember.'

'And where any crime has been committed, it is invaluable, especially if it has not been disturbed and remains exactly the same, for footprints and so forth. How do we get there?'

'We can borrow the hotel motor car in an emergency like this, I am sure Harry will be willing, and perhaps drive us there. I can't yet.'

'But I can, Peter.' His eyes widened at that. Armed with Harry's instructions, which he had read to me earlier, a female at the wheel was to provoke even more stares as well as anxious looks. I was enjoying this new experience. The motor car was easy to navigate and there were none of those sixteen-foot-wide roads, which were forbidden under the law – at least if there were, we were not wasting time getting out and measuring them, I told Peter.

We drove the short distance through Port Bannatyne and down to Kames Bay towards the strand where the man had been found. Parking by the roadside we walked down steps towards the beach and faced our first hurdle. The tide was out, the crime scene now a vast stretch of unmarked wet sand with any visible footprints having been carried away by the twice-daily tides. The disturbance where the finder's dog had scraped away the seaweed, where the doctor had knelt down to examine the body, the footprints of the men from the hospital, all were lost, every possible clue had vanished, washed away into the sea.

'I hadn't thought of that,' Peter scratched his head. 'Sorry, forgot about it being a beach and the tide.'

'Which way was he lying? Can you remember?' I asked. The sea far out now, a faint lace of white waves patterning the land.

Peter stopped, looked round and then with a stick of seaweed lying nearby, he knelt down and drew a shape in the sand. 'Head here – and feet there.'

I thought about that. The fact that he was lying facing the sea indicated that he was running from his attacker but it could also mean that if he was already dead, his body had been arranged in such a position to deliberately create that impression.

'Tell me about him. What was he like?'

Peter thought for a moment and consulted his notebook. 'Mid sixties, I have here. Blood had been washed away, but there was a wound on the back of his head suggesting he had been struck down. However, Rudd said it could have been caused when he fell from the sailing ship.'

He shook his head. 'I think the inspector is keen on the accidental death theory. It makes for less work and interruption of his easy life.'

The same thought had occurred to me as, frowning, he continued: 'The dead man was tall, distinguished-looking, wearing a dark-grey, expensive-looking suit, waistcoat, shirt and tie.' He looked at me. 'D'you know, that was when I first suspected that we weren't seeing one of the drowned passengers. You see, his clothes were all wrong. Not the kind a man would wear for an afternoon outing on a sailing boat – far too formally dressed, clothes he would wear for a business meeting. And his shoes. I always notice a man's shoes, it's part of being a policeman, and his were new and highly polished. They hadn't been in the sea.'

'Well done, Peter.' He grinned as I went on: 'Which suggests that he was dead before he was brought down here. Any identifying possessions?'

'No wallet. A gold watch and chain and a signet ring with odd initials, QVE, sounds like he was a freemason or a member of some secret society. Definitely doesn't sound as if robbery was the motive.'

'I agree, but removing the wallet with some proof of identity is significant.'

Peter shook his head. 'It looked to me as if this wasn't a

planned crime, maybe a quarrel and a fight with someone.'

Not a fight, I thought. Not that blow to the back of his head, unless he was running away. As we walked back to the motor car, my eyes turned in the direction of Vantry. The dead man wearing a dark-grey suit had been tall and distinguished-looking. Now I wondered would the body in the mortuary be the man we had met on the drive after the tour of the house, so frantic not to be seen he had dashed into the bushes. Then there was the other occasion: although I had not had the chance or a reason for a close-up look, the man lurking by the Worths' pony and trap while they lunched in the hotel also fitted the description.

Peter had to go back to the station and while I waited for him back at the hotel, Dr Richards appeared in the lounge. He smiled and said: 'Good, it's you I've come to see – in a professional capacity,' he added wryly. 'Wondering how you were, any ill effects after that accident?'

'The bruises are doing nicely, thank you.'

'Hope you gave the bicycle owner a good telling-off.'

'As a matter of fact, it was the other way round . . .' And I told him about the brake cable having been cut.

He was shocked. 'That could only have happened at Vantry, if the machine was in good order when he last checked it before you.' Silent for a moment, he rubbed his chin thoughtfully and I asked: 'How was your visit? Did you see her ladyship?'

He sighed. 'I did not. A waste of time. And I went just out of goodwill. My father had a heart condition and he was in the same Glasgow hospital where we understood Lady Vantry had been taken and treated after her riding accident. We were very friendly when I came over here as locum.' He laughed. 'I was able to get drugs for her, frowned upon by the good Dr Wills and not easily available without a prescription. In fact, I was always a welcome visitor to Vantry.' A charming smile. 'I stayed several times, she liked young folk around her.'

His expression hinted at more than a little flirtation too, as he went on. 'She was my only reason for nipping across the water from Wemyss Bay after visiting my mother.' He sighed. 'Not exactly popular with the policeman here, our cousin Rudd. Bit of a family feud.'

I knew that already as he went on: 'I wanted to see her ladyship, not only as an old friend but as a doctor I was naturally interested, and I decided it would be worthwhile reporting back on her progress.' Pausing, he shook his head. 'You see, it was quite odd. There had obviously been a mistake somewhere. The hospital had no record of Lady Adeline Vantry as an accident victim, or of treating her appalling injuries. I was interested in sorting it out, decided that it could have been another hospital and that I would call on her anyway when I was in the area.'

His expression was grim as he continued: 'I never got to see her. Beatrice Worth didn't even let me over the threshold, turned me away saying her ladyship was not receiving visitors and hated all doctors for bungling the operation to her face. I was very annoyed. So much for good intentions.'

Peter arrived and Richards, with a look at his watch,

got up to leave. 'I have a ferry to catch and to say goodbye to Mamma before I head back homeward. Been good to meet you, Mrs Macmerry. Enjoy the rest of your holiday.'

I made the usual cordial reply of hoping so. Peter watched him go and I had an odd feeling that there wasn't much love lost there either. And that set me thinking. Neither did Dr Wills like him and the general impression was that nobody was anxious to welcome this one-time locum doctor back in Bute, including his cousin the inspector.

Peter watched the door close and smiled wryly.

'What's wrong with him?' I asked. 'Have you some problem with the good doctor?'

'You'd need to ask Wills.' He sighed deeply. 'First time he's been back since he was locum here. He had a reputation for drinking too much, gambling, and didn't inspire trust in patients.'

Apart from Lady Vantry, I thought, as Peter went on: 'He tried to blackmail a couple of patients. It was all hushed up, one of those incidents that Wills never talked about, but rumours spread like lightning on an island and it left a sour taste after he departed. Shall we go now?'

First time Richards had been back in years, and as I followed Peter, I thought: had he come over to Bute, perhaps prompted by his mother in Wemyss Bay, to patch up that family feud with Inspector Rudd, his visit to Vantry merely interest in Lady Vantry's progress, a sentimental recollection of renewing old acquaintance? Or was there more to it than finding out that she had not been treated in that Glasgow hospital?

The easy explanation was that even the best hospitals can have their past records lost or mislaid, but did the fact that they denied all knowledge of a patient who was a woman of some importance suggest that Richards might have had in mind a more sinister motive for coming back to Bute, some idea or information that suggested it might be a useful piece of blackmail?

CHAPTER TWENTY-FOUR

At the mortuary, a long walk down a narrow corridor into a tiled room, where the acidic chemical smell reminded me unpleasantly of the stuffed animals in the gunroom at Vantry. It made me sneeze and I reached for my handkerchief as Peter spoke to the white-coated man on the door who solemnly ushered us inside and removed the sheet covering the dead man.

I looked down at his face, my worst fears confirmed.

'Did you recognise him?' Peter asked, as we left to return the motor car to the hotel.

'I believe so, inasmuch as I have seen him before but never spoken to him.'

Peter looked at me hopefully and I shook my head. 'I don't know his name or his identity.'

'Tell me what you do know, then.'

So I told him about the furtive man Sadie and I met on the Vantry drive and how I was almost certain this was the same man, identical in height and wearing the same clothes, that I saw waiting for the Worths outside the hotel.

'Our only clue is the initials on that signet ring,' Peter shook his head. 'Some Masonic society, I expect, and that's not much of a clue to go on.'

Suddenly the initials had a new significance. 'It's not a secret society,' I said triumphantly. 'V stands for Vantry and QVE could be the initials of Lady Adeline's estranged husband.'

As we made our way out of the building, I said: 'I have a strange feeling that the corpse we have just visited might well be identified as that remote cousin from England she married.'

Peter whistled and stared at me wide-eyed. 'If you're right, then we have something to go on, a clue at last. Right!'

And as we approached the waiting motor car: 'We'll head to Vantry and when we give the Worths his description, they will be able to immediately confirm his identity. No time like the present, Rose.'

'No, Peter, not so fast.' He began to protest and I said: 'Listen, will you? That would be the wrong thing to do. We have already decided this is a murder and in that case everyone connected with the victim is under suspicion.'

Peter was frowning as I continued: 'You are presuming the Worths and Lady Vantry had nothing to do with Mr QVE's unfortunate end, but if you are wrong and they are guilty, not only will they deny all knowledge of him, but it will put them on their guard.'

Again he began to interrupt and I cut him short: 'Hear me out. What you suggest is entirely the wrong way to go about solving a murder. And I have another reason that you don't know about. A very personal reason. Someone tried to kill me after my visit to Vantry yesterday.'

He gave a shocked exclamation. 'I thought you just had an accident on the bicycle.'

'An intentional one that was meant to be fatal.'

I had made light of it, now he had to be told the details. 'I was there yesterday afternoon, by her ladyship's invitation, and while I was seeing her someone tampered with the brakes cable on my bicycle outside. It's a steep, dangerous hill back to the St Colmac road.'

He nodded. 'I know it well.'

'Then I expect you know that losing control on a bicycle could have had fatal results. I had just ridden about twenty yards when suddenly I needed to press on the brakes. Nothing happened, I had no control, I was whizzing down the hill and I was going to run full pelt into Dr Richards' car coming up the hill, straight for me. The only way I could avoid him was throwing myself off. I went one way into the hedgerows and the bicycle skidded away across the road. Dr Richards gathered me up and saw me back to the hotel with the damaged machine.'

Peter was staring at me, frowning. 'If you don't believe me I can show you some of the bruises.'

'I believe you. But where was Richards heading? That steep hill, it's a dead end, only goes to Vantry.'

'He said he was going to see Lady Vantry.' And I told him about the Glasgow hospital who had no record of treating her after her accident.

Peter was wide-eyed, thinking: 'But that accident of yours. It's serious. You might have been killed.'

'That was the intention. The man at the bicycle shop said that the brakes cable had been deliberately severed.'

'But if that is true, this is incredible. Why should someone at Vantry want to kill you, Rose? You hardly know them.'

I nodded. 'That's true, but if they wanted rid of me then it is because they think I know something that scares them.'

Peter shook his head. 'I don't understand.'

'Neither do I. I have no way of knowing why or what for, but I am determined to find out.' So saying I started the engine. 'However, I will never find that out or if they had any connection with Mr QVE if we just barge in as you suggest.'

'You think the attack – for that was what it was – on you might have some connection with the dead man?'

'I haven't much to go on as yet, beyond a strong feeling that Vantry is the link between my accident and Mr QVE's murder.'

The hotel was approaching and we had already received a fair amount of strange looks: a motor car was one thing but – with a woman at the wheel!

As I parked neatly outside and Peter helped me dismount he said: 'I'll leave you and get back to the station.' He looked bewildered. 'Where to go next? Should we bring Rudd in?'

'Not advisable at this stage. As you've said yourself, he'll probably laugh at you. Wait until we have concrete evidence to offer and need help.'

'You have certainly given me a lot to think about.'

'It's the way most of my cases begin, Peter. So you just have to have patience. It's slow at first, maybe, and then the clues begin to emerge.' I smiled encouragingly. 'Think of it as a bit like going through a labyrinth, a few false starts until you strike the right path.'

He groaned. 'How on earth do you hope to achieve anything positive when you are leaving next week?'

'I might have to stay.'

His eyebrows rose. 'Your husband will be expecting you home again and you have a little daughter. She'll be missing you.'

'Leave that to me.'

And leaving him, I smiled with a confidence I was far from feeling with my additional reason for helping Peter solve this murder. If, as I was almost certain, there was some connection with Vantry, then there might be two mysteries to solve, a link between the murdered man and the attempt someone had made to kill me, all of which, as Peter had pointed out, was going to take more than a few days to solve. The alternative was to sit around and do nothing until it was time to catch the ferry, pretend, except when my bruises and sore legs told me otherwise, that nothing had happened.

I had to find an excuse to stay. If Sadie was now well enough, she could return on her own. I realised I had come a long way from that original plan of proving her innocence, only to be almost certain that my accident and Mr QVE's murder were all linked to Vantry. More than a coincidence.

However, without Sadie as an excuse I also had to find something very plausible for Jack waiting impatiently at Solomon's Tower. The last thing I wanted him to know was that his scornful prediction that wherever I went, murder was waiting, had once again come true.

So I had to think of something – fast.

But nothing happened as planned. There were to be unimagined events and a tragic death – hidden, as yet – which was to bring Sarah Vantry into focus on Rothesay again.

I looked in to see Sadie. She greeted me cheerfully, but when I said: 'Well, all ready to go back to Edinburgh? I need to check the ferries, let Jack know when we will be arriving—' I was aware that she wasn't listening.

'I may not be coming back, Rose. Harry wants me to stay. You remember Uncle Godwin recognised me? And he knows about us,' she added awkwardly. 'Harry and me, that is.'

Two men in the same family of different generations and both had found Sadie irresistible. It was remarkable. I closed my ears to what I could imagine would be Jack's comments. In a few short days, I had not been alone in observing what was happening. They had made no secret of their attraction.

'The dreadful old man has been watching us and he tackled Harry in no uncertain manner.' She gulped. 'It was after he knew he was getting no more money from me and I told him to do his worst. And he did. He told Harry and Gerald that I was Sarah Vantry who had committed a murder and got away with it twenty years ago.'

I was appalled but she went on, smiling now. 'And do you know what Harry said to him? "I don't care who Sadie was twenty years ago. It's the Sadie Brook now that I love – yes, love – and I want her to stay."'

Her eyes were wide and tearful. 'When Harry told me, I cried. I was so relieved. I love him and he loves me. It is just . . . just wonderful.'

I looked at her. I could think of no words. He wanted her to stay, they were in love but there was no commitment. I thought about the difference in their ages, love but without marriage, and Sadie seemed to have forgotten all about her sailor lover whose ship was about to land in Leith any day now and was the reason for luring me to Bute to prove her innocence. She was saying: 'Yes, Rose, I'm in love for the first time in my life – and best of all, with someone who knows my real identity. And doesn't care. Rose, he doesn't care a damn. Do you know what that means?'

I knew. As far as she was concerned there was no longer any need to prove that not-proven verdict should have been not guilty. She could stay here with Harry, perhaps even persuade him to marry her, and not always be haunted by the fact he might get to know.

'Er . . . what about Robbie?'

A shrug of indifference. 'Oh, I told him all about the past, you know – in that letter you posted for me the other day. I had to be honest with him, I owed him that much. Even though Harry hasn't asked me yet,' she smiled determinedly, 'I could never marry Robbie now.'

'You're sure about marrying Harry?'

'Absolutely!' she trilled excitedly. 'Look at this!' She held out an elegant hand, now with a large sapphire. But not on her engagement finger. She saw my expression and must have known. 'It's a bit too big,' she said apologetically. 'A family heirloom, belonged to Harry's mother. Isn't it lovely?'

It was indeed. The rather old-fashioned heavy setting reminded me in size and shape of the rubies worn by Lady Adeline and Beatrice. As Sadie proudly stretched out that beringed hand, suddenly something clicked. A something that needed a great deal of thought, far too nebulous and outrageous to pursue at that moment.

'I must tell you what happened, how it all started.' And she began to eagerly report the conversation, in what sounded like word for word, that Harry had had with Uncle Godwin. After what he thought was dropping the bombshell of Sadie's identity, he was very ready to reveal that he was a great hoarder of old newspapers and especially anxious to produce those relating to the trial with all the details, including a sketch of Sarah in the dock. Like the one I had seen, Sadie said it was almost unrecognisable and would not have convinced anyone, much less her lovelorn Harry, that the sixteen-year-old depicted was also Sadie Brook.

'Harry said he didn't care, that it didn't matter in the slightest. Of course, he's quite a bit younger than me, as I expect you know.' I had counted fifteen years as she paused and added thankfully: 'He was too young to remember anything about the trial, but Gerald knew. Anyway, Godwin went on to ask Harry what were his intentions. And that was the best bit. Harry replied that they were honourable.'

I looked at her. If she was reporting Harry correctly, honourable intentions usually meant marriage.

'Uncle Godwin said that's a pity. Probably thought Harry was like himself, dreadful man – you know he tried to seduce me when I worked here and I knew from the other maids that he had sometimes succeeded to have his way with them because they were afraid they would lose their jobs.'

She paused. 'No wonder his wife left him years ago. Anyway, Harry said, "Finding Sadie is the most wonderful thing that has ever happened to me."'

Eyes shining, she clasped her hands. 'And me, Rose. Just wonderful. I can hardly believe it.'

She wasn't the only one, I couldn't either. I wasn't convinced about the wonderful bit but hoped for her sake it was true.

'What happened then?' I asked.

She smiled. 'Harry just reminded Godwin that he had always complained about him spending far too much time with Gerald, his best and only real friend. Now at last he had found the woman he wanted and said that he should be happy for me. "Happy!", Uncle shouted. "Happy to

259

see you throw away your life and your reputation with a . . . suspected murderess,"' she added in hushed tones. 'Then he said, "You are my heir but I certainly am not going to leave this hotel and everything I possess to you if you associate with this woman. I'm not leaving everything to an idiot, and let me remind you the hotel and all its assets are mine until I die, but if you are determined to include this woman, then my will can be changed."

'Harry then told him, "Your newspapers there recorded the not-proven verdict and I believe her, so what have you got against her?"'

Sadie paused and whispered, 'Harry said he believed it was jealousy, because when I was a maid I had rejected his advances. He couldn't think of a reply to that one.' Laughing happily, she shook her head. 'Hell hath no fury like a woman scorned – seems it can also apply to a man!'

Leaning over, she clasped my hands. 'Oh, Rose, you look so solemn. Be happy for me. I thought you would be glad for me, glad for us both.'

I looked at her, too stunned to do more than nod weakly. 'It's a bit of a shock, Sadie. I really had no idea and I need time to take it in.'

'But you are pleased, Rose, say you are pleased.' She frowned. 'Although this means you'll need to find another housekeeper.'

I laughed. 'That's the least of my worries.' I took those elegant hands and looked at the ring again. 'And I'm sure Jack will be pleased for you too. Am I right in presuming that now you are well again and going to . . . stay here with Harry' – I knew 'marry' was the appropriate word, but neither of us had said it – 'we no longer need to go out to Vantry and try to find the truth?'

When it was too late I was to remember her words. 'Oh no, Rose, surely you understand, I still am determined to prove that I didn't kill Oswald. I owe it to Harry, even though he believes I am innocent. If I am to go on living here, becoming one of the community, the truth is sure to come out, especially if old, spiteful, wicked Godwin has anything to do with it. I will still carry that stigma and it won't do Harry any good either. No, Rose, we must go ahead as we planned and I'm sure Gerald will give us a hand. He knows what it means to me.'

I had been thinking about Gerald, too. 'Is he pleased with this arrangement?'

She laughed. 'Of course, he's devoted to Harry, regards him like a younger brother. And Uncle Godwin can't harm him. He's part of the Clovis family.'

I couldn't think of anything to say, mention of Gerald and the Clovis family had raised new problems. How was I going to fit this in with my promise to help Peter find the killer of Mr QVE?

Sadie watched my expression and laughed delightedly.

'I know how you feel. It's so marvellous, it's quite unreal. I can hardly believe it is happening to me.'

The same thoughts with a grimmer foundation were mine exactly, and I said again: 'What happens next?'

'Of course, I'll let Aunt Brook know that I am moving to Bute for good. That I am to be housekeeper at a grand hotel.'

Umm, I thought, so that was the respectable intention

to be publicly received. It had not been mentioned before.

Sadie went on. 'She will be thrilled and we'll invite her to come and stay.' Leaning over, she took my hand. 'Oh Rose, don't look so solemn. I do beg you, please say you're pleased. I know it doesn't look as if I will be coming back to Edinburgh ever and I am sorry to let you down – and Mr Jack and dear Meg, but I am sure they will understand.'

I could guarantee that they would be as surprised as I was. 'Don't worry about that, Sadie, they will be very happy for you to have found an excellent situation with people who care about you in your native land,' I ended awkwardly.

'Will you find someone to take my place?' she said anxiously.

'I'll do my best, but you will be hard to replace.'

She looked pleased at the compliment. 'Harry realises that my experience as a housekeeper, cooking and so forth will be of great value in the hotel. We have so much in common, Rose.' A sigh. 'It is almost unbelievable that in just a few days one's whole world could change like this.'

I had to agree, in danger of forgetting Shakespeare's words in *Romeo and Juliet* about falling in love at first sight. Strange as it seemed now, I had done it myself much younger than Sadie. I was twelve years old when Sergeant Danny McQuinn rescued my sister Emily and me from one of Pa's villains. I knew I loved Danny then, and when I was grown up I would marry him. I even told him and, determined there was no other man I could ever marry, I followed him to America's Wild West against his wishes for my safety. But we had our ten happy years together and then . . . and then I lost him.

When I came to Edinburgh, Jack Macmerry entered my life. He was the one to fall in love and we married. I hadn't been keen on the idea; being – candid, in current terms – his mistress would have been enough for me. But we were happy now, and we had Meg as an unexpected bonus, but I could not pretend to myself that life with Jack could ever be like the ecstasy and the agony of first love.

And so, Sadie was determined to go ahead with this new love and I went along too. Living together in a solid relationship with Harry was almost as good as 'happy ever after' in marriage, consolation to take back home to Edinburgh while resigning myself to accepting two mysteries as unsolved.

But along with all the 'best laid plans o' mice an' men' it wasn't to work out quite like that.

The day after that conversation between us, I was standing on the landing waiting for Sadie to go down to breakfast. She came out of her room, and looking down into the lobby, I saw a flurry of people gathered and heard anxious voices. 'Who is it? What happened? Do we know him?'

Harry was below, standing anxiously alongside of Dr Wills and Gerald. They were bending over a man's body lying spreadeagled at the foot of the stairs. He was face down, wearing a dressing robe, and his twisted limbs looked ominous – even that I could see from the landing. As if aware of us at the top of the stairs, Harry looked up and saw Sadie.

She put her hand to her mouth. 'Oh, how awful. One of the guests must have fallen downstairs in the night. There was a private party, a lot of drinking, it kept me awake.'

I had heard it too, wakened I thought not from party revellers but from angry voices raised in argument coming from the direction of Sadie's room.

'Poor chap,' she sighed, 'must have been drunk.'

We both stood there, neither of us making any attempt to go down. 'How terrible!' she said.

It was indeed terrible, more terrible than we could have imagined.

The man lying dead at the foot of the stairs with his neck broken was Uncle Godwin and I kept on seeing the expression on Harry's face, and remembering how I had turned sharply to look at Sadie. It was on her face too.

She knew.

CHAPTER TWENTY-FIVE

Sadie didn't go down to him. She ran into her room, sobbing, and I followed her, bewildered, sat down on the bed and put my arm around her.

'What happened?' I asked.

She stopped crying and stared at me. 'You saw it yourself, Rose. What does it look like? Uncle Godwin fell down the stairs. He drinks too much, it was bound to happen.'

I was silent for a moment. 'Bound to happen, Sadie, but with curious timing.'

'I don't know what you mean,' she said coldly.

'I hope you are not the only one and that no one else sees the significance.'

'For heaven's sake, Rose,' she said irritably. 'It must have been obvious to everyone that he'd kill himself someday.'

'Indeed yes, and he's dead, the very day after Harry told you he was going to change his will, disinherit him. A piece of luck for Harry, this very convenient accident.'

Sadie looked at me angrily. An exclamation of horror. 'What a dreadful thing to say, Rose! How could you even think such a thing?' I said nothing. 'It's sheer coincidence, surely you realise that these things happen?'

'Oh yes, they do indeed.'

'And what is that supposed to mean?' she demanded sharply.

'Think about it, Sadie. There are certain implications – which concern you and that surely you recognise – about accidents on staircases.'

She put a hand to her mouth, as if realisation had just dawned. 'No, Rose. No,' she whispered. 'Not me.'

I said as gently as I could. 'Yes, Sadie. It was the first thing that occurred to me, this weird coincidence that the very thing you came to Bute to try to prove your innocence over, should happen again in the hotel where you were staying.'

She stared at me, horrified, and I said as gently as I could: 'Now, suppose you tell me exactly what happened before anyone else gets here.'

'He tripped and fell down the stairs, we presumed it was a guest from the noisy party—'

'Yes, I know that. But I think you knew who it was all the time we stood on the landing, speculating – all this was pretence about a drunken guest. You see,' I said carefully, 'I woke up and heard noises, voices, but they were from your room. I recognised Uncle Godwin's voice, it was always penetrating and he didn't bother to keep it down.' I paused. 'I think you were there when he fell down the stairs, and so was Harry. He sent you back to your room because he panicked and didn't want you involved.'

She was silent for a moment.

'For heaven's sake, Sadie, tell me what happened.'

'All right, I will,' she said weakly, 'but you must promise never to tell anyone else. Harry and I were together – in bed,' she added awkwardly, 'in my room here, when Uncle Godwin just stormed in. Called us all sorts of awful names. Tried to drag Harry away from me. Harry was fighting him off and they were struggling at the door. I ran after them. He was hitting Harry. I tried to stop him, they were on the landing. The next thing . . . the next thing I knew we were on the stairs and he . . . he was falling down.'

She paused, looking at me intently. 'I didn't push him, Rose. Honestly, I swear, it was an accident. He had been drinking – and he just lost his footing and . . . and fell.'

As she was speaking, I was seeing another picture, a twenty-year-old picture, of a girl and a boy struggling on another stair, in Vantry, and the boy falling to his death. And I knew that when this accident story came to light, there would be others who would remember. This was exactly how the police, who had particularly long memories assisted by carefully filed records, as well as anyone else who remembered or cared to read up on the Sarah Vantry case, would see it.

A coincidence, Sadie had called it. I remembered Pa's words that he didn't set store on coincidences, and this one was par excellence, especially when they learnt that the lawyer was arriving this very morning, in a few hours' time, summoned by Wilfred Godwin just a few hours before the accident, to change his will.

While Sadie and I talked, downstairs in the hotel consternation reigned. Wilfred Godwin was taken to the hospital as a matter of routine. Dr Wills accompanied the ambulance but it was hours too late for that and arrangements of a funeral were at the forefront of his mind.

Last night Harry had told the staff that Miss Brook would be remaining at The Heights as housekeeper. I wondered what went on inside the heads of those uncommunicative servants, many of whom must have been victims of the abusive fists of the unpleasant Uncle Godwin, now deceased. They must have heard his angry voice raised in frequent argument with his young nephew as well as Mr Thorn, both men they admired and respected and who were well-liked and honest employers. They must also have been perfectly aware of what was going on between Harry Godwin and Miss Brook to establish her in her new important role on the staff, and their congratulations were doubtless mixed with cautious thought.

'I must go to Harry,' Sadie said. 'He has Gerald, of course, he will stand by him. He knows about us and he approves,' she added defiantly, as if his opinion was all that mattered.

I went downstairs with her.

And so, on that fateful morning, amid the general chaos of trying to continue the amiable smooth running of the hotel in the normal impersonal and efficient fashion, on the stroke of ten o'clock, the swing door opened to admit the Godwin lawyer. Mr Bold was his name, and as is often the case was completely inappropriate to describe the owner, in this case an elderly gentleman of smallish stature, agitated in manner and peering at the world owl-like through large spectacles.

He was suitably horrified at what had happened, stammered sincere condolences to Harry, regarded by Mr Bold and his wife almost as family I gathered later, having known Harry since Wilfred Godwin adopted him after his parents' death in an accident when he was eleven years old. The lawyer gasped out his disbelief several times over that such a dreadful thing could have happened in the few hours since he last communicated with his client.

'I do apologise for coming at such a time and at such an early hour, Harry. I made this my first call before ten o'clock as I was summoned most urgently by Mr Godwin Senior, by telephone from here last night. He told me in his most excitable manner that he had some urgent legal business to be transacted immediately.'

Mr Bold paused. 'He hinted that he intended to make amendments to his will. I hadn't the slightest idea what that implied, but I did know that his health had been failing. Perhaps he realised that the end was in sight, but what a way to go,' he ended lugubriously.

Sadie was at Harry's side and was introduced: 'Miss Brook has recently arrived from Edinburgh and is to be our new housekeeper. Mr Thorn and I are particularly pleased since she was born here in Bute.' In common with most men, young or old, Sadie's particular chemistry affected the old lawyer into a bevy of flattering comments, to which she responded gracefully that it was good to come home again.

Mr Bold smiled, but with a shrewd and thoughtful look at the new housekeeper. Although charming, the difference in their ages was not a matter for concealment and did not provide any clues to their relationship. At well past thirty, Mr Bold concluded that she was unlikely to inspire romantic notions in the young lad he still regarded as a mere boy. And without realising the significance of his words he said: 'Your uncle always hoped that you as his only nephew would marry,' he laughed, 'although you're still a little young and there's plenty of time for that, don't you think so, Mr Thorn?' he added with an appeal to the older man, who had proved himself in the last two years an excellent, reliable friend with his connection to the well-respected Clovis family.

Gerald nodded vaguely and avoided looking at Harry or Sadie as Mr Bold continued: 'Your uncle always had a dynasty in mind for the future, sad that he was not to survive long enough to see a new generation,' and continuing swiftly: 'He much regretted the unfortunate breakdown of his own marriage, which had produced no children of his own.'

Such sentiments painted a more benign picture of Wilfred Godwin than were known to be true by those subjected daily to his disagreeable temperament.

Mr Bold beamed at Harry. 'Back to business now, lad.' He shook his head and said with regret: 'Such a misfortune that your uncle was taken from us so suddenly and we will never know the nature of those amendments that he was contemplating . . .'

As he warmed again to his subject and fell into legal jargon, Harry remained standing stiffly at Sadie's side, unhappy and ill at ease, his hands clenched in desperation to judge by the whiteness of his knuckles, reminiscent of Edgar Worth.

At last Mr Bold's papers were neatly folded, the matter concluded – Uncle Godwin's will to remain in its original form, with his nephew the sole recipient of his estate, which included the Heights Hotel. More condolences on Harry's grievous loss were uttered by the lawyer, with some glowing references to the deceased's character. And then to Harry and Sadie's almost obvious relief, he took his departure. He would attend the funeral, of course, and afterwards in the traditional manner for family lawyers, read the will.

The swing doors had hardly settled when they opened again to admit Peter Clovis. Harry had retreated into the office with Gerald and a vast quantity of urgent matters to sort out, in addition to the menus and luncheon bookings for the day.

Sadie had no desire to meet anyone at that moment. She made for the stairs and Peter rushed to my side and gasped out: 'I have just heard. What a dreadful thing to happen. Poor Harry, commiserations are in order, although,' he added wryly, 'it doesn't surprise me in the slightest: bound to happen sooner or later, the old man always drank too much. I suppose he was on his way downstairs for another illicit raid on the wine cellars again,' he added.

As a friend of Harry, Peter was well aware of his trials and the difficult times the staff had in restraining Uncle Godwin. 'To put it candidly, Rose, I don't think he'll be greatly missed. From what Gerald lets slip, too, the old devil is more than a handful.'

Then with a smile: 'How are the bruises this morning, are you all right? You still look a bit shaken.'

'Hardly to be wondered at, is it? I think despite the poor opinion of old Godwin, we none of us expected to find him at the foot of the stairs with a broken neck.'

He gave me a sharp look. 'You don't think it was deliberate, surely? For heaven's sake don't say that to Harry, he has enough without that kind of rumour.'

I went over and sat down in one of the armchairs. I felt terrible, there had been too many revelations over the past couple of days. Not only had someone engineered an accident for me that might have been fatal, Sadie had confided at last that she was to stay at The Heights as her lover's housekeeper and to crown it all, Uncle Godwin having said he was going to cut Harry out of his will, had a fatal accident, the exact replica of the one Sarah Vantry had been involved in.

'How is Miss Brook today?' Peter asked again, as if he had been reading my thoughts.

'She's making good progress,' I said dully. 'Won't be going back to Edinburgh with me. Harry has asked her to stay on at the hotel – as housekeeper.'

'That's splendid,' said Peter with a radiant smile in which I detected a gleam of hope. He had no idea of the significance of that arrangement or that Harry and Sadie were lovers: 'You will miss her, Rose.'

I hoped that was all to be said on the subject of Sadie, when he changed the subject. 'What I came to tell you was that we've had a visit from the procurator fiscal regarding Mr QVE – came over on the first ferry.'

'And what were his conclusions?'

Peter shrugged. 'That we had the body of an unknown man washed ashore. The sort of thing they find rather depressing. It means that the body will have to remain occupying a space in the mortuary unclaimed, until all avenues of finding an identity are explored. If there is no satisfactory answer, then his remains will be buried in an unmarked grave at the council's expense.'

'Is that all he had to say? What if this unknown man was a murder victim? Did you not mention that?'

He sighed. 'Where is our proof, Rose? This is merely conjecture on our part, and hardly my place to advise the procurator on suspicion or circumstantial evidence, for let's accept that is all we have to go on. For the procurator to be interested we would need to produce reasonable proof, witnesses would be required, or some sort of evidence.'

'What about that bash on his head?'

Peter shrugged. 'Dismissed as quite likely the result of falling off a boat. The procurator was reassuring, said he had no doubt that enquiries would raise some evidence of an accident – perhaps a fellow as yet unknown to the authorities who had gone out with a sailing boat from some other island or the mainland and his absence has not yet been notified.'

'Are you satisfied with all this, Peter? Until the procurator's visit changed your mind, you were convinced that this was murder. Are you now happy to forget the whole thing? If so, then I can return to Edinburgh.'

He rubbed his chin in that now familiar gesture. 'It is going to be very difficult to prove.'

'As are all murder cases at the beginning,' I said calmly.

'What about you, Rose. What's in it for you?'

'I have personal reasons, remember, reasons to believe that the Worths are involved. And that I am close enough for them to consider that I could be a danger.'

'You mean the bicycle incident.'

'I do indeed.' I paused. 'Tell me, what has changed your mind? You were very keen that I should help you solve what you were sure was going to be your first murder case.'

He sighed. 'I was and still am. But you are right about the procurator's visit. That gave me doubts, suggested caution. Taking a step like this, if it succeeded, would be perfect for my promotion to a higher rank.' He shrugged and continued gloomily, 'But if it failed and I had involved the police in what was a supreme waste of their time, I would be not only laughed at, but my whole future would be in jeopardy. We must never forget that the Vantrys are very influential people, and her ladyship a valued member of the community. I can't imagine her—'

'It's not Lady Vantry I suspect,' I interrupted impatiently.

'I am sure whatever is going on she is innocent, but the Worths are a different matter.'

Peter was still frowning doubtfully and I went on: 'However, I can appreciate your misgivings and quite understand that with your future at stake, it's up to you to decide whether we proceed or not.'

And even as I said the words I knew that with or without him, I would go on alone. To return to Edinburgh with this unsolved mystery, a series of questions without answers, would continue to haunt me. I had to prove that the tiny fragments, faint clues lurking at the back of my mind, once set together would somehow solve the mystery.

Peter was watching me anxiously. He came to a decision, perhaps reluctantly as he sighed and said: 'I can't let you down and I want to proceed – with your help, Rose, I certainly couldn't do it otherwise, you know that perfectly well – but where do we begin? It all hangs on the identity of Mr QVE. We've had posters put about; the signet ring is our only clue – we can only hope someone recognises those initials. The procurator was very approving and wished us luck. He won't be pleased at being called back for Wilfred Godwin's accident.'

CHAPTER TWENTY-SIX

And luck we had. Our very first clue. An old jeweller in the town remembered the ring and the initials: Quintin Vantry Elder.

I felt triumphant. My first suspicions had been right, for this from the city records was the name of Lady Adeline's estranged husband who, from what we might now conclude was returning to Vantry hoping for a reconciliation, and died in the attempt.

With the identity established, it now remained to get in touch with any relatives so that they might identify the body and arrange burial.

Peter sighed. 'This is great news – our step over the threshold.'

'I presume you mean into the labyrinth, because there is still a long way to go.'

He nodded. 'Of course, official enquiries and so forth. I'm on my way to Vantry now. Her ladyship must of course be informed and asked to come in and identify her late husband. We can only guess how painful that will be for her. I wish you could come with me, Rose.'

I wished I could and would have given much to observe not only her ladyship's reactions but also how Edgar and Beatrice reacted to the sad news. A couple of hours later when he arrived back with his report, I was waiting eagerly.

'Did you see her ladyship? How did she take it?'

He shook his head. 'It wasn't possible, to see her personally, I mean. Edgar said his aunt was very poorly and she could not be disturbed at the moment, especially with such tragic news. He was at pains to point out that her ladyship had been aware that Quintin was to visit her and that there had been much hope, now destroyed, that after their years apart there might be a reconciliation, the chance of being reunited and sharing what remained of their lives in a few happy years together. He said it had been a severe shock for both of them, but of course it would be worse for their aunt, and hearing that Quintin had died in a fatal accident had been too much for her in her fragile condition.'

He paused. 'Of course, she always refused to see a doctor, Edgar and Beatrice said, and they knew that all she needed was rest and peace. They both sounded so distressed. They really care about her, you know.'

I made no comment and he went on to say that they had instantly agreed to come in, formally identify him on her behalf and make all the necessary arrangements for the funeral.

I said: 'That his widow will attend, of course.'

'I didn't put that to them, insistence would have seemed rather tactless in the circumstances, but I got the feeling that it was all to be handled as quietly as possible and with absolutely no fuss and avoiding any publicity.'

He thought for a moment. 'This emphasis on Lady Adeline being much too frail made me wonder: maybe it was not just that she was physically much too frail, but they were anxious to conceal something else.'

'Which was?'

'Oh, isn't it rather obvious? Her rather odd reclusive behaviour and the way they keep her out of the public gaze suggests to me that she is losing the place a bit, perhaps showing signs of the early stages of senility.'

That idea certainly fitted Lady Adeline's conduct, although it had little to do with my own theories regarding the Worths' behaviour.

Peter went on: 'She only comes into town rarely these days. And when she was at Father's birthday party, if you remember, she just sat in a corner and seemed disinclined for any conversation. The parents noticed that and said she used to be the life and soul of the party before her accident. Mother had doubts too, said she seemed to be getting deaf as well and that the Worths must have their work cut out for them. They must be dreading what is to happen next. Small wonder they are distressed. There isn't a cure for senility, it just gets worse and worse as it progresses.'

Peter was a good man and a good policeman: never ready to jump to conclusions and condemn or accuse, he weighed up the facts and reasoned them out with careful consideration. I, however, had less charitable thoughts: that their distress might be related to the fact that if Quintin's visit and that reconciliation had succeeded, he had returned as a strong, fit man ready to take over the running of Vantry, and they would soon discover that their services would be no longer required.

When I put that to Peter, he said: 'Her ladyship would doubtless have seen that they were suitably recompensed with some sort of allowance or pension for their years of taking care of her. And perhaps Quintin would have been persuaded to let them remain at Vantry.'

'We'll never know,' and I shook my head. Somehow Peter's reasonable theory didn't fit. And most important of all, and what he was now overlooking, was how had the estranged husband come to be found washed ashore? What had he been doing out at Kames Bay, a fair distance from Vantry?

There seemed to be no answer to that, but Lady Adeline would surely want to know why he had died in such mysterious circumstances. And for mysterious circumstances I read Edgar and Beatrice Worth.

I had an idea that I put to Peter. There were no marks on him, apart from that head injury, so carefully explained away. For a body to be washed ashore implies a boat of some kind.

'Did the Vantrys have a sailing boat?' I asked Peter.

'They might have had at one time, but I don't think they were ever keen sailors at any period and any sailing craft had probably been abandoned long before the present generation – or the takeover by the Worths.'

Going right back to our first encounter with Quintin and putting the links together, I said: 'I think he was on his way to see Lady Adeline when Sadie and I met him on the rhododendron drive at the end of our tour of the house. He was in a mighty hurry and for some reason anxious not to be seen.'

'Perhaps he wanted to surprise them.'

'After all those years, that's for sure!' was my comment. 'More likely he just wanted to take a quiet look around and see what changes there had been in his absence and whether they were significant. Anyway, we can conclude he didn't see Adeline on that visit, otherwise why would he have been waiting outside the hotel, the day I saw him standing by the pony cart, while the Worths were having lunch in the restaurant? There was something furtive about his behaviour, secretive and anxious – he didn't want to publicise his visit, otherwise he would have been having lunch with them inside.'

Peter had no comment and I continued: 'My guess is that he was there waiting when they came out. They must have got a surprise, a shock more likely, so they bundled him into the pony cart and took him back with them, ostensibly to meet Adeline.'

'And what happened then, do you think? Did she turn him away?'

'No. the last thing they wanted was for this unexpected arrival, the estranged husband whose presence had been rumoured over the years, to turn up and put to an end their settled existence. They must have been praying that it would never happen, that he was out of Adeline's life for ever. Now here he was, what they most dreaded. I don't think they ever intended the two should meet again. They had to do some quick thinking as to how they would keep him safely away – before they had a chance to meet.'

Peter nodded slowly. 'Obviously they had to dispose of him – at Vantry, immediately after that arrival in the pony cart, while he was waiting to meet Lady Adeline.'

I thought for a moment. 'There was only one safe way, quick, neat and tidy. And that was poison.'

Peter rubbed his chin thoughtfully. 'But that wouldn't account for the blow to his head.'

'Agreed. But let's presume that, in his case, there was an argument, a struggle and a blunt instrument was used. Possibly not intended to kill him. Poison is less detectable. And always available on big estates, for rats and other vermin.'

I remembered something else. 'Vantry has a small private garden – tourists are warned not to go into it – and among those rare exotic and poisonous plants, there are no doubt some from abroad that can guarantee sudden extinction of life and be undetectable to the local doctor signing a death certificate.'

'We should take a look for them,' said Peter firmly. 'Perhaps something that could be slipped into a drink or a cup of tea.'

I smiled grimly. 'Indeed. I was offered one myself. But we'd be wasting our time: it's probably a secret recipe handed down from past unscrupulous members of the family.'

'You make them sound like the Borgias.'

'If I'm right, I'm beginning to think that they might have worthy successors in Edgar and Beatrice. Well, let's assume that the poison worked, they now have a dead man on their hands and they don't want him to be found within miles of Vantry. So how do they get him away?'

Peter thought about that. 'Somewhere like Kames Bay? It's quite a distance. So, they put the body in the carriage when it was dark, late at night or in the early hours when there isn't likely to be anyone around, and dump it in the sea hoping that it would be washed away and Lady Adeline's estranged husband would be lost for ever.'

'They were in a hurry and they removed all means of identification – such as wallet and watch – as it had to look like an accident, that he had fallen in the water. The only identifying thing they couldn't remove without cutting off his finger was the signet ring, worn for years, so they had to take a chance on that.'

'What they hadn't taken into account, either, was the tidal water, twice a day, and instead of being washed out to sea he was washed back ashore,' Peter said grimly.

'Who drove the carriage?' I said. 'Was Angus involved, I wonder?'

'I imagine Edgar could manage on his own. I expect he could drive if needed, although they normally used the pony and trap apart from special occasions.' Peter shook his head. 'I think it is unlikely that they wanted even the faithful servant to know they had killed Quintin.'

'And where was Lady Adeline in all this?'

'I don't think she ever knew about his visit. They had to make sure she never met him. That was the only way,' Peter said. 'We know she's too frail to roam about, cannot go up and down stairs without assistance and rarely even leaves her room.' He paused. 'It's reasonable to believe that the Worths have sleeping powders with the medicines they collect from the pharmacy here each month.'

'So we can presume she was given a heartier dose than usual, drugged in fact, until the deed was done.'

We were silent for a moment.

'What happens next?' I asked. 'We know Quintin's body got washed ashore instead of out to sea as the Worths hoped. That's the first major flaw in their plan – that Quintin has been found and identified, thanks to the help of the jeweller, although Edgar claims that he can recognise him from family photographs at Vantry. After they have formally identified the body, the official channels will be notified and the case closed. All that will remain is for the funeral to be arranged.'

'Will he be eligible for the Vantry vault with his ancestors?'

Peter shook his head. 'There isn't one. It was lost, destroyed long ago under the rubble of the old castle and since the present mansion was built they have been interred in the local kirkyard. As her ladyship's second marriage and its humiliations were rather hushed up, with

Quintin portrayed in the public eye as a ne'er-do-well, no less than a fortune-hunter, I don't expect there will be many mourners – and I imagine there is little chance of her appearing as the grieving widow at the graveside.'

I was glad Peter knew so much about the Vantrys, but I was back to the beginning, the project in hand. 'So what do we do now, how do we prove that Quintin was murdered, as we both believe?'

Peter shrugged. 'I honestly don't know, perhaps it would be better for everyone concerned if we didn't open this particular can of worms. You can go back to Edinburgh in a couple of days, pretend it was all a mistake, accept the procurator's verdict of accidental death and we tell ourselves that these are just theories, after all.'

That seemed the right and proper procedure from Peter's point of view, a safe option. After all, he was just a local policeman and nobody, particularly Inspector Rudd, so anxious for a crimeless existence, would thank him for raising the dust on the name of Vantry.

It was different for me, though, and I had already decided I could go ahead without him, do what I could by putting together my fragments of evidence before I returned to Edinburgh.

I said I might stay around for a few days longer. Peter gave me a hard look when I told him that I'd need to telephone Jack and let him know of my intentions, that there were one or two things to settle for Sadie who was staying in Bute. It was a lame excuse and I knew it.

'You will let me know if I can help, won't you, if there is anything I can do?' said Peter and I knew that it wasn't helping Sadie he was referring to. He had a pretty good idea of what I was up to but he wasn't going to put a foot wrong if he could help it. After all, as aforesaid, he lived here and he had his own future to think of.

Who could blame him?

CHAPTER TWENTY-SEVEN

I hadn't given much thought to the deceased Wilfred Godwin. Back at the hotel the undertakers had been busy and removed the body while Harry and Gerald had taken matters in hand, considering a funeral that was not going to be a wake or a memorial celebration. Godwin had not been popular, and at the news of his decease, there now emerged through the hotel's swing doors a line-up of tradesmen gathering in reception, all waving papers indicating that sums of money had been owed to them. This was yet another headache for Harry and Gerald, particularly the latter who was in charge of the hotel's bookkeeping.

The funeral would be arranged as speedily as possible. It seemed likely that the local minister was in for a busy day with two funerals and neither of the deceased regarded as his parishioners, never – if ever – having set foot in his church.

The Vantrys had their own chapel, rarely used, although at one time in their history they had their own priest. Lady Vantry had appeared in the town church on ceremonial occasions before her accident but she and Quintin had chosen to be married secretly while on holiday from Bute those many years ago.

I had a telephone conversation with Jack. His rank as chief inspector had entitled him to that rare extravagance of a telephone installed at Solomon's Tower. It was just temporary at the moment but an exciting event, nevertheless.

He was a little impatient with the information that I would be staying a few days longer but I almost heard his jaw drop floorwards when I imparted the news that Sadie was to stay on at The Heights as housekeeper.

'What on earth brought that about?' he demanded. 'I wouldn't have thought she had the experience needed for a great hotel.'

'She's formed an association with the young manager, Harry Godwin.'

'And what kind of an association would that be?' my husband demanded suspiciously, although I could hear his imagination running riot.

'I'll tell you all about it when I get home,' I said quickly.

Jack wasn't to be put off. He was curious, as he might well be remembering our entirely efficient and reliable Sadie Brook. 'Surely this is all very sudden?'

'Yes, it is. But remember, she used to live here as a child,' was my inadequate response. 'I'll explain when I see you,' I repeated.

The other reason I needed to stay was one I had no intention of going into or even hinting at, namely that I was now vastly interested in two mysterious deaths and two funerals. If I even mentioned funerals, which implied dead bodies, Jack would immediately leap to the conclusion, quite correctly, that I was up to my old tricks again. That here was some crime involved and that I couldn't bring myself to let well alone, come home and leave these particular mysteries to the local police to deal with. He knew me too well and his prediction about Bute had been right.

I learnt in that brief talk that the Macmerry parents were enjoying their holiday without me and Jack said he believed that he would have no difficulty in persuading his mother to stay until I returned. She had taken a great fancy to Solomon's Tower and enjoyed the novelty of shopping in Edinburgh.

Yes, of course, we would definitely need a new housekeeper and he would get his mother to deal with that problem. Having employed seasonal servants from time to time on the farm, he was sure – although I certainly was not – that she was the right person to find someone to replace Sadie.

I heard Meg at his side. She wanted a word with

Mam. A quick one, then, said her father. We were both emotional, both missed each other – and did I miss Thane too? Then to my surprise Jess wanted a word. She had never spoken on one of these before, not in her whole life, and couldn't resist the temptation. Although naturally suspicious, and not at all sure that she couldn't be seen as well as heard, she put on what Jack called her 'Sunday voice' and pretended there were a couple of domestic issues.

Andrew was in the background, his good humour a steady balance keeping everything in order. He sent his love. Somewhere close at hand, Thane barked as if he wanted a word too.

The line went dead. It was Thane's bark that did it. I suddenly wanted to be away from Bute. I had had enough of Sadie and her problems, now apparently solved by Harry Godwin. Enough of the Worths and Lady Adeline and whatever lay behind those sinister goings-on at Vantry; I was weary of those elaborate theories, constructed by Peter and myself, on what the procurator fiscal had dismissed as the accidental drowning of Quintin Vantry Elder. As for Uncle Godwin falling downstairs in the middle of the night, drunk as usual and on his way for another illicit bottle from the wine cellar, I had let myself be persuaded that this was no coincidence, that it related to the unfortunate case of Sarah Vantry, murderess not-proven, and I was talking myself – with Peter Clovis's assistance – into solving two crimes that weren't crimes at all.

Replacing the telephone and listening to the whirring

silence, I was overwhelmed with frantic longing and homesickness to be back in the Tower, safe with the family. At that moment, I was ready to seize my suitcase and bolt down to the quay for the first available ferry.

I hardly heard Sadie approach. I looked up and she was smiling, looking absurdly happy and excited. 'Would you like to see my new place?'

I nodded, vaguely having wondered with the new arrangement whether she would be moving out of her maid's bedroom and into the private suite of the hotel where Harry and Gerald lived. I had never been invited there and when rather shyly she said that she would be moving her things there right away, I asked did she want help. Yes, she said eagerly, she was most anxious for me to see and approve of where she would be staying.

I followed her upstairs where she opened the door leading to the private apartments, large, airy and pleasantly furnished.

Gerald was writing at a desk by the window of the elegant sitting room overlooking the river. He greeted our arrival with a smile.

There were two bedrooms, one each for Harry and Gerald. She ushered me into the larger of the two with its handsome four-poster bed. When I admired it, she whispered, a little shyly and embarrassed, like a new bride: 'A lot more comfortable than that single bed in my room next to you.'

Gerald tapped on the door. 'Anything you need, Sadie – just ask.'

He did not seem put out by the fact that she would be sharing this bachelor apartment, nor did she by the fact that she would be sharing it not only with her lover but with his best friend.

Later she said to me, as if aware of what I had been thinking: 'Gerald is quite happy about Harry and me, but it might be a little inconvenient and Harry says he has offered to go back to the Clovises. There is plenty of room for him there. It's still his family home, after all, and his mother will be delighted.'

Sadie didn't need me. I could have left then and there on the next ferry, back at Solomon's Tower in time to sleep in my own bed tomorrow night, and in need of comfort and consolation after my adventure, with Jack's head on the pillow beside me. It was wonderfully tempting but even as I went back to my room, pulled out a suitcase and put it on the bed, a cautionary voice whispered in my ear: 'You won't be happy, you know you won't. You'll regret this. You're running away.'

There was no escaping from the truth. I slammed the suitcase shut, thrust it back in the cupboard. I had two mysteries to solve. With the time in hand, it sounded an impossible challenge but suddenly my feet were firmly on familiar ground. I was a lady investigator, a detective and I was in business again.

The next moment, I had my journal – intended originally as a pleasant holiday record of Bute – with all its details, open on the desk before me. I was making notes, working on the theory that had been slithering away, lurking darkly at the back of my mind, taking uncertain shape like an itch sent to plague me and would not give me rest or let me alone until I had given it due recognition.

All I knew was that there was an answer and I had to find it still hidden at the centre of the labyrinth I called my mind, with all its uncertain paths, each holding such promise and leading nowhere. Success consisted of finding the right path by going over in careful detail every encounter I had had with the Worths, both at the hotel and at Vantry, positioning them carefully like puppets on a stage. For that reason, I needed counters labelled Edgar, Beatrice and Lady Adeline.

One, soon after Sadie and I arrived, that first brief introduction to the Worths in the hotel restaurant, as they waited with poorly concealed anxiety for their dinner guest, an important, distinguished-looking gentleman (their lawyer, perhaps?). Arranging the counters, Edgar and Beatrice, without Lady Adeline, on a sheet of paper, I added the Ladies' meeting with Beatrice, how she was dressed etc., her elegant hands so like Sadie's, Gran Faro's mark of breeding.

Two, my first visit to Vantry. With the tourists, conducted by the gardener Angus in the guise of guide. The particular interest given to the notorious staircase while Sadie kept well to the background, afraid of being recognised as Sarah Vantry by Edgar seated in state, writing at the library table and briefly acknowledging the tourists who were rewarded outside by a glimpse of Lady Adeline walking in the grounds with her stick.

A remembered picture of her struggle with the veiled bonnet in the breeze and meeting the fugitive on the rhododendron drive, later identified as Mr QVE, who had met an untimely end. I arranged counters, Edgar and Lady Adeline, no Beatrice this time.

Three, James Clovis's birthday party. My first meeting with Lady Adeline seated regally in an armchair. Told this was one of her rare appearances in public, heavily swathed and looking distinctly frail with veils and stick, her elegant hand extended as she recalled Inspector Faro's visit to Vantry and how she was delighted to meet his daughter, the authoress. I remember thinking that was quite a speech, her voice perhaps throaty with age, hardly above a whisper while Edgar, regarding her anxiously, bitten fingernails nervously clutching a glass of champagne, reminded her of our meeting at the hotel and added rather loudly that the carriage was waiting. This was a brief visit by an honoured guest and Beatrice, suffering from one of her migraines, would be sorry to have missed meeting the authoress as she is a keen reader. Counters for Edgar and Lady Adeline, no Beatrice again.

Four, Edgar and Beatrice having lunch in the hotel restaurant while fugitive man from Vantry drive, later identified as Mr QVE, paced anxiously back and forward beside the pony and trap. Strong suspicion in light of later revelations that they had taken him back with them. Counters for Edgar and Beatrice, no Lady Adeline, who did not normally accompany them on their shopping visits to Rothesay.

Five, my lone visit to Vantry by bicycle. Ignored by so-called fierce guard dog. Ready with authoress research excuse. Gave Lady Adeline time to answer door if, as became apparent, the Worths were elsewhere. Unanswered, went to back door, found it ajar, had that empty-house feeling. Decided wickedly to take chance of exploring. Unkempt kitchens, quick look round ground floor, lacked nerve to go up that staircase, although quite certain no one at home. In limited explorations, intrigued to find former gunroom now a museum. Caught leaving it by Edgar and Beatrice coming in from garden. While making my excuses to Edgar, Beatrice disappears, servants' bell rings. Beatrice returns, says Lady Adeline needing tea, has suggested I return tomorrow and meet her. I had been sure the house was empty. but I did hear that bell and voices. Counters for Edgar and Beatrice, Lady Adeline heard but unseen.

Six, next day visit to Vantry. Met by Angus, who directed me to park bicycle at back door. Invited to cup of tea by Edgar while Beatrice went upstairs to prepare Lady Adeline for my visit. Warned not one of her good days and must not overtire her. Beatrice calls Edgar from upstairs. I hear voices, and follow Edgar up to her ladyship's room overlooking the garden. She is seated in a deep armchair, swathed in shapeless garments and veils, and wearing antique ruby ring, identical to that worn by Beatrice. Briefest interview ever, feeling like a prospective servant, asked a few questions and dismissed, told might borrow book in library for research. Departed on bicycle in fury, and narrowly missed what could have been a fatal accident on steep hill when brakes failed. Later discovered they had been tampered with, i.e. while I was at Vantry. Placed counters. Edgar, Beatrice and Lady Adeline.

There was one important addition and I turned the pages to my detailed meeting with Ellen Boyd, including the significance of her sister Mavis's dying words. Something about it not being Lady Adeline.

I sat back and considered my findings. One interesting fact emerged: I had never seen all three of them, Edgar, Beatrice and Adeline, together, and if I were to make enquiries I could hazard a guess that neither had anyone in Rothesay, not since Lady Adeline's accident when the Worths had appeared on the scene to take over and take care of her.

There was one more counter needed. Dr Tom Richards. Now for the first time he raised his head and played a prominent part in my theory. I had let myself be influenced, based on earlier information from Peter, and I wondered how Inspector Rudd regarded his cousin's visit, and whether any of the other Bute policemen were aware of his dubious past. The suspicion returned. Had he come to the island with the sole mission of looking up cousin Inspector Rudd or had his real objective been to find an explanation for the curious fact that Lady Vantry was not remembered as a patient at the Glasgow hospital. Had he suspected that was worth investigation? I had missed the obvious path by focusing on blackmail, which, if that was his intention, was now of minor importance. Of real significance was why had Beatrice turned him away, refusing to let him over the threshold, and why had he never been allowed to meet Lady Adeline?

CHAPTER TWENTY-EIGHT

I was interrupted by the arrival of Sadie, very excited about her new position as housekeeper and how she was going to enjoy being on the staff. She was flourishing the antique ring, regarding it proudly, although it was too big for her slim hands.

'If Harry doesn't intend to replace this soon, I shall need him to have it altered to fit. He expects to see me wearing it all the time, but I am afraid I might lose it in my daily duties and that would be dreadful.' As she spoke, she again held out her hand admiringly. 'After all, I only regarded it as temporary, and I'm hoping when I tell him, that will remind him that I should have it replaced by another kind of ring' – she gave me one of her intense looks – 'a proper engagement one and in due course, a wedding ring.'

'So you would like to marry him?'

Her eyes widened and she laughed. 'Rose, what a question. Of course I would! I think it's just a matter of time, and when he asks me I'll say yes like a shot.'

I looked at her. 'Do you think that moving in with him until he makes up his mind – or the idea occurs to him – is going the right way about it?'

Her eyebrows shot up. 'Once he realises I am indispensable. He doesn't care about the difference in our ages, he just knows we love each other and that will only get better and better, when we get married.'

'What about children, Sadie?'

'Oh, he loves children, Rose. And I'm sure we will have them. I'm not all that old and lots of women have babies when they are forty.'

A dangerous age for first babies, I thought, and many die in childbirth, regardless of whether the child was the firstborn or – as, tragically, had been the case for Emily and me, losing our beloved mother with a stillborn baby brother when she was forty.

I was curious to know the reactions of one important person in Harry's life.

'How does Gerald feel about all this?'

She stared at me coldly. 'He just wants us both to be happy. Why shouldn't he?'

When she left, her joy over that ring triggered off another of the fragments tormenting me.

That visit to Vantry when I was to see Lady Adeline. Beatrice had left me with Edgar to have a cup of tea, saying it took a little time to prepare her on her frail days. I had refused the tea and he seemed disappointed, I couldn't think why – then. Her elegant hands so like Beatrice's. Despite many afflictions, they had not aged at all, yet according to Gran's bible on the subject, hands could not be disguised and were the one give-away of age.

And Adeline liked jewellery. I remembered on that first visit to Vantry when the tour met her veiled in the gardens, the beringed, elegant hand raised to restore her bonnet, and on my second visit, seeing again the huge ruby she was wearing when I helped her seize the bell rope. Beatrice also wearing a large antique ruby – similar to Adeline's.

No. Not similar. Identical. As were those elegant hands.

And suddenly it all fell into place. The reason why Tom Richards had not been allowed to see her, and the faint echo of Mavis Boyd's dying words to Ellen that 'it wasn't Lady Adeline' took on a new meaning.

I looked over my notes again and the counters. Although I thought I had heard her voice, I still had never actually seen them together—

Because on the occasions when her presence was necessary, it was Beatrice Worth.

There was no Lady Vantry.

I sat back in my chair. So where was she? And even as I thought, I knew the very obvious answer.

Lady Adeline was dead. But when? I decided probably soon after her accident when the Worths gave up their so-called grand estate in England and came to the Isle of Bute to take care of her. Now the question arose, had that riding accident in Glasgow been an invention, for Beatrice's disguise?

And that raised other questions. Had they murdered her, or had she died naturally? Either way the reason for the imposture was now obvious: in order to continue her ladyship's considerable quarterly income, to be collected and signed for, Beatrice had to appear in Rothesay, fragile-seeming, heavily veiled and also able to forge an excusably shaky signature because of age and frailty.

Presuming Adeline was dead and they were guilty of fraud rather than murder, what had happened to the body? Where had they buried her? The ruins of the old castle? But that would have been tricky – old bones have a nasty habit of reappearing, especially murdered ones. A family vault would have been the perfect solution, but it no longer existed, buried in the remains of the original castle.

Her body must have been buried somewhere. I had to have help. And Peter now had a good reason for giving the help he had promised, a good reason and some clues provided for solving his first murder mystery.

He came readily enough and I invited him to my room; I did not want to meet him in the main part of the hotel, not with the information I had to impart. No one must overhear.

He listened and said not a word. As I produced my evidence with the counters for Edgar, Beatrice and Lady Adeline, after a careful study he laid it aside and exhaled heavily: 'I believe you, Rose. As you know, I wasn't happy with only speculations but I'm certain you are right and what you have written here is what happened.' He shrugged. 'Having said that, although I am certain that the Worths are guilty, the tricky point remains of how we bring them to justice. Can we ever prove that they murdered Adeline as well as Quintin?'

I had almost forgotten Quintin in my exciting discovery. 'Well, he certainly did not die naturally, that we do know, but again it has been accepted that he met with an accident at Kames Bay.'

'Edgar has arranged his funeral. We have no witnesses, nothing to prove that he was murdered.'

'But we can make a shrewd guess as to why he was killed. He did succeed in meeting Beatrice in her Adeline disguise and, of course, he knew immediately that he had been tricked. This was not his wife and they had to get rid of him. They used poison, I imagine, the least spectacular way.'

Peter said: 'Did they have the poison on hand, lock him in somewhere until the means could be found?'

'Poison,' I repeated, 'in a cup of tea while he waited. Edgar was very upset on my last visit when I refused tea. Then I had the accident,' I added grimly. 'I might have died because they suspected I was on to them, knew too much.'

I thought for a moment. 'Angus probably provided one of the poisons from the exotic garden, he knew all about them. He certainly was the one who tampered with my brakes.'

Peter nodded grimly. 'So, has he been involved as an accessory to getting rid of Quintin? He could have even driven the carriage and helped dispose of his body at Kames Bay. Edgar would have needed some assistance with that.' He sighed. 'But all we know, without any witnesses or sufficient evidence that would go down in a court of law, is that we believe Quintin died under suspicious circumstances.'

'And to state the case realistically, all that Beatrice Worth can be accused of and arrested for is fraud – withdrawing and securing a substantial quarterly income by using a false identity.'

'But they still have to explain what has happened to Adeline.'

I thought about that. 'Without producing her body, that is going to be difficult, even for them.'

Peter frowned. 'They might try some lies, such as that she died naturally – or from an overdose of sleeping powders – and confess that it was the necessity of keeping Vantry that drove them to the imposture.'

He paused. 'And if she did die naturally, they would not even inherit Vantry. According to the will and the fact that she still had feelings for Quintin, as the sole surviving member of the family, everything – including Vantry – would go to him. The Worths would be left penniless.'

And I was remembering Edgar's nervousness, his bitten nails. No wonder.

First of all, Beatrice's imposture had to be exposed. We thought long and hard about how that could be achieved.

We decided that Lady Adeline had to make an appearance before witnesses, where she could be stripped of her ladyship disguise and revealed as Beatrice Worth.

Peter came back later and said: 'I hope you approve, Rose, but I thought this was going beyond us. I talked to Inspector Rudd and he was very interested. Tom had insisted on seeing him because when he went out to Vantry, the Worths wouldn't allow him to see his old friend Lady Adeline, told him a pack of lies, and that left him with the feeling they were up to something.

'Rudd said Tom was the family black sheep but her ladyship always had a soft spot for him. He wasn't just hurt, he couldn't believe that she would refuse to see him. He made a great fuss as only Tom can, and refusing to take no for an answer he returned to Vantry. He had a feeling that his return caused the Worths to suddenly panic. Beatrice said her aunt was resting just now, but Edgar would give him a drink and show him round the gardens.

'Tom was furious. He didn't want a drink – he's been teetotal since his reformed days – but he wandered round the gardens and waited until Edgar called him and said Aunty, as he called her, was ready to see him now. Tom went upstairs and he knew the moment he walked into her room that, even taking into account the accident and all her shawls and veil, this wasn't Adeline.

'He made some polite remarks about making a mistake and left in a hurry, but on the way back he called in to see Rudd and said he had got this crazy idea that she was being impersonated by Beatrice Worth.'

Peter paused and went on. 'Rudd said that had set him thinking about the Worths collecting her quarterly pension and so forth, so he has been making some enquiries. He thinks there's something crooked going on and that they may have done her in. The only way to prove anything is to go out and demand to see her.'

I decided my share in the proceedings was over; however, not long after having left, Peter again returned. He wasn't alone and introduced me to Inspector Rudd who said: 'Clovis tells me that you are a lady detective and that you have carried out most of this investigation very successfully on your own.' He gave me a searching look and continued: 'Perhaps you would like to accompany us.'

As we walked out to the car, Rudd said he had gathered that my father was famous and that perhaps crime solving was an inherited family trait. He hadn't met a female one before and his look suggested he was rather surprised by this new species. I was also making my own calculations about Inspector Rudd. Based on my observations and calculations, I decided he had the look of a military man and had probably served in HM forces before coming to Bute.

At last we drove into Vantry. Edgar came to the door, with the fierce guard dog locked out of sight but barking fiercely. He seemed more than a little taken aback at this visit by the police inspector with Sergeant Clovis and myself.

Rudd said: 'We are here on official business with her ladyship.' And nodding in my direction: 'It also concerns this lady, Mrs Macmerry. She had an accident leaving here.'

Hearing voices, Beatrice appeared. The situation was repeated to her, she gave me a dagger-like look and I knew they were clearly scared as well as mystified. Beatrice said: 'Her ladyship is not at all well, you will need to come back later.'

It was the usual excuse, but Rudd was insistent.

'Very well, take us up to her room, if you please. We will disturb her as little as possible.'

Glances were exchanged, Beatrice continued protesting about her ladyship's condition, but she had reckoned without her brother, who lacked her staying power in an emergency.

Edgar panicked, stretched out a hand to her. 'It's no use, Bea.' And to the three of us, he shook his head: 'She isn't here, Inspector.'

'Very well, Mr Worth. Perhaps you would tell us where she is.'

Again, miserably, Edgar shook his head. 'We don't know.'

Beatrice, recovered, said: 'She just walked out one day and never returned. Perhaps she went back to Glasgow,' she added desperately.

I said: 'A frail old woman, walking with a stick? She wouldn't get very far.'

A look of hate from Beatrice. 'She was quite strong, really. Very well, we invented that bit. You see, we waited – most anxiously – and when she didn't come back and we didn't hear from her—'

Edgar interrupted: 'That was when we decided that we would collect this considerable pension until she did.'

'With your sister playing the part of Lady Adeline,' said Rudd grimly.

'That was the only way, but it wasn't fraud, really. We were going to give it back to her of course, when she returned.'

'How long ago was this, Mr Worth?'

'About . . . about four years. But the pension people never heard from her,' he continued quickly and added despairingly: 'What could we do? We had no money, no estate in England, we were virtually penniless, except for Vantry, depending on her.'

If he thought this appeal would win the inspector's forgiving heart he was sadly mistaken. There was Quintin Vantry's murder, and the sinister possibility that they served poisoned drinks to unwanted guests like Tom Richards, who fortunately for him was teetotal.

Rudd said sternly: 'We have every reason to believe that Lady Vantry was dead before you took on this role to deceive the authorities and it will be best for you, if she died naturally, to show us where she is buried.'

But they were sticking to their story: she had walked out, they had never heard from her. True, they had helped themselves to her pension, but with every intention of explaining their actions, which she would fully understand and appreciate when she returned.

The inspector looked at them both and knew he was beaten. He couldn't make an arrest for murder without a body, only on suspicion and for fraud.

CHAPTER TWENTY-NINE

I went back to the hotel. I was leaving tomorrow and whatever would be the outcome of this case, I would only hear about it from Peter or read about it in the Scottish newspapers.

I had just finished packing when Peter looked in to say goodbye and promised to keep me informed of the case's progress. He said Beatrice would go to prison and if Edgar was caught and there was proof that a murder was committed, then he would hang.

'If we could prove they'd engineered what could have been a fatal bicycle accident for you, that could be added to the charges against them.'

'I keep thinking about that. It had to be something they

thought I had seen, something that threatened them with discovery, and although I was unaware of it, there was the possibility I might remember.

'So where had I been? I remember being caught coming out of the gunroom room as they came back from the garden. Their consternation and then being asked back to meet Lady Adeline the following day. I remember I had a sneezing fit as I rode home and that Edgar found my handkerchief that I had dropped in the gunroom. It was the acidic smell of stuffed animals that made me sneeze, something like the formaldehyde they use in the mortuary.'

I stopped and gave him a triumphant look. 'The gunroom, Peter. That's where she is.'

We drove out, down the drive and I was wondering how we would get into the house. It looked deserted, silent, with no sign of Angus, who had probably made off with the guard dog before the police had calculated his role as accessory to the Worths' criminal activities.

The front door with its access by the front steps looked as if it had not been opened since the last tourists paid their entrance fee. Our arrival was heard and a uniformed figure appeared from the direction of the kitchens.

Saluting Clovis smartly, he said there would be continual police presence to ensure that the house was protected from vandals. He shook his head, so many valuables, sir, in a mansion this size. He understood that the sergeant was here to have a look round and see that all was in order, and if he did not mind entering by the kitchen premises, he could produce keys for the locked rooms.

And so we walked in and I opened the door to the

gunroom. The acrid smell was stronger than ever and Peter sniffed the air. I sneezed while he regarded the armoury and the stuffed animals with their glassy stare.

'What a collection, the souvenirs of many generations of big-game hunters.'

I wasn't interested in the menacing gaze of lions and tigers, only the robes of past Vantrys, in particular the coronation robes of Lady Adeline, with its accompanying photograph, importantly in a glass case on its own.

'This way,' I said to Peter.

It was sealed. Lady Adeline, in magnificent ermine and velvet, her face hidden under a large wig and an elaborate headdress.

Peter turned to me. 'You think?'

I nodded and he looked for the door. There was no door, this exhibit was sealed in glass and meant to be kept that way.

'How do we make sure? We can't carry it away.'

'A moment,' he said and returned from the kitchen with a large hammer and two large towels one of which he handed to me.

'We break the glass – to make sure.'

He gave it a mighty blow. It shattered and we were gasping for breath, the towels to our mouths overwhelmed by the sickening stench of decay.

We had found Lady Adeline, or what remained of her – a mummified skeleton. As glass tombs go, she was a less attractive sight to us than Snow White must have been to the seven dwarfs.

* * *

But the story wasn't quite ended. I telephoned Jack to tell him I had to delay my departure for another day. Andrew answered. He sounded cautious and said Jack was out but promised to give him the message. I sighed with relief at not having to give the lengthy explanation Jack would have wanted.

As for the Worths. It wasn't just fraud, it was murder this time. Beatrice was in jail. Edgar had run off and left her to face the music. She had screamed when they told her he had been seen scrambling aboard the ferry. The police in Glasgow would be alerted, and of course he would be brought back.

Beatrice called him all the names she could think of and it so transpired that eager to tell the truth now, she wasn't his sister. They had met in England when he was having financial troubles and intending a visit to Vantry as a last resort to endear himself once more to his elderly, reclusive aunt. He needed someone, a female preferably, who could do the cooking, to accompany him. An actor friend with the local repertory company had just introduced him to Beatrice, a good actress but not quite from the right class to be acceptable as his wife by his snobbish aunt. He decided he could overcome this hurdle by persuading her to appear in the role of his young sister.

She maintained that Lady Adeline had died of natural causes soon after their arrival and in desperate need of money, they had panicked and Edgar had decided that she should impersonate his aunt on those quarterly appearances to collect her considerable pension. Beatrice also swore that she had never heard of Mavis Boyd and as for Quintin Vantry Elder she merely shrugged. Edgar had told her he wasn't welcome and said he had send him packing.

I felt that when it came to a trial, this would make interesting hearing, but I had almost forgotten Sadie in all the excitement. She said the hotel was buzzing with it. 'A real murder. Incredible! Harry says it will do wonders for the tourist trade.'

Sarah Vantry had been forgotten. Wilfred Godwin's death safely dismissed as an accident. I thought 'safely', with relief. At the back of my mind was the scene on the stairs that evening, and the unworthy thought – had this accident on the eve of Godwin's intention to cut his nephew out of his will been engineered by Harry and Gerald? Had any suspicions been aroused, then they could point to Sarah Vantry, who would be remembered as a murderess with a not-proven verdict.

I told her I was going tomorrow, but it was not a happy thought. I felt uneasy regarding my suspicions about these two and leaving her future in their hands.

When I promised to send the rest of her clothes and possessions she had left in Edinburgh she assured me that she didn't want them as Harry was to provide her with a complete new wardrobe as well as a housekeeper's uniform.

Just a few hours more and I would be on my way home. Jack and Meg and Thane too would be happy and we would be faced with the prospect of finding someone to take Sadie's place.

It was not to be. Next morning, ready to leave, I was surprised to open my door to her. I held out my arms. She had come to say goodbye.

'Not so, Rose.' And indicating her suitcase at the door: 'I am coming with you.' Closer, it was clear she had been crying.

'A row with Harry? There, there,' I said consolingly – probably something trivial about the uniform.

'No, not with Harry.' She said indignantly. 'With both of them.'

And so it came out, the whole sad story. She had always believed that Harry would marry her but she had reckoned without Gerald, and Gerald objected in no uncertain terms – as the love of Harry's life. They had been together for years and while Gerald did not mind Harry having an occasional fling he was not prepared to take second place permanently.

I listened to as much as I could decipher, between bouts of sobbing, and realised what I had always suspected but for her sake had never put into words. And again they returned, my thoughts from yesterday, of how Uncle Godwin's death had been accepted as accidental but with Sadie's presence a precaution, a premeditated and grim insurance policy.

She had dried her eyes and said wearily, 'Let's go, Rose.'

And so we returned to Solomon's Tower, to all intents and purposes Rose and her housekeeper companion Sadie, after two weeks' extended holiday in Bute, receiving an overwhelming welcome from the family, particularly Meg and Thane. My fears for him had been groundless, he having thrived in his role as an indulged domestic pet at the Macmerry farm but remaining my guardian angel where any dogs – fierce guard or otherwise – were concerned.

Had we enjoyed Bute? asked Jack's parents, preparing to return home once more.

'Did you have a lovely time, even without us?' Meg asked wistfully.

I said yes but it had not been without its incidents, delayed ferries and influenza, but here we were back again, grateful to her grandma for looking after everything in our absence.

This should be the end of the story but fate had a final card to play.

A month passed and I was busy with a couple of new cases. Sadie seemed happy enough, looking after us with her usual efficiency. Jack was glad to have her back, her ironing was splendid too. I smiled. This was one murder case I wasn't prepared to discuss with Jack. Sadie Brook was invaluable and her past would stay our secret.

'We would never have found a replacement,' he said. 'Glad she changed her mind about that fellow.'

She never mentioned his name, or Bute. Both they and Sarah Vantry might not have existed, and then one day, I was looking out of the kitchen window and watched a handsome young man striding purposefully towards the gate.

I opened the door to a captain in the Merchant Navy.

'Good morning, madam. Is Sadie—'

Footsteps behind me.

'Robbie!' And Sadie rushed forward, to be taken into his waiting arms.

As they kissed, I knew another chapter had ended, and another was about to begin.

ACKNOWLEDGEMENTS

Bute is a beautiful island. I fell in love with it on my first visit some years ago and I also knew that it ticked all the right boxes for a crime novel. An apology however is needed to the residents for some fictional locations, such as Vantry, an author's necessary invention for a tale set more than a century ago.

Invaluable sources of information were 'History of Bute, Rothesay' (D. N. Marshall and A. Spiers, 1992); 'Bute: An Island History' (I. MacLaggan and A. Spiers, 2002) ; 'An Archaeological Landscape of Bute' (George Gesses and Alex Hale, 2010).

My grateful thanks are first to the McKenzies for their

ever-welcoming hospitality at Ardbeg; to George, for this book could never have written without his unfailing encouragement, providing essential material and drives around the island; to June, an incredibly kind hostess and a superb cook; and to my dear friend Alex Gray for those memorable ferry crossings from Wemyss Bay.

In Rothesay, thanks to the staff of the Museum and Library, always at hand and ready to answer queries, give directions and useful information, and to Bute's own author Myra Duffy. Here in Edinburgh, thanks to my good friend and agent Jenny Brown and in London, to my publisher Susie Dunlop and her excellent team at Allison & Busby. At home, to the Knight family, Chris and Lucie, Kevin and Patricia, enraptured by their first visit to Bute and always ready with encouragement and support.

Only one final word remains. For the joy in writing this book, thank you, Bute.

ALANNA KNIGHT has had more than seventy books published in an impressive writing career spanning over forty years. She is a founding member and Honorary Vice President of the Scottish Association of Writers, Honorary President of the Edinburgh Writers' Club and member of the Scottish Chapter of the Crime Writers' Association. Born and educated in Tyneside, she now lives in Edinburgh. Alanna was awarded an MBE in 2014 for services to literature.

alannaknight.com

To discover more great books and to
place an order visit our website at
allisonandbusby.com

Don't forget to sign up to our free newsletter at
allisonandbusby.com/newsletter
for latest releases, events and exclusive offers

Allison & Busby Books
@AllisonandBusby

You can also call us on
020 7580 1080
for orders, queries
and reading recommendations